Zemsta

by Victoria Brown

Woodchuck Publishers

For information, e-mail info@woodchuckpublishers.com

First paperback edition May 2012

Cover design by VBMC

ISBN 978-0-9854391-1-8 (paperback)

Boca Raton, FL

For my daughters

Anna Cushman van Tonder
and
Lucy Cushman

Prologue

❖

*I*n that colorless time right before sunset, in the woods bordering the fairway, there was a glint, a flash of light, and the sound of someone struggling. The following morning, behind the country club pool house, they found a young woman beaten so badly she was unrecognizable.

It would be twelve years before they knew who really killed her.

My name is Patty Henry. I'm sixty years old, and this is the story my grandfather told me thirty years ago about his friends Kurt and Charlie and the murder of Catherine Block at Rosewood Hills Country Club on October 24, 1920.

The Early 1900s

❖

At the beginning of the twentieth century, there was a tremendous sense of well-being and satisfaction in the United States and especially in Akron, Ohio, the fastest growing city in the country. After Henry Ford's 1905 deal with Harvey Firestone to supply tires for his Model-A cars, the rubber industry was booming, and each day hundreds of immigrants and "barefoot people"—the poor from West Virginia, Kentucky, and Tennessee—arrived at the railroad station. From 1910 to 1920, Akron's population exploded, growing by over sixty percent to 208,000.

Chapter One

❖

It was November 1914. Three twelve-year-old boys huddled together on a weatherworn bench at the city-sponsored ball field where they had met three years ago. They were best friends.

"The Tribe. Let's call it The Tribe."

"Yeah, I like that. That's great."

So that's what Kurt Becker, Nickels Jablonski, and Charlie O'Brien called their new club—The Tribe. Die-hard Cleveland Indians fans, the club's name was in honor of their favorite team, which had changed its name from the Molly Maguires to the Indians at the end of the season. The team owner asked local newspapers to come up with a new name, and they chose "Indians" after the Boston Braves pulled off a miracle by coming back from last place in July to win the World Series.

After they got back from the ball field and clamored through the kitchen of the boardinghouse, they headed for their hideout under the stairs. They often sat under the stairs between the front hall and the parlor for hours—laughing and scheming like only twelve-year-old boys can.

The war in Europe had begun in July. Sitting in their hideout shoulder to shoulder, they played war and made believe they were soldiers fighting in the trenches. They imitated the stuttering sounds of machine guns and shouted to each other in loud whispers.

"Watch out."

"That was a close one."

Charlie said, "Good thing we didn't get hit. I need a cigarette. Got a light?" They sat back and smoked their imaginary cigarettes. They laughed so hard, they could be heard throughout the boardinghouse.

Someone was playing a record in the parlor. "Can you hear that?" said Charlie. "What a stupid song." Through the wall, they could hear "The Aba Daba Honeymoon" playing on the old Victrola. The tinny sound blended with the sounds of several people talking.

Knowing they could trust each other, the boys agreed that anything they said in their "dugout" was secret, shared only among the three of them. To declare their loyalty and secrecy, they stacked their hands, one by one on top of the other and said together, "Swear."

That was the first thing my grandfather Nicky told me about Kurt and Charlie. He always remembered the dugout and said they spent some wonderful times holed up under the stairs. It was the beginning of their lifelong friendship.

Grandpa said, "Even when we were boys, I knew I could depend on Kurt and Charlie, and as it turned out, I was right."

Chapter Two

❖

When Kurt was seven, his father died of pneumonia. The following year his mother said, "We're moving to Ohio to live with your Aunt Erna and help her at the boardinghouse."

"I don't want to leave Pennsylvania."

"I'm sorry, Kurt, but without your father, I can't make it on my own."

"But this is where we lived with Dad."

"I know, but sometimes life sends you in a new direction. It's not going to be as bad as you think. You'll see."

Kurt missed his father and continued to struggle with his death. Now that he was twelve, he often wanted to talk to his dad, especially about guy stuff he didn't want to discuss with his mother or aunt. He hated living in the boardinghouse and catering to the boarders and believed his life would be different if his father were alive.

Kurt Becker was good-looking and popular, but what everyone first noticed about him were his bluer-than-blue eyes. He was tall and skinny, with wide shoulders and thick, curly brown hair.

He lived with his mother Marta and her older sister Erna in a mostly working-class Akron neighborhood north of the university.

Nothing about Erna Stucke was soft. She was short and fat. She braided her gray hair and pulled it back into a severe bun. Because she was deaf in one ear, she always raised her voice whenever she had something to say. Her sparkly blue eyes were her most pleasant feature.

When they first moved to the boarding house, Kurt said to his mother, "She's so serious. Would it hurt her to laugh sometimes?"

"Once her husband died, a little of the light seemed to go out of her. Give her a chance. You'll see that as time goes on, you'll grow to like her. She adores you. She just doesn't know how to show it."

Marta Becker was short and round and not nearly as fat as her sister. She had brown hair peppered with gray, lively blue eyes, a wide smile that showed deep dimples, and when she laughed, her slight underbite was noticeable. A mild-mannered, genial woman, she was always ready to laugh at herself, and in spite of being plain, she had a kind, happy face that reflected her unfailing optimism.

With two women devoted to him—and the only child in the boardinghouse—Kurt got more than his share of attention. His father was gone, but his mother and aunt treated him as if he were the center of their world.

✧

Stucke House, a home-away-from-home for many of Akron's factory workers, was a three-story Victorian with a large wraparound porch, faded green shutters, and peeling paint.

Inside, the rugs were dingy, the secondhand furniture was threadbare, and the mattresses were lumpy, but the boardinghouse was sparkling clean and neat.

The large kitchen was the heart of the boardinghouse. Marta and Erna always kept a pot of coffee on the cast-iron, coal-burning stove for the boarders to help themselves. And when one of the Stucke House pies came out of the oven, the aroma wafting throughout the house created a warm and homey environment.

The three boys liked to hang out in the kitchen when Marta and Erna made pies. They had a large enameled worktable where they assembled all the ingredients and put the pies together. When the pies came out of the oven, Marta always gave them a piece, which they ate in their hideout.

Running a boardinghouse was hard work. Taking care of chickens and gathering eggs, stoking and feeding the coal fire, never-ending laundry, and meal preparation was only part of it. They were responsible for the bookkeeping, daily shopping, and much more. Five days a week the sisters paid a woman named Nelly to help with the laundry and cleaning.

The sisters charged each boarder three dollars a week for a room, which included a simple breakfast and a weekly change of linens. They charged an extra fifteen cents for the evening meal.

Marta often said, "We work hard all week, and it seems as if we have nothing to show for it. Where does all the money go?"

"Not in our pockets, I can tell you. It's expensive to run this place. I don't know what I would do without the two of you here. I'm afraid I would have had to close the place down."

The boarders rarely saw Marta or Erna without an apron except on Sundays when they refused to work in the kitchen. They prepared Sunday meals on Saturday, so all they had to do was heat the food and serve. They also refused to play cards or dance, and the only book they read on Sundays was the Bible.

Alcohol was forbidden at the boardinghouse. Marta and Erna were rabid teetotalers and members of the Woman's Christian Temperance Union, commonly known as the WCTU. They proudly carried their temperance cards and openly espoused their views by pinning white ribbons on their dresses. Marta liked to announce, "Alcohol has never touched my lips."

The sisters were devout Lutherans, and on one Sunday in late

November, bustled to get ready for services. "Hurry up, Kurt, we don't want to be late," his mother yelled up the back stairs. "Today's sermon is on the evils of alcohol, and both your aunt and I want to sit up front."

Marta was dressed in her best olive green dress. She topped her outfit off with a dark green hat and a spritz of perfume—a gift from her late husband. "Erna, my goodness, don't you look nice today," she said as her sister walked into the kitchen.

Erna wore a burgundy and black polka-dotted dress big enough to sleep two. Her fancy hat had black feathers sticking out in several directions, which made Kurt think of the chickens out back. He made chicken sounds and let out a big belly laugh. Erna scowled. "What are you laughing at?"

"Nothing, Aunt Erna." He turned around so she wouldn't see his big grin.

When they got to the church, the sisters said, "Good morning, Reverend Reiter," as they entered the church. Kurt trailed behind them.

Marta spied a fellow church Guild member. "Hello, Sarah. My, how nice you look today. Will you be chairing the next Guild meeting?"

Sarah didn't have time to answer before Erna leaned in close to Marta and whispered in a voice loud enough for Sarah to hear, "She always thinks she has to be in charge of everything." Sarah turned her back on them.

Marta had to bite her tongue to keep from scolding her sister. She whispered to Kurt, "It's my sister who has to be in charge. She's the bossy one. Erna doesn't realize how often she offends people."

Kurt considered the sermon a form of slow torture and occupied himself by counting. He counted bulbs in the chandelier, hats with feathers, women in the choir with blond hair, and men wearing blue ties. He thought he might die of boredom before the minister's long discourse was over. He wasn't able to stifle his yawns.

The minister concluded with a Proverb. "Wine is a mocker, strong drink is raging: and whosoever is deceived thereby is not wise."

Kurt thought, "When I'm a grownup, I'm not going to church anymore."

Mama and Aunt Erna would have been horrified to know when they passed the offering plate around, Kurt pretended to put his money in, but kept it hidden in his hand.

After they left the church, Marta scolded him for not paying attention.

✧

When they got home, Kurt changed his clothes and dashed outside to find Nickels and Charlie. "Tell them we baked apple pies yesterday and saved each of you a piece," Marta called after him.

The boys didn't go to the same school or live in the same neighborhood, but they'd found a few good shortcuts and knew the quickest way to each other's houses.

By the time Kurt, Nickels, and Charlie were under the stairs, they could hear Erna ranting about Kurt's friends. Erna didn't like catering to immigrants and referred to them as Polacks, Kikes, and Micks. Those who came from other countries she called immi-grunts, and Appalachians were snakes or hillbillies.

The three boys were silent as they heard her say in her too-loud whisper, "They're not our kind. I don't want Kurt hanging around them, and I'm not sure how I feel about them spending time here at the boardinghouse. They're both Catholic, and you know as well as I do that Catholics are heathens. I've even heard that Polack kid speak Polish. We must do something about it."

Kurt was ashamed when Nickels and Charlie heard what his aunt said. "I'm sorry. Aunt Erna is a big grouch sometimes. Don't pay attention to her."

"Don't worry about it," Charlie said, "We've heard it a million times. We know you don't feel that way. Lots of people think the way your aunt does."

Nickels said, "Yeah, that's the way it is."

On most things, Marta went along with her big sister, but she harbored no resentment against others and disagreed with her on the subject of immigrants and Appalachians. Kurt wasn't swayed by Erna's bigotry. His mother had taught him to accept everyone.

Marta scolded Erna. "He's my son, Erna, and I say it's okay. They're nice boys. Leave them alone and stop butting in. They like to play with each other, and they all stay out of trouble. Mind your own business for once."

Erna was shocked. She swung around and left the room in a huff. When she finally came back into the kitchen, she acted as if nothing had happened. Marta was proud of herself for standing up to her sister because it wasn't something she had the courage to do very often.

Kurt was required to do his chores every day. He especially hated cleaning out the chicken coop. He always told his mother that it was so stinky, it made him want to throw up.

And she always replied the same way. "Kurt, you know we can't manage without your help. I expect you to do your chores without complaining, and that includes mucking out the coops and cleaning the bathrooms."

"Why are some people rich? It's not fair."

Marta would shake her finger. "Life isn't fair, and the sooner you learn that, the better off you'll be. Some people will always have more than we do, but some people will always have less. Think how lucky we are to have a home with Erna. I don't know what would have become of us otherwise. God has been good to us."

Kurt was hell-bent on becoming a success and having a lot of money. "When I grow up things are going to be different. I'll buy Mama and Aunt Erna a house and take care of them."

Kurt always looked for ways to earn money from the boarders. One day, a guy on the second floor complained about washing his smelly socks, so Kurt offered to wash them each week for a dime. Other boarders heard about it, and asked Kurt to wash theirs. One of the boarders cleaned gutters around the neighborhood, and on weekends Kurt earned fifty cents a day helping him. After school he ran an errand service, and when word got around he was available, he had more customers than he could handle. At the end of each week, Kurt went to the bank and deposited his earnings.

Grandpa Nicky said Kurt was a born leader and as a young boy was making more money than a lot of grown men. "I knew Kurt wasn't going to settle for a humdrum life. He was obsessed with money and driven to be a success."

Chapter Three

❖

𝒞harlie O'Brien was the shortest kid in his class. He had light brown hair and penetrating green eyes. He loved school and worked hard to get good grades. Fastidious in his dress and habits, he thought carefully about everything he said and did. Even at twelve, he had to have a plan and never did anything haphazardly.

Like many of Akron's earliest Irish residents, Charlie's ancestors helped build the Ohio and Erie Canal in the mid 1800s. For generations, the family had lived in the same Irish Catholic neighborhood that was part of a large area that included many other nationalities, including Hungarians, Russians, and Italians. Their home was a two-story clapboard framed around the log cabin originally built by their ancestors.

In spite of the fact that the family had lived in America for almost a century, there was still a great deal of animosity toward them because they were Irish. Called "white Negroes," the Irish were stereotyped as alcoholics and resented because people believed they took too many jobs away from "real Americans."

"Look at this disgusting cartoon," Charlie's father said one day. "It pictures us as apes to show we're inferior to the Anglo Saxons. When someone calls you a Mick and makes fun of you because you're Irish, I want you to remember Ireland is an old civilization. When we'd been here for a long time, the Anglo Saxons were still heathens." Charlie thought his father had said that to him at least a hundred times.

When Kurt and Nickels asked Charlie to describe his family, he said, "There are nine kids—five boys and four girls. Mary is the oldest, and Michael the youngest. I'm right in the middle. The girls sleep in one bedroom and the boys in another. We call them dormitories.

"We eat at a big picnic table, because it's the only way we can all sit down together. I hate it, because I always have an elbow in my side. I guess it's normal for us.

"Because there are so many of us, if I want something, I have to find a way to earn it myself. My mother always says we have to share. Sometimes I pretend I'm an only child."

Charlie's father Patrick was a nondescript man who worked for the city of Akron. All Charlie knew about his father's job was that he went to City Hall in the morning and came home at night.

His father was a strict disciplinarian who believed in harsh punishment. He rarely showed his children affection.

Fortunately his mother helped make up for what his father was unable to give him. Maureen had brown hair, green eyes, and freckles across her nose. She was warm and loving and knew each child needed individual attention. Her children were the center of her world, and she was known to say, "You're only as happy as your unhappiest child."

Every Saturday was "Children's Day," the day the O'Brien children took turns going on an outing with their mother. It was more than two months between Charlie's days, but it was worth the wait.

When Charlie found out the circus was coming to town, he ran into the house to find his mother. "Mom, I want to go to the circus. Can we? I have some money saved I can give you. Please, Mom, can we go?"

His mother laughed and said she would think about it.

"What's there to think about? That's where I want to go for my special day. You'll like it. It'll be fun, Mom."

"Charlie, I told you I'll think about it. Now run along."

His mother discussed it with his father, and the next time Charlie came to find her, she said, "Good news, Charlie. We're going to the circus."

That Saturday Charlie and his mother took the bus downtown. During the walk from the bus stop to the circus, they passed through a neighborhood where there were several houses of ill repute with risqué posters of almost-naked women on the doors. Charlie's mother crossed herself as she hustled him by. "Mother of God. Close your eyes, Charlie. This is nothing for a young boy to see."

Charlie was used to hearing his mother call on God. He saw the world through Catholic eyes, which left no room to question doctrine, so he didn't have to deal with a lot of things that tempted the other kids. Whenever he was tempted with something the church had taught him was sinful, he said, "I can't because I'm Catholic."

When they were out of the rough area, his mother crossed herself again. Charlie crossed himself, too.

The Ringling Bros. and Barnum & Bailey Circus was a three-ring extravaganza that included death-defying daredevils, scantily clad trapeze artists, wild animals, and freak sideshows. Charlie and his mother arrived an hour before the show, because he heard they might be able to meet some of the clowns if they got there early.

On their way home, Charlie abruptly hugged his mother.

"What's that for Charlie?"

"I love you, Mom. Thanks for a terrific day."

"Glory be to God. Didn't we have fun?"

When they got home, they came into the kitchen through the backdoor. His father was standing there with a scowl on his face. Charlie saw right away that his father was drunk again.

"Oh geez, here we go," he thought.

His father said, "Did you have fun at the *circus*? Spending *my* money? You don't know how difficult it is to provide for a family of eleven. You're damn lucky I can do it." He looked pointedly at Charlie. "What are you lookin' at?" Charlie could hear the slur in his words. He hated it when his father was in one of his moods and tried to stay out of his way—not always easy to do.

Charlie's mother disapproved of her husband's drinking and bore the brunt of his sharp tongue. After one of his father's binges, his mother would sigh and say, "It's my cross to bear." Charlie felt sorry for his mother and thought she deserved better.

✧

Charlie, Kurt, and Nickels were expected to entertain themselves. None of their families had money for expensive toys, and the adults were too busy to provide diversions, so the street was their playground. They enjoyed being outdoors and played baseball every day, and if they weren't at the city-sponsored ball field, they played in a nearby four-corner street.

They had a beat-up ball thrown away by the city league, and every time one of them hit it, it made a funny, whistling sound as it slowly looped through the air. Part of the fun was seeing how far the ball would go before it dropped straight down.

Besides baseball, they played hide and seek, stickball, and marbles.

All the boys—especially Charlie—loved a good practical joke. Three days after the circus, he said, "Come on," and motioned Kurt and Nickels into the dining room of the boardinghouse. "I want to play a joke on Kurt's mother and aunt. Give me a hand. Take the sugar out of the sugar bowls and put in this salt instead."

He handed each of them a small box of Morton's salt. When they were done, he said, "That ought to do it. Let's get out of here."

That night at dinner, when one of the men took his first gulp of coffee, he made a face and spit it back into his cup. A couple more boarders tasted theirs and reacted the same way. One of them said, "This is the worst coffee I've ever tasted."

Marta and Erna were horrified. "What's wrong?" It took a few minutes, but Erna finally figured it out and said, "That's salt in the sugar bowl. You've all been sweetening your coffee with salt instead of sugar."

Marta said, "We're so sorry. We have no idea how that could have happened."

She and Erna apologized profusely and offered the next night's dinner for free. The sisters blamed each other for the mishap, and from then on, checked the salt and sugar each night. Erna said, "We certainly don't want that to happen again. Coffee is too expensive to waste."

Marta chuckled and recited Morton's slogan: "When it rains it pours."

Erna didn't think it was the least bit funny.

Grandpa Nicky said that the next day in the hideout when Kurt told Charlie and him what happened, they laughed so hard they almost peed their pants.

Chapter Four

❖

*N*o one but his mother and father ever called Nickels by his full name—Albert Henrik Jablonski, Jr. Nickels was slim, with brown hair, dark eyes, and full lips. Nice looking, even handsome, he exhibited none of the gawkiness most twelve-year-old boys are known for.

His parents were Polish immigrants who fervently believed in the American dream. But they were proud of their Polish heritage and taught their children to feel the same way.

Located in a predominantly Polish neighborhood, their brick, two-story house had a dark green door and was surrounded by a weather-beaten, wooden fence. Inside, the small rooms were connected off a center hall that led to the kitchen. Upstairs were three bedrooms where gilt-framed holy pictures were hung to remind them of their home in the old country.

Nickels' parents belonged to the neighborhood Catholic Church and socialized mostly with other Poles. Albert, Sr.—Albo—worked the morning shift at the rubber factory and went to his second job in the kitchen of the Rosewood Hills Country Club in the afternoon.

Albo wasn't very tall, but had well-developed muscles from working in the factory. He had a pleasant face, a twinkle in his eye, and a dimple in his chin. He didn't talk much, but when he did, he said something worth listening to.

The boys respected him and enjoyed being around him because

they knew he was sincere when he showed an interest in them.

Nickels' mother was a dedicated homemaker who loved taking care of her family. Her name was Ludmilla, but everyone called her Millie. When Kurt and Charlie came around, she formed a big circle with her arms and said, "Come here. Want hug." They squirmed and acted as if they didn't like it, but each secretly looked forward to her bear hugs.

Nickels' sister Antonia was ten, and in spite of her young age, everyone could already see she was going to be a knockout. She had big brown eyes and long, wavy dark brown hair. Kurt and Charlie were secretly infatuated with her.

Antonia adored her big brother and his two friends, and although she would never admit it, she had a crush on Kurt. She tagged along with the three of them and sometimes was allowed to play with them.

Albo told Millie, "I'm happy Albert, Jr. has made such good friends. They're nice boys, and the three of them have a great time together."

"I agree. I like both Kurt and Charlie, and enjoy seeing how well the three of them get along. They've worked out a good balance. Better than most adults, as far as I can tell."

Kurt and Charlie liked both of Nickels' parents, but had a special affinity for Albo. They were impressed that no matter how hard he worked, he always found time to spend with his children and their friends. He treated Kurt and Charlie as if they were part of the family.

Nickels and Antonia spoke accent-free English to their friends, and insisted on speaking English with their parents, who replied in Polish. It made for confusing conversations, half in English, half in Polish, and with the back-and-forth translation, conversation was often stilted. Kurt and Charlie learned a few Polish words, but Kurt was careful not to use any of them in front of his aunt.

For Kurt, Albo was the next best thing to having a real father. Whenever he had something to say, Albo listened intently and gave him the best advice he could. Kurt talked about his father and explained to Albo how much he missed him.

Nickels translated, and Albo said, "As more time passes, it will bother you less and less. But always remember you have both a mother and an aunt who dote on you. How many boys can say that? Life has a way of giving us what we can handle. I know you can learn to deal with this, Kurt. You're a strong boy who is going to grow up to be a strong, successful man. Trust yourself and your instincts. It will take you far."

"You always know exactly the right thing to say, Mr. Jablonski."

Charlie also had a special attachment to Mr. Jablonski. After becoming friends with Nickels, Charlie found himself frequently turning to Albo. If he had a problem to work out, he talked it out with him instead of his own father. He was amazed at how Albo approached everything. There was no yelling at the Jablonski house. He told Nickels, "Your family pays so much attention to me. In my family, it's tough to get noticed."

When Kurt asked Albo why he left Poland to come to America, he said, "America is the land of opportunity, and that's what Millie and I wanted for our children. You boys don't realize how many wonderful chances you have to become educated and successful at whatever you choose to do. It's all up to you. Work hard, and you'll enjoy the benefits."

To earn money, Nickels was the shoeshine boy at Rosewood Hills Country Club. That's why he was called Nickels—the members of the club nicknamed him that because he charged five cents a shine.

A few of the members referred to him as "the Polack kid," but he ignored the slurs.

One member, a prominent businessman named James Foster, always went out of his way to taunt him. "Hey, you stupid Polack, you speak English yet?" He never failed to mock him whenever he passed the shoeshine stand.

"I didn't let it bother me, because I knew he was ignorant," Grandpa said. "I didn't care what he called me, because I had a wonderful family, great friends, and lots of plans for the future."

The 1920s

❖

*A*t midnight January 16, 1920, the Volstead Act became law and banned the manufacture, sale, and transportation of intoxicating liquors, but not the personal possession or consumption. All breweries, distilleries, and saloons in the United States were forced to close.

Prohibition addressed a serious issue affecting a small percentage of the people and imposed a solution on everyone. A colossal failure, it intended to lessen the evils associated with alcohol, but instead turned millions of former law-abiding citizens into law breakers and spawned gangsters, rumrunners, and speakeasies. With easy money to be made in illegal alcohol and gambling, Prohibition fostered corruption and contempt for the law. While authorities looked the other way, drinking, gambling, drugs, and prostitution flourished. To pass the law meant nothing if it wasn't enforced, and enforcement was nearly impossible.

People began to make liquor out of anything they could ferment. At the boardinghouse, Erna kicked out one of the boarders when she discovered he was making raisin jack in his room. She found out he was cooking the fruit on the stove on Sundays while she and Marta were at church.

For people who didn't buy cases of alcohol in advance or know an accommodating doctor, there were many ways to drink illegally. In fact, the number of establishments offering alcohol and gambling doubled. Owners went to great lengths to conceal speakeasies, which included stores and secret rooms in basements of homes and buildings. People located the speakeasies by word of mouth and to gain admittance, quietly whispered a password through a closed door—thus the term "speakeasy." The Feds raided them, often arresting both the owners and patrons, but it was common for owners to bribe the police and get advance notice about raids.

Corruption was rampant. President Harding's Attorney General accepted bribes from bootleggers. An Ohio bootlegger had a thousand salesmen on his payroll—many were policemen. And in Chicago, Al Capone's organization had half the city's police on its payroll. Capone said, "When I sell liquor, it's bootlegging. When my patrons serve it on silver trays, it's hospitality."

Akron's population was growing, and finding a room wasn't easy. The town was so overpopulated that rubber workers often shared beds in shifts at the boardinghouses. But rubber wasn't the only thriving industry in Akron. Cereal, lamp, toy, and marble companies were also booming.

Advocates of Prohibition thought the law would also help immigrants assimilate better and become more Americanized.

By 1920, there were more people in Akron born in other states or abroad than were born in Ohio. Akron's growing "Tower of Babel" overflowed with Austrians, Hungarians, Poles, Germans, Italians, and people from West Virginia, Tennessee, and Kentucky. The number of West Virginians living in Akron reached almost nineteen thousand—close to ten percent of the population.

Because of the constant flow of immigrants coming to work in the factories, racial tensions were high, and quotas were set for immigrants coming into America. The Ku Klux Klan railed against Negroes, Jews, Catholics, and immigrants. Akron's chapter of the Klan was the biggest in the country, and members included those in high-level political positions, including the mayor and several school board members. With factory workers making up a large part of the membership, the Klan movement was an expression of dissatisfaction with the high cost of living, perceived *social injustices, and the bigotry that was so pervasive throughout the city.*

During the early 1920s, the Klan helped elect sixteen U.S. senators and many representatives, as well as local officials. By 1924, the Klan controlled twenty-four state legislatures.

✧

For young women, the 1920s marked a break with traditions. The Nineteenth amendment gave women the right to vote, and attitudes changed drastically. Long-standing social barriers began to crumble, virtually overnight. Women bobbed their hair and wore short skirts. They used cosmetics, drank alcohol, and smoked cigarettes in public. Nearly every article of clothing was trimmed down and lightened in order to make movement easier. Even the style of underwear changed. Women wanted to move freely for energetic dances such as the Shimmy, the Black Bottom, and the Charleston—something corsets didn't allow.

Young women took part in the sexual liberation, and it was a time of great social change. From the world of fashion to the world of politics, forces clashed to produce the most explosive time in a generation.

The country became smaller. Railroads made long-distance travel possible and were now a central part of American life. Rail lines crisscrossed the country, carrying people, manufactured goods, food, and the mail. The popularity of automobiles and radios had exploded, and new machines such as the washing machine and vacuum cleaner helped eliminate some of the drudgery of housework. The stock market was poised to skyrocket, and you could buy a car for a little less than three hundred dollars.

Akron was an exciting, vibrant city teeming with people and money. The city would experience several years of unprecedented, almost giddy, prosperity. The number of employees in the rubber factories reached seventy thousand with some workers earning up to seven dollars a day— more than most industries paid in a week. People had money, and they were spending it in speakeasies and music halls and on expensive clothing.

Chapter Five

❖

When Russell Hollingsworth Cantrell was a young boy, he was a compulsive—and creative—liar. There was nothing he found more amusing than fooling everyone. Manipulative and able to get people to do what he wanted, he was expert at blaming his bad behavior on someone else.

When he was thirteen, he and a neighbor boy were smoking purloined cigars in the woods next to the Cantrell property when Russell said, "Come on, John, let's set a fire out behind old man Taylor's barn."

"No way. Are you crazy? You can't do that. If you do, I'm going home."

Russell never let anyone tell him what to do. "What a big chicken. Bock, bock, bwwaaaaakkk. Go ahead. Be a baby. Run home to your mommy, Johnny boy."

John rolled his eyes and left to go home. Russell didn't care. He threw a lit match into the woodpile at the side of the barn. He wanted to see how big the fire would get.

The woodpile started to smolder. In an instant, huge flames danced up the barn wall. The fire fascinated him, and soon it was out of control. He watched it for a few minutes and then rushed back to his house and snuck up to his room by the kitchen stairs.

The barn burned to the ground, and later when someone said they thought they had seen him, Russell said, "Oh no, it wasn't me. I saw John Warnick heading in that direction. I bet he started the fire."

When the Warnicks confronted their son John, he said, "I had nothing to do with it. Honest, I didn't do it. Russell did it. All I did was smoke a cigar with him, and when he asked me to help set the fire, I said I wouldn't and came home. I wasn't there when he lit it."

No matter how much John denied it, no one believed him.

When Russell's father Ellwood came home and told Russell's mother Barbara about the incident, Russell listened from upstairs with his ear pressed on a vent in the floor.

"Barbara, I'm not sure I believe Russell."

"Don't be ridiculous, Ellwood. Of course Russell didn't do it. That awful Warnick boy did."

"Well, it doesn't matter. I took care of everything and made sure there won't be any repercussions for the Warnick boy. I promised John's parents I would make certain John didn't end up in a detention center. His parents told me they believed John was lying, and they are going to punish him severely."

Listening upstairs, Russell got a kick out of hearing John was in big trouble. The next time he saw him, he sneered, "That'll teach you. You better learn not to mess with me."

John started to cry, and Russell laughed at him.

Russell's father, Ellwood Hollingsworth Cantrell, was an influential appellate judge known for his honesty and strong code of ethics. He was often described as charismatic.

Russell's attractive and refined mother Barbara was a self-absorbed socialite who was more interested in spending time at the country club with her friends than staying home and spending time with her son. She figured that's what nannies were for. Once a week, his nanny Belinda left a list of things Russell wanted, which his mother promptly instructed one of the staff to buy.

When Russell acted up, even though his father knew his behavior was unacceptable, he refused to acknowledge it to anyone. His mother Barbara thought he was perfect.

Belinda told his parents, "He gonna be a handful. You best get hold of him now. If you don't give him a spank sometime, he be trouble for you. Mark my words."

"How dare you speak to us like that?" said Barbara. "Ellwood, please explain to Belinda what her boundaries are."

Ellwood said, "Belinda, he's our son, and we'll handle him as we see fit. I know you're trying to help, and you have Russell's best interests at heart, but we will determine the best way to discipline him."

Belinda told them she understood and from then on, decided to ignore Russell's bad behavior and let his parents deal with him. "They be sorry, that for damn sure."

After Belinda left, Ellwood said, "Barbara, you know she's right about Russell. He's a magnet for trouble, and as he gets older, it's going to get worse. I don't know what we're going to do with him. He doesn't listen to a word I say."

"Oh for goodness sake, he's fine. He's a good boy. I don't want to discuss this anymore."

✧

Russell Cantrell got his undergraduate degree from William and Mary and went on to Yale for law school. Never a great student, his grades were passable, and there was never any question he would finish and pass the bar. If he had trouble with a course, he paid other students to write his paper or take a test for him. He never hesitated to cheat if he could get away with it.

While at Yale, Cantrell got a girl pregnant. His father paid her family off and convinced them she should have the baby somewhere far away. Russell's father was livid and couldn't hide his disgust. "Russell, this is the last time I will take care of one of your messes. Do you have any idea how many times I have cleaned up after you? It's time you were responsible for your own actions."

Cantrell walked away laughing to himself. "What a fool," he thought. "He doesn't know half of what I've gotten away with."

✧

When Cantrell was thirty-two, he met Elizabeth Barnett, the young daughter of a wealthy Akron financier.

When Cantrell first met Elizabeth, he poured on the charm. He had big plans for the future, and the pretty Elizabeth Barnett by his side would be a big asset. He took her out to dinner, bought her flowers and jewelry, and introduced her as his "very special girl." She was enchanted by him and thrilled when he proposed. They had a big wedding and honeymooned in San Francisco.

After they were married, Cantrell immediately stopped paying attention to her. He merely thought of his wife as a necessary addition to his rising career. He didn't believe in marriage or love. He married simply to create the perception of stability.

Although Cantrell owned a house on hundreds of acres in the country outside Akron, he and Elizabeth lived on his family estate, which was located in the same area where Akron's wealthy rubber barons lived. The neighborhood was situated away from the smoke and soot of heavy industry, and the winding brick streets, rolling hills, and canopy of trees implied big money.

The Cantrell estate sprawled over one hundred acres, and Hollingsworth House had eighteen rooms, polished wood floors, molded plaster ceilings, stained glass windows, and crystal chandeliers. Its rooms were filled with family treasures from around the world. The stable housed five horses, and the family employed twenty-one people.

In 1920, Cantrell was thirty-four years old. He was well over six feet tall with slicked-back, dark hair. He would have been matinee-idol handsome if it weren't for his eyes, which were dark and piercing.

By then, Elizabeth was firmly ensconced in Hollingsworth House. She was bored and sick of being ignored by her husband. "Did you marry me for the wealth and prestige of the Barnett family?"

She loathed his self-interest and considered him a narcissist. "I believe you're amoral and don't have the slightest shred of a conscience. You disgust me. I'm sorry I ever married you."

He put his head back and laughed loudly. "Morality is only a concept, and it's one that doesn't concern me. I do what I want."

A born orator, he spoke with a deep, resonant voice that naturally demanded attention. He took pride in dressing well, and people often commented on his sartorial sense. "Looking good," he often said to himself as he strutted, his Cuban cigar clenched between his teeth.

Cantrell had a successful law practice and many financial holdings. He was on the board of several high-profile charitable organizations, including City Hospital where he made a generous donation toward an expansion. He was also raising money for a much-anticipated baseball field he planned to help the city build within a few years. His charitable endeavors were part of his master plan. He believed the wing in the hospital and the ball field would eventually help him with his political aspirations. He fantasized about the day when he would hear people talk about City Hospital's Cantrell Pavilion and about watching a baseball game at Akron's Cantrell Park.

Cantrell wasn't intimidated by anyone or anything. Used to getting what he wanted, he would do anything if he thought he could get away with it. Witty and charming on cue, his clever veneer masked his true nature. People bought into his charade. They believed he was a good man interested in helping others and in serving his city and country.

Grandpa said the corrupt atmosphere during Prohibition was the perfect time for a man like Russell Cantrell.

Chapter Six

❖

*T*he exclusive Rosewood Hills Country Club was where Akron's wealthy, prominent families congregated for golf, racquet sports, swimming, and social activities.

The gated entry to the private club led to a long, winding drive past the tenth green and up to the impressive clubhouse. The grounds included rolling hills, man-made ponds, and beautiful, mature trees. An elegant dining room offered a view of the rose garden and fountain.

The members took their golf seriously, and a lot of cash changed hands on the weekends when men bet on their ability to sink the money putts.

Besides golf, members relaxed with family and friends at the Fountain Grille, played tennis, or lounged by the pool. They attended black-tie dinner dances in the ballroom, enjoyed outdoor concerts, and gathered for the monthly meeting of the Akron Investment Club. Women played bridge, worked on their favorite charity drives, and gossiped.

◈

Nickels had shined shoes at the country club every Saturday and Sunday during the season for the past six years. By eighteen, Nickels had grown into his looks. Women thought his bedroom eyes and full lips were sexy, and he had a lot of fun flirting with the teenage girls who hung around the shoeshine stand.

Occasionally he was asked to caddy, but was usually too busy shining shoes. Nickels thought his friend Kurt would make a great caddy, because he didn't talk much, was a great listener, and had really good manners. He'd asked him before, but Kurt wasn't interested. Nickels asked him again, explained how good the tips were, and Kurt finally said he'd give it a try.

On a Sunday in late May, Nickels brought Kurt with him to the club. "I'll introduce you to some of the golfers. A lot of them are really nice, although there are a few who think they live at an elevation far above us. Let's see what happens. There's a lot of money in caddying. Knowing you, I could never understand why you didn't take me up on it before. It's right up your alley."

"Thanks. I appreciate it, especially because I'm sick of running errands for the boarders. I really want to start making some serious money. Maybe this is the answer."

The sun was shining, and summer was around the corner. Kurt had never been to a country club before, and he wore his best pants and the only button-down shirt he owned. He didn't have many good clothes, especially clothes appropriate for a prestigious country club like Rosewood Hills. At first he sat with Nickels at the shoeshine stand, but after a while wandered around to check out the place. He looked at the beautiful landscaping and the grand clubhouse and promised himself that one day he would be a member.

As he strolled back to the shoeshine stand, he saw Nickels excitedly waving him over. "Hey Kurt, come over here. I want you to meet Russell Cantrell, one of the members I was telling you about. His caddy cancelled at the last minute today, and there are no other caddies available. His tee time is in a few minutes, and he needs a replacement in a hurry. I told him you're ready and willing."

Cantrell was dressed in a light brown, single-breasted jacket with large side pockets and matching knickerbockers. He wore brown wool stockings, brown and white shoes, and sported a leghorn straw hat.

Kurt thought he looked foolish, but realized that what Cantrell was wearing was the height of style for the golf course. He confidently offered his hand, "Nice to meet you, sir."

"You want to give it a go?" Cantrell asked.

"Well, sir, I'd be pleased to caddy for you, but you need to know I've never caddied before."

Cantrell rolled his cigar around in his fingers, and said, "You just made a big mistake, kid. Never tell anyone what your weaknesses are. That's a lesson you need to learn. But I'm willing to give you a chance.

"These are the rules. Don't talk when anyone is swinging. Don't worry about telling me which club to use—we can figure it out as we go along. And whatever any of us in the foursome talks about is strictly confidential. Can you handle that?"

"Sure can." Kurt wondered what kind of important business he might overhear.

"Okay, good. We have to find some appropriate shoes for you. You can't wear those on the course," Cantrell said, his face registering disapproval as he looked at Kurt's scuffed shoes.

Kurt was fitted with a snug pair of cleated shoes from the club's lost and found, and off he went toward the first tee, Cantrell's big golf bag slung over his shoulder. He was happy and excited to think he might be able to pick up some big-league dough. As they passed the shoeshine stand, Kurt said "Thanks, Nickels. I owe you one."

Cantrell chuckled, "That shoeshine boy is a good kid, for a Polack. Better than all the hillbillies pouring into town, that's for sure. I think we should find a way to get rid of all of them, don't you?"

Kurt was offended and felt a spike of anger. But then he thought about the money he was going to earn and ignored the comment.

Instead, he changed the subject. "Which club do you use on the tee? Hopefully by the end of the match, I'll understand the game a little better."

"The driver. I'm sure you'll catch on quick, kid."

By the end of the front nine, there was "no blood." The match was even. Cantrell played fairly well until then, but on the tenth hole, his game fell apart. His banana hook either landed him in the woods or out of bounds. By the time they were on the fifteenth tee, his opponents were up three. Cantrell pressed, and then doubled the amount of the bet for the last four holes. Now worth a hundred a hole, Kurt was amazed at how casual they were about such a big wager. He couldn't wrap his head around that kind of money. "Jesus, what Mama and Aunt Erna could do with that much money," he said under his breath.

Cantrell and his partner took the next hole, so now they were down two with three holes to go. They had to win the remaining holes if they were to win the match. From that point on, after every shot, Cantrell complained. "Who didn't repair that divot mark? It ruined my shot. Goddamn it, that putt was in the cup. It went in, ringed the hole, and then popped out. Shit." He threw his putter, and Kurt watched it arc and then rotate in wide circles until it landed on the ground near the golf bag.

By the time they were on the eighteenth tee, the match was even, and Cantrell was determined to win the final hole, a par five. They teed off, and his drive ended up in the deep left rough. Kurt shifted the heavy golf bag to his other shoulder. When he got to where Cantrell was standing, he noticed Cantrell had positioned his foot next to the ball as he casually looked around to see what the rest of his foursome was doing. Cantrell slowly nudged the lie, so it sat up on a tuft of grass, giving him an easier shot and a much better angle.

Kurt didn't know much about golf, but he was pretty sure golfers weren't supposed to improve their lie when no one was looking. He tried to keep his face impassive the way all the other caddies seemed to do, but his feet were beginning to ache, and the borrowed golf shoes were rubbing against the big toe on his left foot. He was sure when he took the shoes off, he was going to find a big blister.

Cantrell hit the shot fairly well, but Kurt thought it rolled into the water hazard. Cantrell charged ahead to look for the ball, but couldn't find it. "Damn, it must have ended up in the water," he mumbled to himself. Cantrell furtively dropped another ball, turned around, and was surprised to see Kurt standing right there watching him. "Hey, look. Here it is. Thank God I found it. Now get my nine iron," he snapped.

Kurt was starting to think his friend was fooling with him by setting him up with Cantrell. But Nickels had promised that Cantrell was a big tipper, and if there was one thing Kurt liked, it was money.

Cantrell won the hole with a birdie. One of the men eyed Cantrell and asked about his third shot. "I was pretty sure I saw it roll into the water."

Kurt was quick to answer. "No sir. The ball was right where we thought it was, and it was definitely outside the red, water-hazard line."

Cantrell smiled smugly, pleased with Kurt's lie. "The kid picks up the lingo fast," Cantrell thought. Aloud he said, "I think I better keep him around. He's my new good luck charm."

On the way up to the clubhouse from the eighteenth green, Cantrell casually handed Kurt fifty dollars. "You earned it, kid," he said with a knowing wink. "Here's another five. Use it to buy some new golf shoes." It was more money than Kurt had ever earned at one time in his entire life.

Kurt pushed away thoughts about how he lied for Cantrell.

Grandpa Nicky told me Kurt never forgot how he helped Cantrell cheat that day.

Chapter Seven

❖

*N*ickels knew he didn't want to spend his life working at the rubber factory or in the kitchen of a country club. He had the utmost respect for his father, but it wasn't what he wanted for himself. He enjoyed writing, and at the beginning of his senior year, after he turned in a paper for his senior English assignment, his teacher asked him to stay after class. "Albert, you have a special talent, and I encourage you to pursue it. Try to write as often as you can about anything and everything. You'll find the more you write, the easier it will become. Then bring what you write to me, and I will critique it and help you rewrite and edit."

Her compliment launched his lifelong love affair with the written word. He told her, "I'm doing what you suggested and writing as much as possible. There are so many things I'm interested in and want to write about, and I'm writing every day. The more I write, the easier it becomes, exactly like you said."

He continued to show his work to Miss Owens.

One day after a review of his work, she told him she had something for him. She handed him a journal bound in leather. After that he carried the journal everywhere.

He learned to take a mundane idea and turn it into something interesting and began examining issues from different perspectives. He wrote about family, friends, and current events. The more he wrote, the more he knew it was what he wanted to do for the rest of his life.

Miss Owens encouraged him to submit his work to various publications. "Your chances of getting published are slim, but it's worth a try. You never know what's going to happen. And nothing will happen if you don't try."

In May, when he walked into the house, his mother told him there was a letter from *Sports Today* on the table in the front hall. He read it and yelled, "Mama, they're going to pay me for the article I wrote about what it means to be a Cleveland Indians fan." He was jumping up and down.

The next day, he took the letter to school and showed Miss Owens. She said, "I always knew you could do it. You should be proud of yourself. Not many eighteen-year-olds can say they're going to have an article published in a national magazine. Good for you."

After seeing his name in print, he never contemplated any other career. He wanted to be a journalist and work at a big-city newspaper. And he was willing to start at the bottom and work his way up, if that's what it took.

After graduating from high school, he applied for jobs at newspapers in four Ohio cities—Columbus, Cleveland, Cincinnati, and Akron. When he made the appointment for his interviews at the newspapers, they asked him his name. Without skipping a beat, he said, "Nick Henry."

Nickels was offered a job in the mailroom at the *Cleveland News Tribune*. It wasn't a prestigious title or position, but it was a start, and that was what he needed. He planned to work at the newspaper during the day and attend college classes at night.

When he told his parents about his new job, they were proud of him. He hesitated to tell them about his name, but he knew he'd have to explain it eventually. "Sorry, Papa and Mama. Jablonski is difficult to remember and too Polish sounding, so I used my nickname Nickels and combined it with my middle name Henrik. I thought it would make a good pen name that wasn't indicative of a nationality or ethnic group."

His parents were upset he wasn't going to use his real last name. "It's a good Polish name, and we're proud of it." His father sighed.

"I know, Papa, and I'm proud of it, too, but as a writer, it's to my advantage to have a name no one can associate with any particular group." Albo said he understood, but Nickels could tell he was disappointed.

His father and mother were sorry he was leaving home and moving to Cleveland, but they accepted he was a grown man and had to follow his own path. It was exactly why they came to America—so their children would have many opportunities.

Nickels was excited about his new job, and shared his dreams with his parents, "Someday I'm going to be a well-known writer. Every day thousands of people will read my opinions in the newspaper. If they're interested in what I write, it might be instrumental in helping them change their views on a particular topic. It's going to be wonderful to do something I really like and get paid to do it. The mailroom is only the beginning."

Later he told Antonia about his job. Naturally she was disappointed he was moving to Cleveland, but was really happy he was going to do what he wanted. He planned to tell Kurt and Charlie when they went to a baseball game in Cleveland in a few days.

✧

Kurt, Nickels, and Charlie got together as often as possible, and although their lives were going in different directions, they still thoroughly enjoyed each other. They met at The Canal, a local restaurant, where they always sat in the same red-leather booth against the wall, near the back and away from the door. The owner Sam knew them by name, and every time they came in he gave each of them a friendly pat on the back. He always said the same thing, "Where have the three of you been? You need to stop by more often. Eat. Enjoy."

None of them was ever flush with cash, so when they ate at The Canal, they made a habit of throwing whatever money they could spare in the middle of the table. They ordered as much as they could and shared the meal.

Nickels said, "Maybe this place isn't as cozy as our old hideout under the stairs at the boardinghouse, but it's still a good place for The Tribe to meet."

"I don't think the three of us could fit in the dugout anymore," Kurt said.

"Yeah, a bit of a tight fit, for sure," said Charlie.

They laughed at the thought.

Over the years their friendship had matured, and their bonds had become stronger. Their fascination with baseball and their beloved Indians was as solid as ever, and they never tired of discussing the ins and outs of each game. And if one of them had a problem or conflict, the other two were always there to help him work it out. They trusted each other completely.

By eighteen, Charlie hadn't gained much in height, but his personality was so dynamic, he seemed much taller than he actually was. In April, he joined the police force and began training with a group of senior officers who administered a verbal exam to determine his responses in certain situations. He passed with the highest possible score. At the time of the exam, one of the officers said, "You're exactly what this department needs. We're lucky you decided to join us." After the written exam, Charlie had no trouble passing the department's physical fitness requirements.

A career in the police department was ideal for Charlie because he liked to play by the rules. Training was intense, but by August, Charlie—along with ninety-eight other uniformed Akron policemen—was walking a beat downtown. When the Akron Police Department named the first Chief of Detectives and assigned twelve men to his team, Charlie decided he wanted to be a detective someday.

Charlie was the first man in his family to join the police force, and although he respected men like his father who got up every morning and went to their office jobs, he knew it would drive him crazy to sit behind a desk all day.

Sitting in The Canal with Kurt and Nickels, Charlie said, "You both know that watching my father fade deeper and deeper into boredom, and ultimately the bottle, was the only catalyst I needed to do something exciting with my life. From that first time my school class visited the police department, I wanted to be a policeman.

"Each day is totally different and definitely never boring. I look forward to going to work every day, even if it is hard work. I have to be alert at all times.

"When I'm on a case, I won't give up until I solve it." He laughed. "The guys at the station have started calling me Bulldog."

Kurt and Nickels got a kick out of that and told him it was the perfect nickname.

✧

Kurt wanted to move out of the boardinghouse, but knew his mother needed his help. When he told his mother he wished he could move out, Marta said, "Kurt, we really need your help here. I hate to say it, but we're getting older. Both of us have arthritis, and we're definitely moving a little more slowly. We're both so tired of the day-to-day routine. We cook, wash dishes, clean, go to market—only to do it all over again. If we didn't have you and Nelly to help us, I don't know what we we'd do."

Kurt said, "You can count on me. You've always been there for me, and I won't leave you when you need me so much. I won't move yet. Working the night shift at the rubber factory and taking a course at Akron University takes up a lot of time. And tuition is expensive, so I guess I really couldn't afford to move out. I suppose it's better to stay put and save the cost of rent."

Over the years, the three of them found a way to live together that was supportive. His mother indulged him. She couldn't help it. After all, he was her only child and the light of her life. She saw his successes as if they were her own. He knew no matter what happened outside the home, he always had a place of safety to come back to. Kurt had even adjusted to his aunt's thorny personality and thought of her as his second mother.

Kurt was one hundred seventy-five pounds of drive and ambition and was determined to rise above the socio-economic class into which he had been born. He continued to deposit every penny he earned into his bank account, and whenever he opened his passbook, he was pleased to see how much he had saved. Unfortunately it wasn't going to be enough to pay for his fulltime college tuition.

Kurt never shirked hard work, but sometimes cut corners to get ahead. And it always involved money. On the golf course, he looked the other way when Cantrell cheated because it meant a bigger tip. When he found some money on the porch of the boardinghouse, instead of giving it to his mother or trying to find out who dropped it, he put it in his pocket. He figured if they were dumb enough to lose it, it wasn't his problem. Down deep he knew it was wrong, but whenever he felt a twinge of conscience, he ignored it.

Grandpa said money was Kurt's god.

Chapter Eight

❖

In 1920, the Cleveland Indians captured their first American League pennant, and Kurt, Nickels, and Charlie could talk of little else. Charlie bounced around with a newspaper in his hand. "Cleveland clinched it. I read all about it in the newspaper. What a gem of a game. Now all we have to do is win the Series."

Getting tickets to any of the World Series games was difficult, and they were amazed when Charlie told them that through a connection in the police department, he had managed to get four tickets to game five. He said, "Who cares if we have nosebleed seats in the bleachers? I'm excited we got tickets. We have to keep our fingers crossed that there will be a fifth game."

On Sunday, October tenth, in a car Nickels borrowed from one of the members at the country club, they headed up to Cleveland's Dunn Field for game five of the World Series.

Charlie invited Antonia, and she was delighted to join her brother and his friends. And although Kurt mentioned it to no one, he was happy Antonia was coming with them. He thought she was as gorgeous as a movie star, and whenever he saw her, he felt an intense wave of attraction. Antonia was only sixteen, and Kurt knew they were too young for anything serious, but that didn't stop him from thinking about her all the time.

Kurt really liked the way she talked, her cheery personality, and how caring she was about everyone around her. She was sweet and kind and would do anything for anybody. One of the things Kurt liked best about her was that she always saw the good in people. She never said a bad word about anyone.

Kurt studied Antonia's flawless skin and pouty lips. Her long, wavy chestnut hair was tied back with a blue ribbon, and curls framed her face and accentuated her beautiful brown eyes. She looked happy and carefree in her pretty yellow dress and blue sweater, and he got a kick out of how she giggled at everything he said. He was completely infatuated.

Antonia had plans to go to college and become a teacher. She told Kurt, "I love books and read all the time. Lately my favorite novelists are Edith Wharton and Thomas Hardy. Do you like to read?"

"Sure. I enjoy a good book. I think it's great you like to read. My mother and aunt only made it through the eighth grade, and the only book they read is the Bible. I love them both, but I appreciate an intelligent, well-read woman."

Antonia said, "Well, I can honestly say, no one has ever called me a woman before."

Kurt was embarrassed, but when Antonia laughed, he laughed along with her.

It was a pleasant day, around seventy degrees with clear skies. The Model-T touring car with its fold-down top and open windows was cranked up and ready to go. Nickels said, "Can you believe we're on our way to a World Series game in Cleveland? I never would have guessed we'd be so lucky to get tickets to the game *and* be able to borrow a Tin Lizzie. This is great."

Filled with deep ruts, the road wasn't any better than a farm road, but they didn't care. They talked and laughed for the entire drive from Akron to Cleveland and only had to stop twice to repair and pump up the tires. At one point, after Kurt got up his courage, he whispered to Antonia, "Toni, I want you to know that someday we're going to be together."

She felt a tingle creep up her body. She always got that feeling when she was around Kurt. She smiled at him and said in a hushed voice, "I'm going to hold you to that."

She thought he was handsome and couldn't believe he was interested in her.

Nickels told them about his job and pen name and informed them he was moving to Cleveland by the end of the month. They were surprised, but happy he was going to do what he wanted. "We'll have a going-away party," Antonia shouted from the back seat.

"We'll miss you, Nickels," Charlie yelled over the loud clattering of the engine's fan belt.

Nickels said, "I'll come home as often as I can. We'll stay in touch and meet at The Canal. It really won't be much different."

Once they got to the stadium, they parked the car and climbed up to their seats. They got hot dogs, peanuts, popcorn, and coca-colas. "This is my definition of a perfect day. I'm at a World Series game in Cleveland with my best pals and the prettiest girl in Akron," said Kurt. "What could be better?"

Antonia blushed.

At the beginning of the game, they spotted Russell Cantrell with his entourage, including his wife Elizabeth and a young woman with auburn hair. Nickels said he had seen her at the country club and thought her name was Marion White. Cantrell didn't see them, and Kurt and Nickels agreed he probably wouldn't have acknowledged them anyway.

Game five was a huge day in Cleveland baseball history. It was a great game, and by the fourth inning, the score was seven to zero with Cleveland leading against the Brooklyn Dodgers. As they sat in the bleachers and watched the game, they witnessed an unassisted triple play by Bill Wambsganss. It was the top of the fifth inning, and runners were on first and second, when Wamby caught a line drive, touched second base, and tagged the runner coming from first base.

Like the rest of the crowd, Kurt, Nickels, Charlie, and Antonia were momentarily stunned. There was complete silence for a few seconds, and then the entire stadium erupted with everyone jumping up and down and screaming. In the midst of spilled snacks and drinks, they grabbed each other and hugged—especially Antonia and Kurt who held on to each other the longest.

Nickels said it for all of them, "This was a once-in-a-lifetime experience, and I can't believe we were here to see it in person. Can you believe the game set three World Series records—the only unassisted triple play, the first grand slam, and the first home run by a pitcher?"

The Dodgers manager was later quoted in the Cleveland newspaper: "I've been in baseball forty years, and I never saw one like this."

Two days later the four of them were over the moon when Cleveland triumphed in game seven and won the World Series.

Antonia's going-away party for her brother never happened.

Chapter Nine

❖

When Albo first started working at the factory, he explained his job to Millie. "The BF Goodrich complex is huge. It's like a big city. Believe it or not, it covers almost forty acres, and there are sixty-five buildings with over one hundred fifty acres of floor space. The factory is so big we have our own fire department, post office, and police station.

"I work in the Vulcanization Department. That's a fancy word for curing. Rubber tires are cured in a high-temperature, high-pressure process. I put the uncured tire into a mold to form the tread and sidewall. Working in the curing department is smelly and dirty, and I have to be careful because there's always a risk of being burned."

On Saturday, October twenty-third, almost two weeks after game five of the World Series, Akron was in the midst of an Indian summer, and the three-hundred-fifty-degree heat of the curing presses transformed the warehouse-sized room into an oven. Add in the heavy, nauseating smell of burning rubber, and working conditions were brutal.

But Albo's mind wasn't on the monotonous and dangerous work. He was thinking of his family and how much better their life was in America. Making the decision to move from Poland to the United States hadn't been easy. He was working two full-time jobs, but it was going to pay off. His children would go to college and never have to work as hard or as much as he did. He was proud of what he and Millie had accomplished.

At the end of his shift, Albo showered and changed into his clean white shirt and pants for his job at the country club kitchen. His factory clothes were impossible to keep clean, and Millie threw them out when they got so dirty she couldn't get the stains out. He had two sets of work clothes for his job in the kitchen, one clean and one dirty. Millie washed a set on her wooden wringer washer every day.

After arriving at Rosewood Hills, Albo made a beeline for the back entrance to the kitchen and dropped a change of clothes into his locker where he had tacked up a sign that Antonia had made for him: "Albo, The World's Best Papa." It made him smile each time he saw it.

The chef was already elbow-deep in what he was preparing for the day's menu. He wasn't a very nice person to work for, but Albo kept to himself and tried to stay out of his way. It wasn't easy work, but it was a snap compared to working at the factory. He washed dishes, mopped floors, peeled potatoes, and did anything else the chef asked him to do.

At the end of the night, exhausted and ready to get home, he caught the last bus about eleven. By the time he got home, he was so tired, he stripped off his clothes and rolled into bed next to Millie. She woke up long enough to give him a kiss and say, "Dobranoc. Kocham cię." *Goodnight. I love you.* He had to get up early the next morning to get to the factory on time.

Russell Cantrell's wealth opened doors and automatically afforded him influence. When he threw money around, he loved seeing people's reactions, like the first time he tipped Kurt. The look on the kid's face was priceless.

Cantrell had trouble establishing and maintaining emotional closeness and used sex to feel validated and complete. Sex was like a drug to him. He experienced a high by acting out his sexual fantasies, and always felt an emotional letdown afterward.

Over the years, he had become a practiced charmer and serial womanizer. Bedding women was his compulsion. He told a woman whatever he thought she wanted to hear and lied so easily, he slipped in and out of double-speak without thinking.

He usually played with a woman for a while and then grew tired of her. Often physically rough, he felt no remorse and rationalized his behavior. Many times he was forced to pay for a woman's silence.

He was having affairs with three women.

One of the women Cantrell was stringing along was Catherine Block, the daughter of a prominent local businessman. She was a petite woman with dark hair and beautiful hazel eyes. When they first met, she was recovering from a broken engagement and was especially vulnerable to his flattery. Catherine was aware he was married, but was so crazy about him that she continued to see him anyway. She believed every word he said because she needed to believe him.

Cantrell was afraid Catherine was head over heels in love with him. "I'm going to have to break it off with her soon. She's getting way too attached. It's a shame, because she's terrific in the bedroom."

That Saturday, Catherine slipped away from her parents and cornered Cantrell. Puffing on his cigar, he loomed over her and had trouble hiding his contempt.

"Russell, please, we need to talk. We have something important to discuss. We have some decisions to make."

"Be quiet or someone will hear us. Will you be here tomorrow?"

She said that she would.

"Then I'll see you tomorrow, and we can talk about whatever you want to then. Now scoot. Hurry back to your parents. I don't want them to see you talking to me." He watched her walk back to her parents and was relieved no one had seen them together. Cantrell was irritated with himself for letting the situation with Catherine get so out of hand.

Chapter Ten

❖

As Cantrell became more successful and well known, he decided
to hire an "assistant" to help with his illegal activities. He had defended
Louis Voigt on an assault and battery case two years before, and they
had been together ever since. Voigt fronted as Cantrell's chauffeur, which
Cantrell thought was the perfect smoke screen.

Voigt, a physically powerful man, stood well over six feet and
always dressed the same—white shirt, black tie, black pants, and black
shoes. Stocky and barrel-chested, he looked as if he were too big for his
own clothes, and his hands were so large he couldn't find a pair of gloves
that fit. He had pointy teeth, slicked-back, mouse-brown hair, and flinty,
close-set eyes. When he spoke, he sounded as if he had something in his
mouth.

Voigt never knew his father, and his mother died when he was eight.
When she died, he was glad she was gone because she beat him all the
time. He had rope-like scars to prove it. After his mother died, the state
of Kentucky sent him to an orphanage where he was horrified to find
the headmistress was meaner than his mother. Miss Kruger finished the
job of instilling in Voigt a lifelong hatred of women.

He hated the orphanage. He hated the other boys. He hated the
food. He hated the faded brown, one-size-too-small overalls he was
required to wear.

And most of all, he hated Kruger. He hated her big nose, her bulging eyes, and how she always licked her lips. And he hated the way her tongue darted in and out of her mouth when she talked.

"Come over here, Louie," she'd say. "I want to check behind your ears." He tried not to look at her mouth. Then she would cuff his ears until he wanted to yell at the top of his lungs. But he didn't. He knew if he made a sound or begged her to stop, the beating would last longer and get much worse.

Sometimes Kruger took her father's old belt off a hook and told him to turn around and pull up his shirt. "If I could take the belt, so can you," she said.

The belt was black and had a large silver buckle with the raised letter "K." She would swing it around in a wide arc and release it, so that when it hit him, it left a deep gash. Between his mother and Miss Kruger's abuse, it was difficult to find a place on his back without a puckered scar. One day when she whirled the belt around, she lost control. She watched it fly through the air and hit him on the side of his head. When he screamed, she was irritated to see the buckle had sliced off the top of his ear, and it was bleeding profusely.

"Goddamn it. Shut up, you idiot. Take this, and hold it really tight on your ear," she said as she handed him a dirty rag. "Sit down over there and don't move. Keep pressure on it." He did what she told him, and when she checked again in about fifteen minutes, the bleeding had stopped, but he had bled all over his clothes.

She haphazardly bandaged it. "That will teach ya, you little prick. Now get outta my sight, and put on clean overalls before anyone sees the blood," she said as she picked up the overalls from a stack on a chair in the corner. She threw them at him and waited for him to undress while she watched.

He vowed to take care of her someday.

Voigt was the orphanage bully, and the other boys had learned to stay out of his way. Sometimes they weren't able to.

One day when Voigt was thirteen, he grabbed a boy named Freddie on the way out of the dining hall. He dragged him over to an alcove under the stairs and pinned him down on the floor. Voigt yelled, "Say it. Tell me you know you're a pussy, and your mother was a whore."

Freddie cried, "Leave me alone." The more he struggled, the more Voigt enjoyed it and wanted to torture him more.

"Say it," he said as he stomped his boot on the back of his neck.

Freddie sobbed and choked out the words, "I'm a pussy, and my mother was a whore. Please, Louis, let me go."

Voigt relished hearing him whimper. "You're so pathetic," he said and then released him.

He didn't know why he wanted to hurt Freddie so much, but told himself Freddie deserved it for being such a coward.

✧

A year later, when he was fourteen, his back raw from the belt after a particularly nasty run-in with Kruger, he decided it was time to take care of her. He waited until the building was quiet, and then pulled the kitchen knife he'd stolen the month before out from underneath his thin mattress.

He crept up the stairs and down the hall to her door and slowly turned the knob. He quietly opened the door. Carefully inching over to her bed, he watched her sleep for a minute and listened to her snore. "You made a big mistake messing with me," he said aloud.

She began to stir, and by the moonlight streaming through her window, she saw Louis standing in front of her. She pulled the covers up under her chin. "What the hell are you doing in here?"

"I'm here to set things straight, you ugly bitch."

"Get out of my room this instant. I'll take care of you in the morning. You're going to regret this. You're in big trouble now."

"No, Kruger, you're the one in big trouble," he sneered. He brought the knife out from behind his back.

When she saw the knife, she gasped, "What the hell?"

He yanked the covers off, and without another word, plunged the knife into her stomach and wrenched it upward. Her back arched, and he heard her gurgle as she tried to get oxygen into her lungs. Her eyes bugged out, and he wondered if she could still see him.

As she took her last breath, he watched her insides spill out onto her bed. A wave of tremendous satisfaction washed over him.

"Now you can never touch me again, you fuckin' dog."

The police were called in to investigate, but no one was able to figure out who killed her. Louis had gotten away with murder.

By the time he was sixteen, Voigt left the orphanage for good. He had numerous run-ins with the law—mostly for petty theft—but somehow always managed to wiggle out of trouble.

When Voigt came to Akron in 1913, he was twenty years old. He knocked about town and worked odd jobs, never finding a place where he belonged. He lived in an abandoned warehouse, and continued to have scrapes with the law, but was able to stay out of jail.

In 1918, Voigt beat up a guy in a bar fight and was arrested for assault and battery. The man was hurt so badly he ended up spending two weeks in the hospital. As Voigt sat in his jail cell, he realized he wasn't going to get off and would have to serve some jail time.

A judge who was a friend of Cantrell's father asked Cantrell to take a look at Voigt's case. When Cantrell walked into the visiting room, he was taken aback by how big Voigt was. Exuding almost palpable anger, Voigt remained seated and didn't offer his hand. He looked up at Cantrell. "What do you want, fancy pants?"

Hearing Cantrell bellow with laughter puzzled Voigt at first. But when Cantrell said, "I think we're going to get along fine," Voigt relaxed.

They talked for close to an hour, and Cantrell agreed to handle his defense. He posted Voigt's bail and cautioned him, "Stay out of the bars. Stay out of trouble. And definitely stay away from alcohol until I can get this settled."

Voigt said, "No problem."

Voigt got no jail time and only two years probation. Over the course of the negotiations with the District Attorney and attorney-client conversations, it began to dawn on Cantrell that Voigt was the kind of man he needed as his assistant. Cantrell had a feeling they would work well together, and he needed someone exactly like him. Cantrell asked Voigt if he would be interested in coming to work for him on the QT. Voigt couldn't believe his good luck and immediately agreed.

Cantrell said, "Ladies and gentlemen, welcome to double trouble."

Voigt laughed and thought, "There's a lot more to this man than his fancy clothes and fat wallet. This is gonna be interesting."

Voigt saw working for Cantrell as his big opportunity. He decided that nothing Cantrell asked him to do would be off limits.

Cantrell still loved getting away with something. It gave him a rush, and was the next best thing to sex. Cantrell had cheated many people over the years, but had been careful to cover his tracks. So far he'd been lucky not to get caught. He figured with Voigt on board, he could continue his dirty tricks, and his chances of getting caught would be much less likely because he could always make Voigt the patsy.

Voigt hated the police and looked forward to working for Cantrell and pulling one over on them.

Grandpa Nicky said Cantrell and Voigt together were a deadly combination.

Chapter Eleven

❖

*K*urt had caddied for Cantrell since that first time in May. Between working part-time at the factory and caddying, he was earning more money than he ever thought possible. He was making a lot more than he could have running errands at the boardinghouse.

On Sunday, October twenty-fourth, Kurt headed out the back door. "Where are you going?" his mother asked. "We need some help today."

"Mama, I'm sorry, but I can't today. I'm caddying for Mr. Cantrell, and I'm running late. It's terrific money, and my bank account is really growing. I'm working hard to save enough to go to college full-time."

"What does a big boy like you need with more schooling? Erna thinks you're old enough to work in the factory full time."

"Mama, it doesn't matter to me what Aunt Erna thinks, or what anyone else thinks for that matter. What's important is what I want, and you can tell Aunt Erna I'm going to college and law school, and I *will* be a lawyer some day."

Marta hesitated, and then said, "Okay. If that's what you want, I'm behind you, but you're going to have to help us around here. We can't handle it without you."

"Of course I will. You don't ever have to worry about that. I'll help you as soon as I get home this afternoon."

Marta sighed, "I think Mr. Cantrell is such a nice man. You're lucky he's taken such an interest in you."

"Trust me, Mama, he isn't always so nice. There's another side to him, but I don't let it bother me. Goodbye, Mama," he yelled as the door slammed behind him.

The sun was out, and it was a perfect day for golf. The temperature was unseasonably warm and was expected to reach eighty degrees. Everyone at the country club was happy to be outside on what was sure to be one of the last good golfing days of the season.

By the time Kurt got to the country club, it was late morning. As soon as he got to the caddy shack, he noticed Cantrell excitedly waving him over. "Shake a leg, kid. I have a match to win." Kurt picked up his golf bag and followed him to the first tee where the men in Cantrell's regular foursome were already standing. "I shouldn't play today, because I have to prepare for court tomorrow morning. Damn it all, I'll have to go to the office tonight," Cantrell mumbled.

"Christ, he's in a terrible mood," Kurt thought.

Cantrell said, "Double the bet, gentlemen?" The men in his foursome agreed. They chatted while they waited for the foursome in front of them to move ahead so they could tee off.

One of the caddies approached Kurt. "I guess your guy lost big in last night's poker game. I heard he was furious and stomped out of the game room in a big huff. Your buddy has a temper, especially when he's been drinking." Kurt barely acknowledged him. He didn't think it was a good idea to discuss Cantrell with the other caddies. But after learning why Cantrell was in such a bad mood and that he had a hangover, he thought it was a good idea to stay out of his way as much as possible.

Cantrell's game fell apart on the front nine, and no matter how hard he tried to concentrate, he couldn't get it back together. By the eighteenth tee, he and his partner were down by five. Cantrell rarely spoke during the round, and Kurt studied him. "Boy oh boy, he sure hates to lose. I'm surprised I can't see steam coming off his head."

Cantrell and his partner lost the last hole, and after they walked off the green, Cantrell counted out the money to pay off the bet. He threw some cash on the ground in front of Kurt and grunted, "See you next time." Kurt guessed Cantrell had a lot on his mind, and was sure it wasn't golf. When he picked the money up and counted it, he realized Cantrell had only given him ten bucks. "Crap. I know my tip depends on how well he plays, but I was really hoping for a good tip today."

Trailing behind Cantrell on the way up to the clubhouse, Kurt shouted, "Better luck next time, sir." Cantrell turned around and frowned. "Don't throw platitudes at me, kid. I don't like it."

Cantrell entered the Fountain Grille and sat down with his foursome to have a drink. He sure needed it. "Thank God the law exempts whatever inventory the club had on hand the day Prohibition went into effect. Damn those teetotalers. What a pain in the ass."

Kurt went to the main kitchen to say hello to Albo. Nickels was working in Cleveland, and Kurt missed hanging out with him after caddying for Cantrell. Albo was busy and asked him if he would do him a big favor by taking some silverware up to the Grille. Kurt was happy to help him out, and besides, he enjoyed wandering around the country club.

When he got to the Grille, a young woman with tears streaming down her face ran by him. He thought he recognized her as Catherine Block, the daughter of one of the members. He looked over and saw Cantrell sitting at a table next to where Catherine had been sitting with her friends.

Kurt gave the silverware to the headwaiter. He saw Cantrell get up from his table and head off in the same direction as Catherine. When Cantrell passed Kurt, he looked directly at him and waved him aside as if he were a nuisance.

Kurt thought, "Where's the fire? He's sure in a big hurry."

Cantrell was having what he thought was a casual affair with Catherine. He knew she was in love with him, and now she told him she was pregnant. It would be a disaster if anyone were to find out. He was going to sever all contact with her and try to convince her to have an abortion. Earlier he asked her to meet him out by the ninth fairway to discuss what they were going to do. He knew everyone would be off the course by then.

When he joined her, she said, "I hate it when you ignore me. You wouldn't even look at me in there. You can be so mean, Russell."

"I don't want anyone to know we are together, Catherine. You know that's all it is."

Catherine had been hounding Cantrell about what he intended to do about the baby. She refused to get rid of it and insisted he divorce Elizabeth and marry her. He could see she was already worked up.

"Catherine, please. Let's discuss this calmly."

"It's easy for you to be calm. You're not the one who is pregnant. Why won't you agree to leave Elizabeth and marry me? You don't even have children with her," she screamed.

He tried to remain calm, but was disgusted with her for getting pregnant. "I can't do that Catherine. It would ruin my career. But don't worry. You know I'll take care of you. We'll figure something out."

"What's there to figure out? I'm going to have a baby, and I want to be married to my child's father. I've told absolutely no one I've been seeing you and I'm pregnant because it's what you wanted. But now I'm giving you three days to decide what you're going to do. Leave your wife or I'll tell my parents everything. And believe me, Russell, I'll tell them *everything*." The more she talked, the more provoked he became.

"I told you I will work something out. You need to start thinking about an abortion. I'll take care of whatever it costs," he hissed. "But we have to get out of here. *Now*. No one can see us together. Move over here, out of sight," he said as he put his hand on her arm. He had been so careful to keep this affair under wraps and was enraged that he had to handle this complication.

Something caught his eye. Just inside the woods on the edge of the fairway was a club someone had neglected to put back in his golf bag.

Instantly, he knew what he had to do. He slowly led her into the woods.

Catherine said, "Russell, I absolutely refuse to have an abortion. I already love our baby."

When she covered her face with her hands and began to sob, he leaned down and grabbed the golf club. He swung it toward her as hard as he could and heard a loud crack as it hit the side of her head. Her face registered utter amazement as a blaze of excruciating pain shot through her. She collapsed to the ground. Cantrell leaned over her and swung the club over and over again. When he finally stopped, the only sound was the hum of the nighttime bugs.

He dragged her farther into the woods and walked away. "That takes care of that problem."

As he made his way back to the clubhouse, he felt relieved. All that was left to do was some clean up, and his man Voigt could handle that.

He entered the men's locker room and felt luck was with him when he saw no one was there. He examined his clothes and saw blood had spattered all over his shirt and pants. He quickly changed into clean clothes he kept in his locker and wiped the blood off his shoes with some towels. He stuffed the bloody clothes, towels, and golf club back into his locker.

As he was leaving, he literally ran into Kurt. "Oh, it's you. Sorry, Kurt. I'm late for dinner with my wife and have to dash."

Kurt thought Cantrell was acting strange. He had never seen

Cantrell sweat so much. "I thought you had to work."

"Where'd you get that idea? I'm going out to dinner with Elizabeth."

Kurt decided not to tell Cantrell that he got the idea when he said it on the first tee that morning.

In the Grille, Cantrell rejoined his foursome. He ordered another bourbon and slugged it back. The drink calmed him, and he said, "Sorry, but I have to get going. I'm late for dinner with Elizabeth and have to hurry to make it on time." He said goodbye and nonchalantly walked out.

Cantrell figured the Polack who worked in the kitchen was the perfect scapegoat for the murder. He barely spoke English, and Cantrell knew no one would believe him when he said he didn't do it.

Voigt was waiting for him in the parking lot. After listening to Cantrell's instructions, he trudged down to the woods, picked up Catherine Block's body, and threw her over his shoulder. Making sure no one was around to see him, he walked to the back of the pool house and tossed her behind a tall hedge as if she were a sack of flour.

He walked to the back entrance of the men's locker room and stood where no one could see him. As soon as he was sure no one was in the locker room, he hurried in and took the bloody towels and clothes out of Cantrell's locker. He put them in a bag and slid the golf club up under his jacket.

While Kurt waited for the bus, he saw Voigt get into the car where Cantrell was already sitting. He wondered where Voigt had been. They sped right past him and never made eye contact.

No one other than Kurt had seen Voigt.

In the car Voigt said, "All done. I'll come back later to finish."

Cantrell said, "I'm glad that's taken care of. Drop me off now. Wipe the golf club down so we don't leave any fingerprints. And don't forget to destroy the clothes you took out of my locker."

Voigt said, "Consider it done, done, and done."

Cantrell said, "That Becker kid watched us as we drove out. I ran into him in the locker room. I hope he's not going to put two and two together."

"Do you want me to take care of him?"

"Oh God, no. That's all we need. Two murders right on top of each other, and both connected to the country club. No, we'll have to deal with Becker in another way."

Around midnight, Voigt snuck into the country club by the back service entrance. He picked the lock to the door of the staff lockers and planted the bloodied club and towels in Albo's locker. "Good thing he has a sign on his locker. That's one more Polack out of the way," he muttered. "Like Russell says, if the cops have a suspect, they'll never look for anyone else."

Chapter Twelve

❖

On Monday morning, a grounds keeper discovered Catherine Block's body. The police were notified and arrived en masse. The Pro Shop provided a list of member tee times from Sunday, and police interviewed each member who played that afternoon. No one saw anything.

They also interviewed the staff who worked that day. Their search for evidence included the clubhouse, the pool house and grounds, and the parking lot. The one place they didn't search was the golf course. Instead, they mistakenly assumed she was killed near the clubhouse or pool house.

They talked to each of the women who participated in a tennis tournament with the victim on Sunday. They said Catherine seemed really upset about something, but none of them knew what it was. One woman said, "She was very quiet during the match and played horribly, which wasn't like her. We knew something was wrong, and we asked her about it, but she refused to tell us. She said we would find out about it soon, and she hoped to have some exciting news to tell us."

When they talked to the men in Cantrell's foursome, each of them said they were puzzled by the brutality of the crime. One of the men said, "Who would do something like this? From what I could tell, she was a very nice person, always friendly and pleasant.

"This is a tragedy and reflects poorly on our club. How can

we attract new members if things like this happen here?"

Cantrell was looking forward to talking to the police. He thought it was going to be fun. They asked him if he saw anything unusual on the previous afternoon, and whether he had any thoughts on who would want to murder her.

"Not really. I didn't know her other than to see her here with her parents. I played a lousy round of golf yesterday, had a drink, and then left for dinner with my wife. I did notice a few of the kitchen staff standing outside the back door." He was pleased to hear they were in the process of searching the employee lockers.

"Is there anything else you need from me? I'm happy to help in any way I can."

"No sir, you're free to go."

As Cantrell walked away, the policeman heard him laugh and was puzzled by how odd it was. He wondered what humor Cantrell could possibly find in the situation.

The police searched the employee lockers, and it didn't take long to find the bloody towels and golf club tucked in the back of Albo's locker.

"Over here," one of the officers shouted. "Looks like we found what we're looking for." The officer jerked Antonia's sign off the front of the locker. "Albo, The World's Best Papa." He waved it at the detective walking over. "We've got a real family man on our hands."

"Get someone in here who can tell me who the hell this Albo character is," the detective growled.

They learned it was Albert Jablonski's locker and that he was working the morning shift at the rubber factory. They left immediately to arrest him.

The police had already established that David Hawkins had reported a missing golf club on Sunday afternoon. They interviewed

Hawkins again, showed him the club, and asked if it was his. He said it wasn't. Afraid they would think he was the murderer, he chose not to tell them that it was his missing golf club. The officers took him at his word.

✧

At midday, four policemen arrived at the factory and were directed to the curing department. Albo looked up and saw the police talking to the foreman who was pointing in his direction. As they strode toward him, he wondered what was going on. Everyone in the room was looking at him.

"Albert Jablonski?"

"Yes, I am Albert Jablonski," Albo said in heavily accented English.

"Step away from what you are doing." Albo moved away from the equipment and was sure he heard them say, "Albert Jablonski, you are under arrest for the murder of Miss Catherine Block."

He couldn't believe what he was hearing. "What you talking about? I never murder nobody. You have wrong person."

"No, we definitely have the right person."

Albo was bewildered and frightened. "I want my son. He know what to do."

"We'll have someone inform him after we get you processed and locked up." Albo was wearing overalls with no shirt, the standard clothing for most of the men in the department. One of the officers shoved him and told him to put his shirt on.

Albo reacted instinctively and pushed back. In seconds, four policemen were on top of him trying to restrain him. He screamed, "Spadaj. Zostaw mnie w spokoju." *Get off. Leave me alone.*

"What the hell is he saying?" said one officer.

Another said, "Not a clue, but this guy is strong. Four of us against one, and we still had trouble getting control. Now stand up and turn around, Jablonski. We expect you to cooperate."

They cuffed him and informed him they found the bloody towels and the golf club stashed in his locker at Rosewood Hills.

"Geez, it's freakin' hot in this stink hole," said one of the cops. "Come on, make it fast. I wanna get outta here."

They led a dazed Albo out of the factory.

Two policemen were sent to the Jablonski home. When Millie saw them walking up the front steps, she was scared to death Albo had been hurt at the factory.

She opened the door to the two police officers standing on the front steps. "Mrs. Albert Jablonski?"

"Yes, I am Mrs. Jablonski." Antonia heard the fear in her mother's voice and came to the front hall. "What is it, Mama? Who's at the door?"

Millie moved aside and Antonia saw the policemen.

"Officer, my mother doesn't speak English very well. I'll translate for her. Is something wrong?"

"We're looking for Albert Jablonski, Jr. Is he here?"

"No. He's in Cleveland. What is this about?"

"Tell your mother she needs to come down to the jail with us. We've arrested your father."

Antonia couldn't believe what she heard. She quickly translated, and Millie said in English, "What? What he arrested for? What are they saying, Antonia?"

They told her he'd been arrested for murder and about the evidence they'd found in his locker. Antonia explained in Polish what the police had said. Millie grabbed Antonia for support. "It is a lie. Not my Albo.

"We must be strong, Mama."

To the police she said, "I'm going to contact my brother, so he can get down here from Cleveland. It may take him a few hours, but I don't think my mother and I can handle this without him. When he gets here, the three of us will come to the jail."

She hated to leave her father alone for so long, but Millie was in no condition to go to the jail without Nickels, and Antonia didn't want to leave her alone.

When Millie, Antonia, and Nickels arrived at Summit County Jail, it was almost dark. Built near the turn of the century, the brick building on South High Street was three stories high and housed the Summit County Jail, the Akron Police Department, and Akron's Municipal Court.

A police officer escorted Albo into a room where the family was waiting. He was handcuffed and looked confused. And he had dark purple bruises on his face and neck. A policeman stood in the corner while the family talked. Nickels wasn't concerned about what they said because they spoke in Polish.

Millie hugged Albo, and wouldn't let go. Antonia put her arms around her father. For his sake, she refused to cry.

Albo said, "I did nothing. I don't know what they're talking about. I didn't murder anyone. The police marched into the factory, and in front of all the other workers, they arrested me. They humiliated me by pushing me to the floor and handcuffing me. I was so confused, and I didn't understand what they were talking about. Why is this happening? This is America. This shouldn't happen here," he said as he looked down at the floor.

Nickels said, "Papa, look at me. We know you. We know you didn't kill that girl. And it's beyond comprehension that anyone else would think you did. But you must not say anything to anyone until I can locate a lawyer for you. Can you do that?"

"Yes, but they tried to make me say I did it. They wanted me to say I killed her." It was the first time Nickels had ever heard his father raise his voice.

Millie looked at Nickels as if to say, "What do we do now?"

Nickels said, "Say absolutely nothing, Papa. Trust me, it's important to wait until we have an attorney."

The officer told them their time was up. They hugged and held onto each other until the cop said, "Come on, Jablewski, move it."

Nickels snapped, "It's *Jablonski*."

"Whatever it is, Jablewski, Jablonski, it's all the same to me."

Nickels was disgusted.

Antonia said, "Be strong, Papa. We love you. We'll come again tomorrow."

Grandpa Nicky said after he left the jail, as soon as he was alone, he cried like a baby.

Chapter Thirteen

❖

*A*fter Albo was arrested, Nickels asked around town for the best local defense attorney, and the same name kept coming up. William Oxnard. Oxnard had a reputation as someone who refused to lose. He was methodical, thorough, and prided himself on his integrity. Word was he would never do anything underhanded to win a case. Nickels learned Oxnard was an outstanding attorney who was honest, professional, and tenacious.

When Nickels contacted him about defending his father, he explained that his father was innocent and wanted to vigorously defend himself at trial.

When they got around to discussing payment arrangements, Nickels was shocked to hear how much Oxnard's fee was. "That's more than we can pay at one time. I don't know how we can manage it, but we'll work something out."

"I always take financial circumstances into account and often allow clients to pay in installments. There's no reason why I can't make the same kind of arrangement for your family."

They talked it over, and Oxnard agreed to let the Jablonskis pay monthly until the debt was settled.

Nickels thanked him and said, "Unfortunately, it's going to take us a long time."

"I don't see that as a problem, as long as you pay it."

It was a lot of money, but Nickels was relieved to have a defense attorney with such a good reputation.

Oxnard and Nickels went to the jail to talk with Albo. When the guard brought him into the room, Oxnard noticed Albo looked him directly in the eye. Over the years, Oxnard had learned to trust his instincts, and he sensed Albo was a proud man. His initial, gut feeling was that Albert Jablonski was innocent.

"I want to hear what you have to say, and then we can decide together how to proceed."

When Albo tried to explain what happened in broken English, he got so upset, he started to talk rapidly in Polish. Nickels put his hand on his father's shoulder and asked him to slow down. "It would be easier on my father if he spoke Polish. I'll translate."

Albo explained he had no idea how the incriminating evidence got in his locker, and although Albo had nothing to say that would help in his defense, Oxnard believed him.

"My first reaction is that you're taking the heat for someone else. It's way too pat." Oxnard stood up to leave. "Mr. Jablonski, I'm going to review the evidence tonight, and then I'll come back tomorrow, and we'll discuss your situation further. But you must listen to me. Under no circumstances are you to speak to anyone without me present. Do you understand?"

Nick translated, and Albo nodded. "Tak."

They met again the next day, and Oxnard asked Albo to go over everything again. While Albo talked, Oxnard watched him intently. The attorney had thought about it overnight. He wasn't sure why he believed Albo so completely, especially because nothing specific supported his innocence. But Oxnard was convinced that Albo was a gentle man who would never hurt anyone. Despite the fact that he wasn't a person of substance, he had a presence about him that commanded respect.

"The fact that someone has gone to great lengths to make you the fall guy for this murder really bothers me, and we're not going to let him get away with it," said Oxnard. "I'll take your case, and I'll do my damnedest to make sure we either get the charges dropped or get an acquittal."

When Albo heard what the attorney said, his shoulders relaxed.

Oxnard recognized it was going to be a high-profile case. With a prominent businessman's daughter as the victim and a Polish immigrant as the defendant, every detail was going to play out in the press. This case was going to be a career-maker and possibly bring him national recognition. On the way out of the jail, he made a snap decision. "Nickels, I'm going to take your father's case on a pro bono basis. I believe he's being railroaded, and we're going to prove he is innocent."

Nick couldn't believe it. "I can't tell you how much this means to me and my family. I'm overwhelmed by your offer. My mother and sister will be so relieved we don't have to scrape the money together. As it stands, we've lost the income from both my father's jobs. We have talked of little else and had no idea how we were going to find the money to retain you. Mr. Oxnard, on behalf of my father and my family, I can't thank you enough."

"Please. Call me Bill. Now go tell your mother and sister about our arrangement, and when you see your father tomorrow, tell him we're going to get him out of there. Let me start by talking with the police. Then I'll talk to the members and staff of the country club. We'll get together again within a few days. How long will you be in Akron?"

"The *News Tribune* gave me two weeks off to deal with what I told them was a personal family matter. After that, I'll make the trip from Cleveland as often as I can."

"Okay, good, that will give us enough time to begin formulating our strategy. What I'm going to do now is see about bail, so we can get your father out."

At the bail hearing, Albo stood up and waited to hear how long it would take before they released him. He was amazed to hear the judge say, "Bail is denied. The prisoner will await trial at Summit County Jail. The trial is set to begin November fifteenth."

Oxnard objected, but the judge refused to budge. "Your client is charged with a brutal murder, and the court believes because he has family in Poland, he is a flight risk."

"Your Honor, Mr. Jablonski has no money for a ticket, and his wife and children are here in Akron. There is no chance he will attempt to flee."

The judge shook his head. "I'm sorry, but they're going to have to visit him in jail. Next case."

Albo startled at the sound of the gavel. Oxnard steadied him, and whispered, "I'm going to see what I can do about this. Be patient."

But Oxnard wouldn't be able to do anything. Cantrell had already gotten to the judge.

✧

The week of the murder and Albo's arrest, Cantrell told Kurt he had a surprise for him. "I'm going to stop by the boardinghouse next Saturday afternoon around two. I have something I want to discuss with you. Make sure your mother and aunt are there.

"What's this about?"

Cantrell winked at him. "Listen, kid, don't ask so many questions. Set it up for next Saturday, and you'll find out then. I can tell you this much—you won't be disappointed."

"Why such a secret?"

Cantrell didn't answer. He was perturbed he had to make sure Kurt kept his mouth shut. He would rather get rid of the kid, but if there were another murder that could be connected to someone at the country club so soon after the girl, it would look suspicious. He didn't want the authorities looking more closely at Catherine's murder. But he also thought because Kurt lied for him in the past, he might be useful in the future.

Marta and Erna were flustered about having such an important man come to Stucke House. "I wonder what he wants," Marta said to her sister. "I'm surprised he's willing to come to this part of town."

"What's wrong with where we live? This is a perfectly nice neighborhood. Why wouldn't he want to come and visit us after all the time he spends with Kurt? I'm looking forward to meeting him."

"Me too, but we have an awful lot to do to get ready for his visit. What should we bake for him? Should we have coffee or tea? Maybe we should have both." Marta was so excited she couldn't stop talking.

For five days, Marta and Erna cleaned the house from top to bottom, paying special attention to the common rooms where they planned to visit with Cantrell. They beat the rugs and put fresh doilies on the tables. They baked several kinds of cookies and two pies—apple and strawberry-rhubarb. Signs went up in the kitchen and on the bathroom doors. "No one is permitted in the parlor or first-floor lavatory on Saturday from two o'clock to four o'clock."

When Cantrell arrived, the smell of his cigar preceded him into the parlor.

"So nice to finally meet you, Mr. Cantrell," Marta said as she waved away the cloud of smoke. "We've heard so much about you." She thought he was extremely handsome.

He was unconcerned that the smoke bothered her. "It's my pleasure, Mrs. Becker. I'm looking forward to having some of the Stucke House baking I hear so much about."

Marta giggled.

Erna came in from the kitchen, introduced herself, and placed a tray with an assortment of baked goods on the table next to the coffee pot. Erna told Cantrell they made everything especially for him. "I assure you I'm flattered," he said.

The sisters were so discombobulated neither could stop chattering. Cantrell thought they were two of the silliest women he had ever met. And he couldn't believe how fat they both were.

Erna bustled back into the kitchen and returned with cream and sugar. Marta asked what everyone wanted.

Cantrell said, "You wouldn't have some whiskey for a thirsty man, would you?"

Erna gasped and unconsciously touched the temperance ribbon pinned on her dress. Marta quickly said they didn't serve liquor, but she would be happy to make him a Welch's grape juice highball. He stared at her in disbelief. "No thanks, he said. "I'll settle for some coffee, thank you. Cream and sugar, please."

Marta served the coffee, and no one spoke. The four of them looked at each other for a long, awkward pause. Marta and Erna fidgeted. Kurt broke the silence by asking Cantrell if was planning to play in the President's Cup, the last golf tournament of the season.

"If I have time to work it in, I will. But let's talk about something your mother and aunt can understand. Let me guess. Neither of you is a golfer, isn't that right?"

Marta and Erna tittered and Erna said, "We've never even been on a golf course."

"You'll have to join me and my wife sometime for dinner at the country club. I think you'd like it there. The food in the dining room is better than most restaurants in town." What he really thought was, "I wouldn't be caught dead with either of them."

"We'd love that," said Marta. "How kind of you to offer. But we have so much work here at the boardinghouse, it's almost impossible to get away. Akron has grown so fast, and we're filled to capacity."

Erna chimed in. "With a bunch of snakes from Appalachia."

Kurt interrupted, "Aunt Erna, please."

Erna glared at him.

Cantrell laughed. "It's all right. I can't stand the hillbillies. To tell you the truth, I think all these people pouring into Akron are a real problem. You can't go anywhere without bumping into them. We're getting lost in a sea of immigrants and Appalachians. We have to remember we're a country of white Protestants. We have to stick together and protect who we are and what we stand for.

"After all, we're the 'real Americans.'"

"I'm so glad to hear someone as important as yourself say that," said Erna. "But I don't know what we can do about it."

Cantrell shook his head and said, "It's a real problem, but we'll have to discuss it another time. I don't have much time today, and I want to get to the reason I'm here."

The sisters sat up a little straighter.

Cantrell began. "Kurt may have told you my family contributes to causes and individuals we think are worthy. When you're as well off as we are, it's important to help those who aren't as fortunate."

Erna and Marta were sitting so still Kurt thought they looked like statues.

Cantrell continued, "Let me get right to the point. I came by today to explain how I'm going to help Kurt, as well as the two of you."

Kurt hoped he knew where this was going.

"I intend to pay for Kurt's college education and eventually law school, if that's what he wants. I also want to pay off the boardinghouse mortgage and provide some funds to fix up Stucke House, which needs some paint and general upkeep. You're both widowed, and Kurt has told me how hard you work. I think with help from the Cantrell Foundation, your lives can be a little easier."

Marta was completely overcome. Erna was equally stunned and for once, had nothing to say.

Kurt spoke first. "As you can see, we're completely overwhelmed. There are no words to express our gratitude." This was so much more than he had hoped for. He turned to his mother and aunt and said, "What do you have to say?"

Marta and Erna both spoke at once, "We're so grateful. Thank you. Thank you. God bless you. You're a good man." They never stopped to think how strange and out of the blue his generous offer was.

They discussed the details further, and Cantrell asked Marta and Erna to provide him with the proper papers the following week, and then he would go to the bank and take care of the mortgage.

He explained he had already spoken to Student Account Services at Akron University and would pay Kurt's tuition directly to the college. When Kurt decided where he wanted to go to law school, he would make arrangements to pay the tuition the same way. "But," he told Kurt, "there is one condition. When you finish law school and pass the bar, you'll work for me. You can have your own practice, but I'll be your principal client. Do you agree?"

"Of course, but I need to know the specific details."

"Already thinking like a lawyer. Good for you. I'll send a contract over, so you have all the information you need to make a final decision. All you have to do is sign, and your education is taken care of."

Kurt couldn't believe he was going to get everything he ever wanted. A college education and law school would open doors to the kind of life he had always dreamed of. He couldn't wait to tell Antonia.

After Cantrell left, Marta and Erna danced in circles around the parlor. They were dizzy with excitement. "This is a gift from God," Erna exclaimed as she clapped her hands together. "I never thought in a million years anything like this would ever happen to us."

Marta said, "Sissy, this is unbelievable. How did we get so lucky?"

"I don't know, but I thank the Lord for our good fortune. Thank goodness our Kurt had the opportunity to caddy for Mr. Cantrell and make such an impression on him."

They decided one of the first things they were going to do was have the house wired for electricity. Marta also insisted they buy some new furniture and paint the house as Cantrell had suggested. They went on for hours about how they were going to spend the money.

Kurt was happy for them, and although he was relieved, he was a bit more pensive. Later, Marta asked, "Why aren't you turning cartwheels, Kurt?" This is more than we could have ever asked for."

"I'm thrilled, Mama. I can't believe I can enroll in college full time and never have to worry about how to pay for law school. Of course it's wonderful."

He didn't want to dampen their enthusiasm. They deserved to be happy. But he wondered about the timing of the offer. He had only known Cantrell a few short months, and Kurt thought it was strange he had made such a substantial contribution to his family. He wondered if something specific prompted Cantrell's generosity, but didn't want to dwell on it or jinx whatever luck had come their way.

When Kurt told Charlie and Nickels about Cantrell's magnanimous offer, Charlie said, "Congratulations Kurt, I'm really happy for you and your family."

Nickels was silent. He was happy for Kurt, but at the moment could think of nothing but his father. He was frantic to find a way to prove his father was being framed.

Kurt said, "Nickels, I know you're upset about your father. We all are. But aren't you happy for me?"

"Well, of course I am, but there's something about Cantrell that bothers me. I'm not sure what it is, but there's something…below the surface."

"You may be right, but I'm not going to question it. Nothing is going to ruin this for me."

Grandpa said, "Kurt thought he was getting everything he ever wanted, but what he didn't realize was he had made a deal with the devil."

Chapter Fourteen

❖

*T*he decadent society of the 1920s worshipped wealth and status. Russell Cantrell dressed and played the part of an upstanding, philanthropic citizen contributing to society. In addition to his law practice, he had forged a career in finance, making a fortune as a stock market and commodity investor and investing in real estate and a diverse range of industries.

But he was leading a double life. He wore no diamond rings or gangster clothing, but he was a hoodlum at heart.

Cantrell knew Oxnard by reputation and had met him briefly a couple of times. He knew he was fearless when it came to defending his clients, and Cantrell was concerned that when Oxnard delved into the evidence, it wouldn't hold up to intense scrutiny. He looked up Oxnard's court schedule, and the day after the bail hearing, Voigt intercepted Oxnard on his way out of the courthouse.

"Come with me," Voigt demanded as he towered over Oxnard and pointed toward the back of the building. "This way."

"Who are you? I don't know you, so why in the world would I follow you?" Oxnard wondered who this large man was. He could barely understand him. He sounded as if he had pebbles in his mouth.

"I'm Russell Cantrell's chauffeur. He wants to speak to you. Come with me."

"Why didn't you say so?"

He followed Voigt around to the back of the building. "Why are we behind the courthouse?" Cantrell opened the back door of the car, and motioned Oxnard to get in. They shook hands and formally introduced themselves. Oxnard began to praise him and all the work he had done on behalf of others and the city of Akron.

Cantrell cut him short. "I'll get right to the point. You're going to get Albert Jablonski to plead guilty to the murder of Catherine Block."

"What? I am most certainly *not* going to do that. I believe he's innocent and already have people looking into the shoddy evidence. I believe the evidence was planted in his locker by the real killer, and we're going to prove it."

"No you're not. You're going to do what I tell you. Because if you don't, I'll ruin your reputation. I think you know I have the power and connections to do it."

"My God, Cantrell, you can't be serious. You're a respectable man. Why would you do this?"

"Why is not your concern, but you'll do what I say, or I will make your life miserable. And to make sure you cooperate, I'm giving you a large sum of money. Consider it a bribe. Voigt will deliver a package filled with cash to you as soon as we hear Jablonski has pled guilty, and you'll sign for it. It's my insurance policy."

Oxnard was confused. "First of all, why do you want me to make sure he goes to jail? Obviously, it makes me wonder if you had something to do with that poor girl's murder. Secondly, I'm not going to do what you want. It's not right. Jablonski is innocent. I'm sure of it. You can't browbeat me into doing this, because I'm an honest man, and this is preposterous. I'm getting out of the car now, and we'll forget we ever had this conversation."

Cantrell had a funny smile on his face and motioned to Voigt. "Show him how serious we are."

Voigt grinned. He grabbed Oxnard by the neck. At the same time, he twisted Oxnard's little finger backward until they heard the bone crack. With Voigt's vice-like hand wrapped around his neck, Oxnard couldn't breathe. Voigt released him right before he passed out.

When Oxnard caught sight of the look in Cantrell's eyes, he realized how crazy he was.

He shrieked with pain. "You broke my finger. Oh my God, you're both deranged."

"That's just a little taste of what we can do to you. And if that isn't convincing enough, I can always have Voigt pay a visit to your lovely family." He stopped talking long enough for Oxnard to digest what he had said.

Oxnard kept shaking his head and saying, "I won't do it. You must think about what you're doing. Leave my family out of this."

"Let's go for a little drive, Louis. I think he needs some further persuasion."

They drove away from the courthouse. Cantrell waited for a few minutes and then said, "Maybe we'll grab your little blond daughter outside that fancy private school you send her to. She's quite a pretty thing. Louis would love to spend some time with her, wouldn't you, Louis?"

Oxnard was speechless and kept shaking his head back and forth. "I can't believe this is happening. Please don't hurt my family."

Cantrell was enjoying Oxnard's reaction. "We watched your boy yesterday. We can snatch him any time we want. I personally don't want to harm your family, but Voigt would take great pleasure in hurting them. Perhaps I should tell you exactly what he'd do to them."

Oxnard was in shock. He sputtered, "Isn't there some arrangement we could come to?"

Cantrell said, "You have thirty seconds to agree to my demands, or we drive to your house and get your wife."

"No, please stop. It's against everything I believe in, but I'll do whatever you say to keep my family safe."

"I knew you'd agree." Cantrell's laugh was maniacal.

They drove back to the rear of the courthouse, and Cantrell shoved Oxnard out of the car. He leaned his head out the window. "I won't warn you again. If you try to cross me, I promise Voigt will come after your family."

As the car sped away, William Oxnard began to shake. "I'm so sorry, Albo. To save my own family, I have to ruin you and yours." Oxnard threw up on the side of the street. He was devastated that he was forced to throw the case, but when Cantrell threatened his family, he had no choice. He was powerless.

He had to do whatever it took to protect his wife and children.

His reputation was well earned, but he didn't care about it now. And for an honest man like Oxnard, it was anathema to accept Cantrell's bribe. He would stash the money somewhere and never touch it, not even a dollar.

Oxnard went to visit Albo in jail. He dreaded the meeting, but knew it had to be done. Albo entered the attorney-client room with a big smile on his face. "You have good news, yes?"

Oxnard asked him to sit down. "Albo, I have carefully weighed the evidence they have against you and have spoken at great length to the District Attorney. I'm afraid we are in quite a bind. The evidence is solid. I have gone over and over the evidence and tried to find a way to defend you, but in my opinion, there is no way around it. I believe you were framed, but if we go to trial, you will most certainly be convicted. In my estimation, the odds of an acquittal are next to nothing.

"I have a recommendation—plead guilty to second-degree murder. The District Attorney has agreed to a sentence of twenty-five years. If you stay out of trouble in prison, your first opportunity to come before the Parole Board will be in ten years."

Albo was very quiet.

Oxnard continued, "I have tried on several occasions to get the District Attorney to lessen the charge to manslaughter, which would mean less jail time and an earlier release, but the DA refuses." Oxnard didn't know that the DA played poker with Cantrell once a week.

Albo felt down deep it was futile to fight it. He knew he was the fall guy and didn't like the plea deal, but ultimately decided to agree to it for his family's sake. Albo didn't want his children affected by a long, drawn-out trial that ended in a conviction and possibly a life sentence. After much deliberation and discussion with Oxnard, Albo agreed to plead guilty.

Albo explained in broken English, "I trust you, and believe you have done your best. Do not tell family this talk. I not want them to know what we say. I no talk good English, and my children be shamed in public. I will not let happen. Better for my family no trial."

After the agreement was signed, he worried about how his family would react and what he would say to them. They were going to be angry.

Oxnard was distressed that he deceived Albo. It went against everything he stood for, and he could think of little else. He refused to take on any other capital cases and began to think about whether he could continue to practice the law.

When Nickels, Antonia, and Millie visited Albo, he told them he had pled guilty and had agreed to a twenty-five year sentence. Nickels was furious and told him he was "szalony." *Crazy*. "You didn't murder her, Papa. What the hell were you thinking? Please don't do this," he begged.

They wanted him to fight the charges, but Albo explained that Oxnard didn't think they could win the case. Albo said he thought it would be easier on everyone if they didn't go through the humiliation of a trial. He got twenty-five years instead of life and would get out early for good behavior, most likely in about ten years. "I'm only forty-three years old and will be out by the time I'm fifty-three. I have decided. It is done. We won't discuss it again."

The big, bold headline in the *Akron News Journal* was: "Jablonski Pleads Guilty to Country Club Murder." The article stated that Polish immigrant Jablonski had been caught red-handed with evidence found in his locker. It went on to say he was sentenced to twenty-five years, with eligibility for parole in as early as ten years.

The Block family was quoted as saying, "Our daughter is gone forever, and we will never see her grow up and have children. We'll never hug her again. Although this brings us some closure, we're not happy with the plea deal and think Jablonski should have been given life without parole."

No one questioned the evidence. They were glad to have a quick resolution.

By the time the plea agreement was settled, Albo had spent close to a month in the cramped Summit County Jail.

✧

On Albo's last day in Akron before being transported to the Ohio State Penitentiary, Kurt and Charlie walked into the jail to visit. They were upset about Albo's sentence and didn't believe for a minute that he was guilty. Charlie was in uniform, so they were taken back to see Albo right away. Albo's attorney William Oxnard was with him. Albo introduced them, and Kurt noticed the attorney seemed ill at ease. Oxnard excused himself and quickly said his goodbyes to Albo.

Kurt and Charlie were surprised at how composed Albo was. Once he had made his decision, he was resigned to his fate. They hugged each other and sat down to talk. Kurt said, "Mr. Jablonski, we want you to know how sorry we are this happened to you. We both know you're innocent. This is a travesty."

Charlie added, "We'll come to visit you as much as possible."

"I not want you to come. You remember me at home with family in good times."

Kurt said, "Please don't say that. Do you realize how important you are to us? We can't imagine not being able to talk with you and get your advice. Think about it once you're in Columbus. I think you'll need to see friendly faces. We'll give you some time and then ask again if you'll allow us to visit."

Kurt was a little embarrassed in front of Charlie, but knew this would be his only opportunity to tell Albo how much he meant to him. "I want you to know how important you are to me. When I lost my father, I missed him so much, I thought I'd never get over it. Then when I met Nickels and you, it was as if I came home again. You're like a father to me, and I want you to know I'll always be here for you. If you need anything, I'll do whatever I can to help you."

Albo was obviously touched, but didn't say a word. He took Kurt's hand and held it.

Charlie said, "You were always there when I needed you. When I couldn't talk to my father about anything, either because he was drunk or angry, I talked to you. The words 'thank you' aren't enough. Please keep yourself safe in prison. When you change your mind, we'll come and see you."

When Kurt and Charlie got up to leave, they had tears in their eyes.

After they left, Kurt said, "That was one of the hardest things I've ever had to do."

Charlie couldn't speak.

Later the same day, when Nickels walked into the room for the family's last visit, his mother and Antonia were already there. He couldn't believe this was happening. It was like a bad dream.

"Papa, we're sad and angry for what's happened to you. We want you to know that until you return, we'll be fine. We'll do our best to make you proud of us. You'll be with us again sooner than any of us realizes. We love you."

"I'm sorry my prison sentence is a sentence for the whole family. I worked hard to provide for all of you, but now my life is not my own. We're a strong family. We've survived in hard times and difficult situations, and we'll survive this. Be brave, my dearest Millie. You have my heart." As they led him away in his drab gray prison jumpsuit, he didn't turn around to look at his family.

On November 24, 1920, Albert Henrik Jablonski, Sr. was transported to the Ohio Penitentiary in Columbus to serve his twenty-five year sentence. It was the day before Thanksgiving.

When the prison transport bus bounced into the compound and past the ominous gun towers and razor-wire fences, Albo wondered how he had ended up at the state penitentiary. When he heard the sound of the heavy metal doors close behind him, cutting him off from the rest of the world, it was almost unbearable.

Along with the other prisoners arriving that day, Albo was processed in the basement holding room. "Strip naked, and get over your modesty, because there ain't any in here," said the guard. "You're gonna take a shower and then we're going to search every inch of you." As the guard's rough hands moved over his body, Albo thought it was one of the most uncomfortable feelings he'd ever had.

They marched single file into an auditorium to listen to the warden speak. He warned them to behave and follow the rules. After the warden's orientation, a guard walked up to Albo, stood three inches in front of his face, and yelled, "Move it, Number one-two-two-seven-three. It's time to move into your lovely new home."

Chapter Fifteen

❖

*A*t the start of Prohibition, Russell Cantrell recognized the high demand for alcohol and the limited supply and realized it was a great way to expand his vast fortune. By day, Cantrell was a successful lawyer and legitimate businessman, but at night he smuggled liquor.

In early 1921, Cantrell had asked Voigt to set up the operation, and within a month Voigt reported back. "I've recruited a group of men to hijack the whiskey from Canada. On moonless nights, we'll bring it into the U.S. by boat across Lake Erie. Then the team will drive the supply down to Akron in vans camouflaged as produce trucks. We'll deliver it to the speakeasies in quart bottles packed in suitcases. No one will have any idea who's running the show."

A few weeks after they were up and running, Cantrell asked, "How's it going, Louis? Any problems?"

"Smooth as ice. This is a sweet little game."

"Well done. I knew I could depend on you."

Voigt said, "Why do you want to do this?"

"For the money, of course. To me this is simply one more business."

Through his network of nefarious connections, Voigt threatened or schmoozed until they had the biggest percentage of the bootlegging business in Ohio. By 1922, Cantrell was making more money from bootlegging than he ever thought possible—literally millions. But no amount of money was enough. It was the game that counted and the thrill of getting away with something.

There was no question Cantrell was in charge of the big picture, but Voigt had the last word in day-to-day decisions. Cantrell figured the fewer details he knew, the better.

Cantrell paid Voigt a big salary and kept track of the finances. He made sure Voigt knew it, because he didn't want him tempted to skim the profits.

Cantrell didn't like Voigt much, but recognized he couldn't manage the bootlegging business without him. Voigt, on the other hand, had grown to resent Cantrell. He felt as if he were doing all the work and wasn't getting enough of the rewards, and it was beginning to irritate him.

Cantrell went from running illegal booze to making it. Hidden in the woods on the property out at his country house he'd had Voigt assemble several stills. It was a large enterprise that included manufacturing, warehousing, and distribution. Retailing was left to the speakeasy owners.

Voigt brought in factory day workers to work the stills. They worked all night with no light other than the moon. He picked them up each evening, and they loaded the supplies into the camouflaged trucks. Voigt never bought the supplies in one place, and if it was a big order, he divided it among several suppliers.

On the ride out to the stills one night, a couple of the new men asked how they made the liquor. Voigt explained the distilling process. "First we combine fifty pounds of rye meal, fifty pounds of barley meal, eight hundred pounds of sugar, and water. Then we pour two sacks of wheat bran on top of it all to hold in the heat of fermentation. This is what we call 'mash.' We boil the mash, and the alcohol is released as steam, which we cool back into liquid. Following me?"

They murmured yes.

Voigt continued. "We use submarine stills, because they're the biggest and can hold up to eight hundred gallons of mash. Any questions?"

One guy asked, "Is it any good?"

Voigt laughed and said, "The best damn hooch you'll ever have the opportunity to guzzle."

In mid-1922, City Councilman Stephen Lyle contacted Cantrell and informed him he had something serious to discuss. Cantrell wondered what it was about, but because of Lyle's position, agreed to meet with him.

Lyle was a skinny man with thinning hair, a sharp nose, and a pasty complexion. He swaggered into Russell's office with a smug look on his face and offered his hand. "Good morning Russell. How are you today?"

"I'm doing well, thanks," Cantrell said. "What can I do for you?" Cantrell's immediate impression was that Lyle was a fool.

"Well…I thought you would be interested to know that I figured out you have some…er…some side businesses. I know you're smuggling booze into the country from Canada, and what you don't run across the lake, you make at your bootlegging operation out in the country. I even know where the stills are located."

Cantrell kept his expression neutral and tried to keep his temper in check, but he couldn't hide the red flush inching up his neck. "I have no idea what you're talking about."

"Yes you do, and here's what we're going to do about it. I want seventy-five thousand dollars in cash by tomorrow afternoon, or I'll turn you in to the authorities. Those revenuers sure are anxious to find out where your stills are and who's behind the whole thing."

Cantrell inwardly fumed, but he knew what he had to do. "Who have you told about this? I want the name of your source, or there will be no deal."

"I haven't told anyone, and I won't if you give me the money. You don't need to know how I found out. No one knows I'm here. Listen, I know you're respected and well connected, and I understand you're planning to run for office. Your reputation is a good one. You wouldn't want to ruin it, would you?"

Cantrell glared at him for an uncomfortable minute, and then said, "You have to give me a day to get the cash. Meet me at the south entrance of Hollingsworth House at four tomorrow. Do you know where that is?"

"I know where it is. I'll see you there tomorrow."

Cantrell said, "Don't tell anyone where you're going."

"Of course not."

Lyle walked out of the room thinking how surprisingly easy that had been. He was finally going to be rich, and it would be the easiest buck he ever made. When he first discovered Cantrell was behind the illegal operation, he thought he'd hit the jackpot, and now it looked as if he were right.

The next afternoon Cantrell and Voigt watched Lyle drive into the back entrance of the estate. On the ground next to Cantrell was a satchel filled with newspaper and a few tools, including an ice pick Voigt had thrown in. Lyle got out of his car and walked toward the two of them. He spied the bag. "Is all the money in there? All seventy-five thousand?"

Cantrell stared at him.

As Lyle walked toward the two of them, he thought what an unlikely pair they made. Voigt was dressed in his standard uniform of white shirt and black pants. He stood with his legs spread wide apart, and his hands on his hips. Behind him, Cantrell nonchalantly puffed on a cigar. Lyle noticed Voigt had a strange look on his face, and when he saw Cantrell nod at Voigt, it hit him that he had walked into a trap. Lyle turned and bolted into the woods.

Voigt took off after him. In spite of his size, Voigt was quite fast. As Lyle turned around and saw that Voigt was closing the gap between them, he tripped on a root and fell. "Don't hurt me, please don't hurt me," he begged, as he scrambled to get up.

Voigt lunged and clamped his huge hand around Lyle's ankle. Lyle felt the bones break and screamed, "Holy crap. You broke my ankle."

Cantrell was aroused as he watched the scene play out. Having control over life and death stimulated him. But before they got rid of Lyle, they had to find out if anyone knew he had come to the Cantrell estate and whether he had told anyone what he knew about the bootlegging operation.

"Bring him over here, Louis."

Voigt dragged Lyle back to where Cantrell was standing, tied him up, and sat him down on the ground next to his car.

"We're going to ask you a few questions. Answer truthfully, or it will be even more painful for you."

Lyle thought Cantrell looked menacing and not at all like his public image. He was terribly frightened. His ankle throbbed, and he had soiled himself.

Cantrell positioned his face inches from Lyle's and said very quietly, "Does anyone know you're here?"

Lyle sniveled and shook his head no. "I told no one. I swear."

"How did you find out I was involved? I want the truth and will know if you lie."

Lyle refused to answer, so with Cantrell's signal, Voigt picked up the bag Cantrell had dropped on the ground and took out the ice pick. Voigt had an evil grin on his face.

Lyle's eyes grew wide.

Voigt grabbed Lyle's wrist, flattened his hand on the ground with fingers fanned, and punched the ice pick through the middle of his palm. He waited a second or two for Lyle's brain to process the pain and then twisted the ice pick around. Voigt and Cantrell snickered at Lyle's agonized howls.

Lyle's howls dissolved into whimpers. "Take it out. I'll tell what you want to know if you don't hurt me anymore."

Voigt pulled the ice pick out of Lyle's hand. Lyle moaned.

"I suggest you start talking," Cantrell said.

Speaking fast, and in a higher-than-normal voice, Lyle said, "I learned about the rum running and stills from my brother-in-law. You deliver booze to his speakeasy. He saw Voigt one time and mentioned to me that he thought it was curious that he looked so much like the guy who chauffeured for you. After my brother-in-law told me about it, I began to put two and two together.

"I made sure I was at the speakeasy during one of the deliveries, and saw one of your camouflaged trucks. Once I knew which trucks were yours, it was easy.

"I tailed them to your place out in the country a few times until I got a sense of the scope of the undertaking. I caught sight of Voigt a couple of times and knew he was your driver. I looked up the property and found out it was yours, and that's what gave me the idea to turn it into a nice big payoff."

"Have you told anyone about this?"

Lyle, snot running down his face, sobbed uncontrollably. "No. All I wanted was the money, so I didn't dare tell anyone. I've never broken the law before."

Cantrell was convinced he was telling the truth. "Take care of him, Louis. You know what to do."

Lyle pleaded, "No, I'll do whatever you want. Please don't kill me. Please. I have a family."

Voigt grabbed Lyle by the neck and strangled him as Cantrell watched in fascination.

Cantrell said, "Good riddance to this piece of shit. This is a wake-up call, and we have to be more careful. We're going to have to start watching his brother-in-law to make sure he doesn't catch on to the size of the operation. If this jerk figured it out, someone else might be able to as well."

Voigt threw Lyle's body in the back seat of his car.

Cantrell said, "Make sure you ditch him and his car somewhere far away. Somewhere where no one can find it."

Cantrell watched them drive away. He was pleased with the outcome. "Good riddance, asshole. That will teach you to blackmail Russell Cantrell."

Kurt was going to Akron University full-time, and other than occasionally caddying for Cantrell on weekends, he had very little contact with him. Kurt was doing well in his junior year of college and worked hard to get good grades. He liked his classes and had made many new acquaintances who might prove useful later on in his career. He had researched law schools and decided he wanted to go to Western Reserve in Cleveland.

Kurt had no idea about Cantrell's dirty dealings and would be horrified to know Cantrell and his badger Voigt had tortured and killed Councilman Lyle. He didn't like Cantrell, but he had no idea how nasty he really was.

Voigt asked Cantrell what was going on with the Becker kid. Voigt said, "I find it interesting you don't want to get rid of him. It's two years since the girl's murder. No one will make the connection."

Cantrell said, "No, I don't want to kill him. I'm not sure if he suspects I killed Catherine Block, so I realize I have to be cautious around him and keep him close enough to watch him. But like I always said, Becker might prove to be useful to me in the future. I'm looking forward to having a bright young lawyer at my beck and call. I enjoy having control over his life. And I find it interesting that I don't intimidate him. At least the kid has backbone."

Chapter Sixteen

❖

*W*ithout Albo's paychecks, the family was having a tough time. For the two years since Albo went to prison, they'd been able to squeak by with money Albo and Millie had saved, but it was almost gone. Six weeks after Antonia turned eighteen, she and Millie went to work in the factory. "Don't tell anyone we work in the factory," Antonia said. "I don't want anyone to know. Respectable women shouldn't have to work outside the home, especially in a factory. You should be keeping house and planning meals, and even though you don't think it's necessary, I want to attend college full-time."

"Antonia, your father and I taught you that life has many twists and turns, and we make the best with what we have. We were lucky to get these jobs, no matter where they are."

"I know you're right, but I can't help it. I'm ashamed to work at the factory."

On the days they worked at the factory, they got up at five, drank a cup of black coffee, ate a bowl of oatmeal, and rushed out the door to catch the bus at the end of their street.

On a Tuesday in August, as the bus pulled up outside the parking lot of Goodrich-owned Miller Rubber Company, Antonia looked at the dirty brick building and the kids playing on the train tracks. The smokestack spewed a constant stream of smelly black smoke that covered the city of Akron in a layer of black soot.

"Mama, we're running late."

Charging past the gateman, they punched the time clock and hurriedly changed into their green and white shop aprons. The company didn't provide uniforms, so they paid for them out of their earnings. They bought two each and rotated them between the factory and home, so they could always start the workday in clean clothes.

Antonia and Millie worked in the Miscellaneous Department, which was the finishing area for bushings and valves, both used in the manufacture of cars. The factory was clean, but in the summer, it was stifling, and workers were required to drink oatmeal water to stay hydrated. There was no air conditioning, and with up to one hundred women on the floor, at least one of them fainted every day from the heat. By the time the day was done, Antonia and Millie's clothes were dripping wet, and they smelled like sweat.

Antonia used a big machine to grind the flash off the cured bushings and then packed them in boxes, which she maneuvered up onto a high shelf. She told one of the other girls, "That fifty-pound box feels as if it weighs more than I do, and sometimes I'm not sure if I can get it up on the shelf before it falls on me. It's a miracle I can lift those damn boxes all day long."

She pointed to her upper arm. "Check out my muscles."

Millie's job was to inspect the valves, pull out the bad ones, make appropriate notations in a ledger, and then move them to another workstation where they were packed for shipping.

Their supervisor Ralph was nice enough, but while eating lunch, Antonia said, "His personality is about as lively as a Lake Erie rock. It's the unskilled women who do the work that requires manual dexterity, because men aren't as agile as we are. This is how I describe Ralph's job: 'Make sure the women are working and not talking.' All he has to do is to watch us, and he probably gets paid three times as much."

At three in the afternoon, Antonia and Millie punched out and headed home. Antonia made about ten dollars a week, her mother, twelve, and even though they were required to clock in and out, they got paid by the piece, not for how many hours they worked. The company offered no pensions, no medical insurance, and no paid vacations.

Once seated on the bus with her mother, Antonia said, "Everyone in this town smells like burning rubber. The smell is disgusting. It's in my hair, on my skin, and my clothes are permeated with it. I'll say it again. I'm ashamed to work in the factory."

"Heavens above. Stop it and don't be so foolish. In this family, we hold our heads high."

"Believe me, I try, but I loathe working there and I hate what has become of our family." She stared out the window. "I shouldn't complain. Papa has it so much worse. Our lives are easy compared to what he's going through. I'm sorry, Mama."

Millie took a deep breath and put her arm around Antonia. Antonia rested her head on her mother's shoulder, and neither of them spoke again for the rest of the ride home.

When they got home, Antonia bathed, gobbled down some dinner, and raced out to make it to night school on time. She usually ended up getting about four hours of sleep a night, and by the time she got to the factory each morning, she was already exhausted. Every once in a while she was able to grab a few winks in the supply closet, and when Ralph came around, one of the other girls covered for her.

Millie was amazed Antonia wanted to go to college and didn't understand what a woman as beautiful as Antonia would do with an education. She worried a college degree would make her unfit for marriage and motherhood. But Antonia wanted to be a teacher.

"Why do you need all that schooling? What you should do is get married and take care of a husband and babies. I see how Kurt Becker looks at you."

"Mama, please. We're just friends." But in her heart, she knew there was more to their relationship than friendship.

She wanted her mother to understand why school was so important. "I've always loved books and learning about all sorts of different things. There's a huge world out there to discover, and I find it exciting to learn about it. When I become a teacher, I want to help my students have the same love of learning."

Antonia had four close girlfriends. They studied together in the library, and when Antonia could find the time, she went out with them together in a big group that included some of the guys they knew. She didn't have much time to spend with them, but she knew they were available if she needed them. Antonia appreciated that they valued her for her intelligence, not just her good looks.

She had known one of the girls since kindergarten. When they were younger, Antonia and Rosemary played dress-up and followed her brother and his friends around. Antonia cherished their friendship and felt Rosemary was the kind of friend who knew everything about her, and liked her no matter what. They still laughed together like when they were little girls—a nonstop, belly laugh that came from way down deep and made them gasp for air.

One day when they were studying in the library, Rosemary said, "I want you to join my sorority. Rush starts next week, and I'd love it if you came by the sorority house to see what it's like. For girls like us who live at home, the sorority house is a great place to spend time and get together with friends. You can even study there when you want to."

Antonia was happy when Rosemary asked her to join. "I would like that. I think it would be a lot of fun to be part of a close-knit group of women who feel the same way about things as I do. I hope I'm asked to join."

The process of rush and pledging took a little over a week, and Antonia had to take time off from the factory to take part in pledge week. She was elated when she was invited to join the sorority.

When she told her mother, Millie looked sad. "What's the matter, Mama?"

"Nothing, honey. I only wish your father could see how happy you are."

"I'm going to write him a letter right now and tell him all about it."

Chapter Seventeen

❖

*I*t was 1922, and Albo had been in prison for almost two years. The prison was a dark, damp, and cheerless place. Living in a small cell, eating disgusting, tasteless food, and without sufficient exercise or air, Albo lost weight, and his mental health deteriorated. Some nights, in the privacy of his cell, he couldn't stop the tears, and though he tried not to dwell on it, the fact that he was innocent haunted him.

Albo's cell was off the main corridor and on an upper tier where the cells had a bit more privacy. He had a fold-up bunk, a toilet, a desk, a chair, and a sink.

Most of his fellow prisoners tried to beat the system, but Albo didn't want to jeopardize his chances for early release. He worked hard to be a model prisoner, exactly as Oxnard had instructed. It wasn't uncommon for other inmates to break the rules and get caught. Afterward, they considered their punishment an honor.

Brutality was a constant part of life in the prison. It hardened both the guards and the inmates. The prisoners hated the warden and the guards, which in turn made them suspicious and alert, resulting in even more aggression. No matter how much he tried, Albo couldn't entirely escape it. He was kicked, beaten, verbally abused, and degraded, but he kept his mouth shut and did his damnedest not to react.

To the other inmates, it didn't matter whether Albo was guilty or innocent. As a convicted murderer, he was automatically granted elevated status, and his reputation as a killer helped persuade the other convicts he deserved their respect.

Although basically a loner, Albo had befriended an inmate in the next cell who had four years left on his sentence for armed robbery. Gary was a big man, well over six feet tall, and because the guards were afraid of him, they left him alone. Albo trusted Gary and talking to him made the days go a little faster.

"I tired all the time. When I think of my family and try to imagine what each one doing, it help. I make time go faster by keeping track of the days, the hours and the minutes, until I am out of here."

Gary said, "I do exactly the same thing. It can't go fast enough for me. I hate this hellhole."

His alliance with Gary helped him more than once. One day in November, just short of Albo's two year mark, Gary whispered from the next cell, "Hey Al, keep your eyes open and watch out. Some of the guards are riled up and looking for a fight today." Albo saw a guard who had it out for him heading in his direction. The next thing he knew, Gary yelled, "Over here, asshole."

"What did you call me?"

"I didn't call you nothin."

"That's not what I heard."

The guard had forgotten about Albo and walked over to Gary's cell. "Who do you think you're talkin' to? Keep your mouth shut and stop screwing around or next time you'll be sorry."

Watching the guard walked away, Gary said, "What a sap."

Albo appreciated Gary's help. "That guard not leave me alone. You helped me today. Thank you."

He couldn't wait to see Millie and to speak Polish. She was visiting the next day.

✧

Millie remained steadfastly loyal to her husband, and at least twice a month made the arduous trip to Columbus by bus.

Millie was allowed to bring him food, though the guards had to thoroughly inspect it before she could give it to Albo. On the weekends before she visited, she cooked whatever she could carry with her on the bus. She made enough for the guards and each time gave them a big package of cookies so they wouldn't confiscate it like they did the first time she brought her husband food.

Albo had refused to talk to Millie about prison conditions, but on this visit, he finally broke down and told her what life on the inside was really like.

He explained his routine. "Each morning they wake me at six. After I clean my cell, I'm required to stand at attention. Then the cell doors open, and I walk to the mess hall in single file with the other prisoners. They give me twenty minutes to eat, and afterward I line up for my work assignment. It's the same every day, and it makes me want to scream.

"I hate the counting. When I hear the keys clinking as the guards come down the corridor, I know they're counting again. They count us in the morning, at noon, and at night. They count us when we get up. They count us when we eat. They count us when we work. And they count us when we sleep.

"I'm told when to eat, when to sleep, and even when to move. I've learned to detach myself from the outside world and to concentrate on survival on the inside. I walk around the perimeter of my cell over and over again. I can't stop doing it. I know every inch of that stinking cube. I've tried my best to adjust to life in prison, but in spite of living with so many others, it's lonely. I miss you. I miss Albert. And I miss Antonia.

"To the administration I'm known as Number one-two-two-seven-three, but the guards refer to me as 'The Polack' or 'bohunk.'

"During the day I can hear the clanging of the heavy metal doors. It never stops. I hate the sound of it. Thank goodness it's much quieter at night.

"But night presents its own terrors. Last week, I was awakened by the sound of the new night guard walking down the corridor between the cells. I stayed completely still even after I heard him stop and put his key in the lock of my cell. 'Wake up you dumb fuck,' the guard said. He banged his riot stick against the rim of my metal cot.

"I told him I was sleeping and asked him what he wanted.

"He mocked me. 'You don't even know how to speak English, you dumb Polack. What do I care if you're sleeping? You need to know I'm in charge here now. Understand? You do whatever I tell you no matter what. Now sit up, ya lazy bum.'"

Albo said, "The guard came in my cell. I sat up, and he kicked me with his steel-toed boot. It really hurt, but I refused to give him the satisfaction of seeing me react, so I bit my lip to keep from making a sound.

"He told me that was a small taste of what he could do to me and that now he owned me.

"After the guard left, I touched the big welt on my leg and felt the stickiness of the blood that had begun to clot. As I lay on my bunk in the dark, I realized my survival depended on getting along with the guards and not provoking them."

When he finished, Millie was crying. She said, "You're strong, Albo. You can handle this. Just keep thinking about your family and how much we love you."

He said, "It's the only thing that keeps me going.

"I try to follow three unspoken rules. I don't show weakness. I mind my own business. And I never snitch on another prisoner."

Millie thought he looked terrible. He had bags under his eyes and had lost too much weight. He seemed sad and broken. She gave him the food she got past inspection that day. "Eat it. All of it. You need to put some meat on those skinny bones."

Millie's visits made a huge difference to Albo. When she left, he immediately began to yearn for the next visit.

Millie was sad whenever she came back from Columbus. When Millie returned from her visit, Antonia asked her how she was. Millie said, "What a horrible place that prison is. I can't believe your Papa is stuck in there. Some days it's so depressing I want to crawl into my bed, and sleep for the next eight years. But I have to stay upbeat for him, for you, and for your brother. The only thing that keeps me going is knowing he'll be back home with us someday."

Antonia asked Millie to tell her about Papa. Her mother didn't want to tell her the complete truth. "He finds great comfort in knowing we're getting along without him. I think he's handling life in prison better than any of us could expect. And though he's not here with us, he'll always be the rock of our family. He's the best husband and father in world. That will never change. Your Papa is a brave man, and he's holding up very well. He misses us more than he can say and sends hugs and kisses to everyone."

"Mama, every day I get down on my hands and knees and pray Papa is safe, and that time passes quickly until he gets out. If it weren't for your strength and positive attitude, I'm not sure if I could handle it. You're the best mother in the world, and I love you."

Nickels later told Antonia that Mama had confided in him that their father's health was deteriorating, and they had to find a way to help him regain his strength.

❖

Although Kurt and Charlie tried to visit several times, Albo didn't want to see them. Finally, in December, he asked Nickels to tell Kurt and Charlie he was willing to see them if they still wanted to come. "I miss those two boys, and want them to come and see me. I have eight more years here, and each visit is what keeps me going. I can't seem to remember why I didn't want them to come."

Kurt asked Antonia if she wanted to join them, but she said it was a good idea for them to go alone. "I'm glad he agreed to see you. Seeing you and Charlie will be good for him."

When Kurt and Charlie drove into the prison, they were amazed by how big it was. The barbed wire was intimidating and they thought it was symbolic of the loss of freedom. A guard led them to the room where they would visit with Albo. It was dark and dreary, and Kurt suddenly wished he hadn't come. He didn't want to see Mr. Jablonski in this place.

Charlie stared at the drab wall. "I'm used to working with prisoners in Akron, but this is the first time I've come down to the state pen. This is dreadful, and I feel sorry for Mr. Jablonski. He doesn't deserve this. I still can't believe he pled guilty."

"Yeah, that was a huge surprise to everyone."

They walked into the room and both greeted him with a hug. "Mr. Jablonski it's so good to finally see you," said Kurt.

"Call me Albo. You both old enough now."

They spent over an hour with him, and at first talked about everyday events and incidentals. Eventually Kurt got around to the subject of Antonia. "Albo, I hope it's okay with you if I'm dating Antonia. I'm doing well in college and working hard. It would mean a lot to me if you approve."

Albo grinned and said he was pleased he and Antonia had finally admitted they were together. "We know for long time you two a couple."

"Thank you. That means a lot to me. I'll tell Antonia what you said. I know it will make her happy."

"Good. Now tell me how Mama and Aunt doing."

Kurt told him they were fine and working as hard as ever. "The boardinghouse is buzzing with activity, and there isn't enough room for all the lodgers who want to move in. But they both agreed not to offer hotbeds." Albo asked him what a hotbed was.

"It's when a night worker sleeps during the day, and a day worker uses the same bed at night. My mother and aunt think it makes it too confusing to keep track of everyone. They pride themselves on creating a home-like atmosphere, and feel when there are too many people, it's more like a hotel than a home.

"They're both getting older, and I worry about them. I want them to move out of the boardinghouse, but they insist they can handle it and want to wait."

Charlie was conflicted about seeing Mr. Jablonski in the penitentiary, and was surprised to find he was overcome with emotion. The big, strong, confident man he remembered looked so insignificant and defeated. Albo had stubble on his chin, his hair was unkempt, and he was thin and frail.

"Albo, I thought you would like to know that one of my superiors recently told me I'm in line to make detective within the next couple of years. I remembered what you always told me, and I've worked hard. So far everything is going according to the way I planned it."

"I knew you be successful at whatever you decide. I proud of you."

"You don't know how much that means to me. You were always more interested in me than my own father, and I want you to know how important that was to me. When my own father didn't have time for me, you were always there. You had a lot to do with what kind of man I am today."

Albo was quiet for a minute, and then said, "I always try to be there for you boys."

As Kurt and Charlie were getting ready to leave, Albo said, "You like family to me."

"We *are* family," Kurt said.

On the way home, Kurt said, "I'm glad he let us come and see him. I really missed him these last couple of years."

"I agree. It's good for Albo to be in touch with someone besides his family. Let's try to make the trip down here as often as we can."

"Charlie, there's something else. We have to do something to find the real murderer. Can you get some of your guys to help? "

"I've already talked to a couple of the guys. We've begun looking into the case on our own time."

Chapter Eighteen

❖

he radio was on its way to becoming a national obsession. Marta and Erna bought a brand new RCA-Westinghouse radio and wooden cabinet for the parlor, and every evening after dinner Marta, Erna, and the boarders gathered to listen to music. It was standing-room-only when the announcer described plays during an Indians game.

Marta and Erna continued to work as hard as they always had, but were no longer weighed down with worry about heavy debt, so they were happier and more carefree. One night when Kurt paid a visit to the boardinghouse, he heard loud laughter coming from the kitchen. When he walked in, he saw Marta and Erna dancing with each other and giggling like schoolgirls.

"What are you doing?"

Marta swung Erna around one more time, and Erna plopped herself down with a big flourish on one of the sturdy kitchen chairs. She sighed and said, "We're having fun. But I'm afraid Sissy has exhausted me."

"You were the one who wanted to dance. Don't blame it on me," said Marta.

Kurt laughed. "It makes me feel good to see you happy and having a good time."

After Nickels' father was sent to jail, he was no longer welcome at the boarding house. When Albo pled guilty and went to prison, Erna put her foot down. Kurt pleaded and argued, but Erna wouldn't budge. "That Polack is a cold-blooded killer, and I won't have his son in my house." Kurt tried to tell her Albo was innocent and had been framed, but Erna wouldn't listen. He enlisted Mama's help, but they couldn't change Erna's mind.

"I never did like that boy," Erna said.

Kurt didn't want to tell Nickels he couldn't come to the boardinghouse anymore, and so far had been able to arrange to meet somewhere else. Nickels knew about Erna's mandate, but didn't want to jeopardize their friendship.

It also bothered Erna that Kurt and Antonia were dating, but Marta forbid Erna to interfere. After several heated discussions, Erna reluctantly agreed to stay out of it. "Okay, but I don't want him bringing her around here."

It wasn't only Erna who didn't want Kurt and Antonia together. Cantrell had never met Antonia, but he was unhappy they were seeing each other. He wanted to control every aspect of Kurt's life and took every opportunity to comment about Kurt seeing Antonia. But Kurt was adamant. "She's my girlfriend, and you'll have to get used to it. Frankly, I don't think it's any of your business. With all due respect, sir, you don't own me."

"Listen, kid, don't talk to me like that. I don't like it, and after everything I've done for you and your family, I think it's disrespectful."

"I apologize, but you have to understand she's important to me and part of my life."

Kurt believed it was his right to keep some parts of his life private and was frustrated by Cantrell's proprietary attitude. He didn't care what Cantrell thought about Antonia. He planned to live his life as he saw fit, and that included dating whomever he wanted.

❖

A few days after his discussion with Cantrell, Kurt called Antonia.

"I heard about this terrific new spaghetti place. Let's go there for dinner and then a movie afterward. The Valentino film is playing. Do you want to go?"

"Of course I do."

"I like telling people you're my girlfriend."

"And I like saying you're my boyfriend."

He heard her laugh over the phone, and the sound exhilarated him.

Antonia stood at the window and watched Kurt walk up the front steps. It hit her again how handsome he was. She loved his broad shoulders and dreamy, pale blue eyes. Whenever she saw him, her heart beat a little faster. She saw Kurt as her future. She loved him and he loved her, and that was all that mattered.

Antonia wore a royal blue and black, straight-line chemise, topped with a close-fitting cloche that emphasized the lines of her face. She was glad the corset was no longer in style. Women like her mother and Kurt's mother and aunt continued to lace up, but like other women her age she liked the freedom of the new clothes. When Kurt saw her all dolled up, he whistled and told her how beautiful she was. She reached up and ran her fingers through his curly, thick hair.

When they arrived at the restaurant, they were shown to a small table in the corner with a red-checkered tablecloth topped with a single red rose in a small vase, and a flickering candle. They could see each other, but not much else. "What a great place, Kurt. It feels as if we are the only ones here."

"I thought you might like it. You look delicious in this candlelight, Toni. I can't believe what a lucky guy I am."

"I'm the lucky one."

When they ordered, the waiter winked at them and asked if they wanted *coffee*. Kurt knew that was hush-hush for booze. "Sure, we'll have some." He and Antonia chuckled at the ruse.

The waiter returned with coffee cups brimming with muscatel. Antonia said, "Why would they serve a sweet wine with spaghetti?" For some reason, it struck them as funny, and they laughed so loudly that everyone in the restaurant heard them. When the bill came, the wine was listed as "special coffee."

For twenty-five cents each, they saw a movie starring Rudolph Valentino. It was a romantic tragedy about a married bullfighter who took a lover. After a bull gored him, his wife nursed him back to health, and he returned to the ring. While looking up at his lover in the stands, the bull charged him, and he was fatally wounded. He died in the arms of his wife.

When the lights came up, Kurt noticed Antonia was teary-eyed. He put his arm around her and pulled her close.

As they walked out of the theater, he said, "I'm not ready to take you home yet. Let's walk." He took her hand, and they meandered toward the park.

Antonia noticed Kurt was fidgeting.

Kurt said, "Toni, stop and sit on this bench for a while. I have something I want to ask you."

"Why are you acting so strange?"

"Sweetheart, please sit down. This is important."

"I'm going to finish college in another two years and then go on to law school."

"I know that, silly."

He took her into his arms and kissed her neck, slowly making his way to her mouth. They both began to breathe faster as they shared a deep, passionate kiss. They kissed again and again, and she pressed her body close to his. Nuzzling her neck, he felt as if he were losing himself in her. He loved her smell and the way she felt in his arms.

His need for her was intense, but she had never been with a man, and he wanted to wait. He pulled away and looked at her.

"Is there something wrong?"

"Nope. Everything is exactly right."

Kurt took both her hands in his. "I love you, Toni. I've never loved anyone else. I think I've loved you ever since that day we went to the World Series game. I want to make it official."

She couldn't believe what she was hearing. "What are you saying?"

"When I graduate from law school, I want to get married. I know it's too soon to become formally engaged, and I don't have a ring, but how do you like the sound of Mrs. Kurt Becker?"

"Oh my goodness, what a surprise. I wasn't expecting this so soon. Of course I'll marry you. It's all I've ever wanted. I think I've loved you since the first time you came over to my house with my brother."

They sat there for more than an hour, hugging, kissing, and making plans for their future together. Neither of them could stop smiling.

Later when they reached her house, they stood on the top step and wrapped their arms around each other. The curtains fluttered and Kurt realized Mrs. Jablonski was watching. "Your Mama is peeking out at us."

They began to giggle uncontrollably again. Antonia laughed so hard, she was doubled over, clutching her stomach. Kurt laughed right along with her.

She said, "Oh my, I better go inside."

After she closed the door, Millie asked her what happened. "You look like the cat who swallowed the canary."

"Maybe."

"Antonia, tell me what's going on."

"It's nothing…only that he loves me, and he asked me to marry him when he finishes law school. It's five years away, but I can wait forever for Kurt. Oh Mama, I'm so happy. I never thought it was possible to be this happy after what happened to Papa."

Millie jumped up and down, held out the hem of her dress, and turned pirouettes around the kitchen.

Antonia watched her and thought how great it was to have some good news for once.

"Mama, you'd think you were the one who just got engaged."

"That's exactly how I feel. I'm overjoyed for the two of you. I hoped this might happen someday, but not so soon. It's wonderful news."

During her next visit, Antonia told her father about her unofficial engagement. He said, "It's so good to have some really happy news. Kurt is like a son to me."

Chapter Nineteen

❖

*K*urt, Nickels, and Charlie still got together at The Canal as often as they could arrange it with their different schedules.

On this night in early 1924, after they'd eaten, they sat back in the booth and drank their "coffee." Kurt looked at his friends and said, "When you're growing-up friends like we are, there's a bond that runs deep and never goes away, no matter where you are in life."

"I know exactly what you mean," said Nickels. "Whenever we haven't seen each other for a while, we only have to spend a few minutes catching up because we know each other so well."

"Listen to you two. Don't get all girlie on me," said Charlie.

After they stopped laughing, they discussed the baseball season in earnest.

✧

Nickels had been promoted to copyeditor and was happy to escape from what he called "the bowels of the mailroom." He liked working at the newspaper, but was frustrated he hadn't been assigned anything to write yet. "I edit and proof the work of other writers, but I don't get to write anything myself. I want to write, and I don't care what the topic is. Hell, I'd write about the Ladies' Garden Club if they asked me to," he said to Harriet Weaver.

He had begun seeing Harriet six months before. She was petite, golden-haired, and had a smile that lit up a room. They met one night on the way out of their college classes when they literally bumped into each other, dropping all their books and papers on the floor. Scrambling to pick them up, they looked at each other and instantly felt a connection.

The next time Nickels went to his class and came out into the hall, he didn't see her at first, but when he turned around, she was staring directly at him. They laughed because they realized they were looking for each other. They went out for coffee that same night, and began dating exclusively from then on. They made each other laugh and found they had similar views on almost everything. When they did disagree, they enjoyed their heated discussions, which usually led to a romp in the bedroom. They had been dating for almost a year. The more time they spent together, the deeper they fell in love.

Harriet asked many times about his family, but he always dodged her questions. He wanted her to meet his mother and sister, but he hadn't yet told Harriet his real name was Jablonski, so he had kept her away. He wanted to wait until the right time. Telling a woman your father is in jail for murder wasn't an easy thing to do.

But he had decided Harriet was the girl he wanted to marry, and felt he couldn't put it off any longer. If she were the person he believed she was, when he told her about his father, it wouldn't change what they had together.

Nickels found it difficult to begin. He said, "I have something important to tell you, and I'm not sure how you're going to react." He took a deep breath. "My real name isn't Nick Henry."

She looked completely surprised. "My goodness. What is it? I don't understand why you haven't told me this before."

"This isn't easy for me. When I'm finished, you'll understand why I haven't told you before.

"My parents came to America from Poland because they wanted

their children born in America. My name is Albert Henrik Jablonski, Jr."

"Oh my God." Neither of them spoke for a few moments, and then Harriet said, "Wait a second. I think I read something about someone with that name a few years ago. Is your father…?"

Nick interrupted. "Please, Harriet, don't say anything else until I finish.

"Yes, Albert Jablonski, Sr. is my father. He pled guilty to Akron's country club murder in 1920, but he's innocent. Someone did a really good job of setting him up." He studied her reaction and noticed she was listening carefully.

"I know everyone who is convicted of a crime says they're innocent, but in this case, it's the truth. My father's attorney didn't think he could get an acquittal and convinced my father to plead guilty to second-degree murder. He's serving his sentence at the state penitentiary in Columbus for a murder he didn't commit.

"The entire ordeal has destroyed my family. We'll never be the same. We're counting on the parole board to release him when he comes before them for the first time. So far he's stayed out of trouble, which isn't easy."

"When is the first time your father will come up for parole?"

"Six years. It seems like forever, but I try to tell myself it will be over before we know it. It's difficult to explain how I feel. I miss my father every day, every hour, and every minute. He is without question the best father and a wonderful man who wouldn't hurt anyone. Some days when I think of him in that hellhole, it makes me physically sick.

"The prison is overcrowded to a shocking degree, and the conditions are horrendous. It's hard to imagine my father trying to survive in there. I wouldn't treat a dog the way inmates are treated, and even though he tries, the warden is unable do a thing about it.

Sometimes when I visit Papa, he has cuts and bruises and refuses to talk about it. He insists on talking about good things and doesn't want us to dwell on his life inside the prison.

"The last time I saw my father and complained about the situation, he told me to be patient and work hard, and life will get better. That's the way he is—always positive and looking on the bright side."

Harriet reached over, pulled him to her, and hugged him. Her chin was quivering, and she had a lump in her throat that made her voice sound hoarse. "Nicky, I'm so sorry about all of this and what it's done to your family. My heart breaks for all of you."

He told her he was writing an exposé on the state penal system. It wasn't an assignment, but he explained that he hoped after the editors read it, they would run it. "My dream has always been to be a columnist, and maybe this will put me on the right track. But the article has to be perfect if it has a shot at being published. Do you want to read it before I show it to the editors?"

"Definitely."

He explained about the article. "Prohibition has created many new laws, which create a heightened demand for more aggressive prosecution and longer sentences. With these rising conviction rates, the Ohio Penitentiary is close to twice capacity. As I researched the Ohio State Penitentiary system, I found conditions are much more deplorable than I originally thought, and the treatment of prisoners is literally draconian."

He handed her the article to read.

Throughout written history, there are many accounts of prison cruelty. Within Ohio's state penitentiary in Columbus there is a system of brutality and cruelty that is a way of life for the inmates. Publicity, public indignation, investigation, removal of officials, and reform methods have all been ineffective at correcting the problem.

Our attitude toward a criminal is different than other members of society. We think he is different, but we are not concerned with why he is different, or to what degree he is different, or even whether the difference is one that is basic to the man. We merely believe he is different. This belief is common, and unfortunately, it is shared by prison administrations.

Further, we do not distinguish between the thing a man has done and the man himself. We interpret a single act to be the whole man, all but forgetting his past. We assume the crime and the man are synonymous."

Nickels went on to cover the lack of training for personnel and gave many examples of brutality and the ghastly conditions his father had finally told him about, and he had seen first hand.

He concluded with:

The goal of reform is to eliminate the atrocious aspects of our penal system and to make cruelty nonexistent. We must demand a new attitude that emphasizes the social aspects of human life by developing initiative and cooperation, thereby creating a new reality for all inmates."

Harriet read the article without comment. Afterward, she hugged Nickels. "This is excellent, and I can't imagine why they wouldn't publish it. Good job, Nicky."

He thanked her and then slipped the typed pages in an envelope. The next day at work he walked up to the managing editor and handed the envelope to him. "I'm not sure if you know who I am, but please allow me to introduce myself. I am Nick Henry, and I work here at the *News Tribune* as a copyeditor. I wrote an article on a topic I feel strongly about—prison reform. After you read it, I hope you'll publish it."

Nick heard nothing for two weeks and was ready to give up hope that they would publish his article. Then the editors called him up to the front office. They were going to run his piece as a Sunday feature. He was so excited he found it difficult to pay attention. "Nick, this is great stuff. We think you have tremendous potential."

One of the editors had penciled in some edits. He handed the manuscript to Nick and said, "Your research is impressive. I don't know how you got all this information, but it's excellent. Rework the sections we marked, and get it back to me by Wednesday."

Nick couldn't stop grinning. That night when he saw Harriet, he said, "I can't believe I'm going to have a byline in the paper. Wait until I tell my father."

Three weeks later, "Prison Cruelty: The Time For Modern Reform," ran in Sunday's paper with the byline "by Nick Henry." It had a lead-in above the fold. The editors were so impressed with Nick's writing, as well as his initiative, they gave him a regular assignment—Ohio politics.

He and Harriet went out to dinner to celebrate. He told her, "After waiting four years for a desk in the city room, I am finally right where I belong. I love listening to all the sounds—the staccato of fingers typing, rustling papers, and the hubbub of several people talking at once."

Harriet tapped her glass with a spoon and said, "Congratulations Nick Henry. This is only the beginning, and I'm proud of you." She handed him a gift-wrapped box.

He tore open the paper and opened the box. In it was an expensive fountain pen with his name engraved on the barrel.

"That's for taking notes when you're out on assignment." Harriet could see he was touched.

✧

Nick and Harriet were spending all their free time together, and by March, they were engaged and planning to marry. Nickels asked her if she was ready to meet his father and invited her to go with him to visit his father in prison.

They drove to the penitentiary in Columbus that Saturday. Nick introduced her to Albo, and while she spent time talking with him, Nick went to find the warden and give him a copy of his newspaper article.

On the way home, she told Nick she could see why he adored his father. "He's the most upbeat, optimistic person I've ever met. It's hard to fathom why he doesn't complain, especially knowing he's innocent."

The following week when Nickels was with his mother and sister, he told them about Harriet. Mama was surprised, but thrilled he had found his life's mate. Antonia wasn't happy that he had kept her a secret, but she understood why.

Nickels said, "I know Harriet will always be there for me. When I told her about Papa, she didn't flinch. She believed me when I told her he was innocent, and after she met him, and I listened to her reaction, I knew I had chosen the right woman."

Antonia said, "If you love her, I know we're all going to love her. She's going to be the sister I never had, and I can't wait to spend time with her and get to know her. The next time you're both in Akron, after you spend some time with Mama, let's go out on a double date—you and Harriet and Kurt and me."

The wedding took place on a beautiful spring day in May. Millie and Antonia took the trolley from Akron to Cleveland. Millie was dressed in her best dress—the tan one with red piping she always wore on special occasions. Her only concession to the fashion of the times was to wear a red, beaded felt hat that came down over her forehead. She carried a woven handbag with a silver clasp she brought with her from Poland.

Antonia was glad to see her mother look so happy and relaxed. "You look smashing, Mama."

"I can't believe my little Albert is getting married. I think Harriet is the right girl for him and will make him happy. Oh my goodness, maybe I'll be a grandmother soon."

"Mama, don't think too far ahead. They're not married yet." They laughed, and the mood was light on the ride up to Cleveland.

When they arrived at the church, Harriet's parents, sister, and brother were standing out front. Everyone introduced themselves and commented on what a beautiful day it was.

Nickels and Harriet had decided on a small wedding and only invited their immediate families, and of course, Kurt and Charlie. Nickels told Harriet he considered Kurt and Charlie family, so she readily agreed they should be included.

Once everyone was seated, Nick and Harriet joined each other at the altar. As the ceremony was about to begin, Antonia was watching the door and wondering where Kurt and Charlie were. It wasn't like them to be late. Just as she turned around to face the front of the church, Kurt and Charlie quietly slipped in and took seats behind Millie and Antonia. Kurt tapped her on her shoulder and leaned over the pew. He whispered, "Sorry we're late. We had a little problem with the car. I'm glad we made it in time."

She turned around and smiled at him. "I knew you and Charlie wouldn't miss it."

After the ceremony, everyone was in high spirits. Nickels immediately approached his two friends. "I'm glad you made it. It wouldn't be the same without you."

When they were all seated at the restaurant, Kurt and Antonia sat next to each another. It didn't escape anyone how close they had become. Harriet's mother asked, "Are you two next?"

"Someday, but not for a few years," said Antonia.

"We've known each other for a long time, but we're going to wait until I finish law school," Kurt explained.

Nickels kissed Harriet, stood up, and raised his glass. "First I want to say we're missing an important person today. My father. But I think he's with us in spirit. Thank you for sharing this special day with us. I found myself a good woman and couldn't be happier." He looked at his new wife. "I look forward to growing old with you. I love you, Mrs. Nick Henry."

Harriet stood up and gave him a kiss. Charlie whistled, and everyone clapped. She said, "Thanks to all of you for joining us today. It wouldn't be the same if we weren't in the company of our dearest family and friends." She smiled at Kurt and Charlie and raised her glass.

She continued, "Nicky, I want you to remember this is only the beginning of our grand adventure together. I'm so happy to be Mrs. Nick Henry. There isn't anyone in this world more perfect for me than you. I love you."

When Grandpa told me about his wedding, he said, "The day I married your grandmother was one of the happiest days of my life."

Chapter Twenty

❖

Cantrell was aware Kurt was in love with Antonia, but he had other plans for him. Long-time family friends had a daughter whom he thought was a much more appropriate match. When Russell mentioned to Marion White how terrific Kurt was, she wasn't the least bit interested. "I can find my own boyfriends, Uncle Russell."

Cantrell made sure Kurt and Marion ran into each other from time to time, and he could see a spark of interest on Marion's part. One day, after chatting with Kurt, Marion told Cantrell, "I really like his easy manner, and he sure is handsome. I could get used to looking at those blue eyes. But he doesn't seem to notice me at all."

Cantrell said, "Let's see what we can do about that."

Marion wasn't a classic beauty, but with her dark auburn hair, big brown eyes, and lush lips, she had tremendous sex appeal and an earthy magnetism. One thing was sure: She was an expert at attracting men.

A woman of the '20s, Marion wasn't going to let the government tell her what she could or couldn't do, and at twenty-one years old, she was self-confident and took great pride in being a liberated woman. A little over five feet, she dressed in short skirts, wore makeup, and smoked cigarettes.

She was definitely a little crazy, but it only added to her allure. Her friends affectionately called her Tiger, because "any man who catches Marion White has caught a tiger by the tail." Her temper was legendary, and if she didn't get her way, there was hell to pay.

She had no fear, and she loved riding in fast cars and taking risks. When she was sixteen and had never driven before, she convinced a bunch of her friends to go for a ride in her father's new car. She hadn't gone a mile before she plowed into a tree.

When her father found out, he scolded her. "Marion, I'm relieved no one was hurt, but what were you thinking? It was such a foolish thing to do. You should be ashamed of yourself."

"Oh stop it, Daddy. It was such a little thing, and nothing to get upset about. All you have to do is buy a new car. You can afford it."

Marion's family was what everyone called filthy rich, and as the only girl, her parents spoiled her. She was used to getting what she wanted, and what she wanted was a handsome husband with a promising future. She preferred men who were a little rough around the edges because she thought they were more interesting and had a lot more depth.

Marion was aware Cantrell was going to retain Kurt after he finished law school, and from what he had told her about him, she sensed Kurt wasn't going to let anything get in the way of his success. Each time she came in contact with him, she was surprised to find she was becoming more interested. Apparently he was in love with some other girl, but that only made him more appealing. Marion loved a challenge. "I need to find out if we click because I'm positive we'll look good together."

Cantrell told Marion he planned to take Kurt on a trip to New York City as a graduation present. She decided she wanted to join them and went to talk to her father. She found him in his den. "Daddy, I want to go to New York for a few days with Uncle Russell. His protégé Kurt Becker is graduating from college, and Uncle Russell is giving him the trip as a present. He invited me to go with them. You know I adore

New York. Please say you'll let me go."

What Marion's father didn't know was that she wanted to seduce Kurt. She thought if she could get a few days with him, he'd fall for her.

"Russell is paying for the trip, but I know you'll give me a lot of spending money. Right, Daddy?"

He didn't hesitate. "Whatever you want, Baby."

"Thank you. You're my hero." Her father shook his head and chuckled as Marion walked away.

After Kurt was thrown together with Marion a few times at Hollingsworth House, he caught on to the idea that Cantrell was trying be a matchmaker. Kurt wanted Cantrell to know he was committed to Antonia. "When I finish law school I'm going to marry my fiancée Antonia. I'm not interested in other women, including Marion White. I love Antonia."

"How many times do I have to tell you to dump that Polack? It won't be good for you to be seen around town with her. You need someone who can open doors and help you with your career. Once you're my attorney, you'll have to attend fancy social events, and Marion is the kind of woman you should have on your arm. I want you to look and act like the clients you're going to represent."

It infuriated Kurt that Cantrell thought he could orchestrate his life and that this was the price he had to pay for the money he had accepted. He ignored Cantrell's bigoted slur and walked away.

By June Kurt had graduated from Akron University and was accepted at Western Reserve Law School, one of the oldest in the country. Cantrell wanted him to go to Yale and had offered to pull some strings, but Kurt wanted to stay close to home so he could continue to see Antonia and get back and forth to Akron without a problem. Cantrell was pleased with how well he had done in college and told Kurt his graduation present was a big surprise.

"What is it? I hate surprises."

"You have to wait to find out. Be at Hollingsworth House by noon on Friday. Bring a suitcase and pack a good suit and enough clothes for a few days. We're taking a trip."

Kurt was annoyed he didn't know where they were going, but thought it might turn out to be fun. He had never been anywhere other than Pennsylvania and Ohio, and the most he had ever travelled was by trolley bus to Cleveland, if you could call that travelling. He had to buy some new clothes, because he had nothing acceptable for the trip.

When Kurt showed up at the mansion, Marion was standing next to Russell. "Oh shit. I should have known this was going to be a set-up. Oh well. I don't really care if she's coming with us. I'm taking a real trip for the first time in my life, and nothing is going to ruin it. Not even Marion White."

When Cantrell reintroduced them, Marion was once again surprised by how attracted she was to Kurt. She was enthusiastic about the trip and said to herself, "By the end of this little jaunt, Kurt Becker isn't going to know what hit him."

Between Cantrell and Marion's parents, no expense was spared.

When Cantrell told Kurt they were taking the train from Cleveland to New York City and staying at the Waldorf-Astoria, he was thrilled. New York City. Wait until Mama and Aunt Erna heard he travelled to New York on the train and stayed at a deluxe hotel like the Waldorf.

The three of them piled into Cantrell's Packard for the trip to Cleveland where they would catch the eastern-bound New York Central Railroad train.

Cantrell had reserved two deluxe Pullman staterooms with

sleeping compartments. He and Kurt would share one, and Marion had one to herself. Kurt marveled at the furnishings. The stateroom was elaborately decorated. Chairs and couches were soft. Carpeting was plush. This was definitely the right way to travel. He had never seen such opulence, but he was sure he could get used to it.

Cantrell had planned ahead and snuck some booze onboard. Neither Kurt nor Marion knew it was distilled at Cantrell's country place.

They sat in Russell and Kurt's suite and had cocktails before dinner. Cantrell said, "Tonight you're going to experience a true gourmet meal. They go all out on these trains, and the food is better than some of the best restaurants in the country."

In the ornate dining car, they sat at an elegant table set with starched white linens, bone china and sterling silver. A white-gloved, Negro waiter served roasted pheasant, rice pilaf, and green beans with sautéed almonds. Dessert was cherries jubilee, which the waiter flambéed at the table. Kurt had never seen anything like it.

After dinner, Cantrell excused himself and said he was going to another passenger's stateroom where he had been invited to a card game. He enjoyed gambling and had promised Marion he would give her some time alone with Kurt.

"It's just you and me now," Marion said. "What shall we do?"

Kurt was surprised to find he was not immune to her wiles, and the air sizzled with the sexual tension between them.

She chattered about their plans for New York and about some of her girlfriends. It really didn't matter what she was saying, because when she gazed at him, he felt an energy bounce back and forth between them. Their chemistry was so powerful that he found it difficult to pay attention to anything she said. He noticed how she seductively batted her eyelashes, and thought, "She's good at this."

When he walked her back to her stateroom and stood at the door, she moved very close to him and slowly massaged his back and arms. He got an immediate erection.

She stood on her tiptoes and kissed him passionately on the lips. He kissed her back, and they stood at the doorway kissing for a long time.

"See you tomorrow, Kurt."

"Um, yeah, see you tomorrow, Marion."

She rubbed against him and felt how hard he was. She said, "I have a feeling this trip is going to be a lot of fun."

Early the next morning the train came into Grand Central Terminal. They found a porter and entered the main concourse. Kurt turned around in a circle to take it all in. "This is unbelievable. It is so much bigger than I could have ever imagined." Marion and Cantrell were already twenty yards ahead of him and didn't seem to notice their surroundings.

Cantrell waved at him to hurry, "Come on. We need to catch a taxi and get to the hotel."

Cantrell had booked the grand luxury suite in the Waldorf-Astoria Towers. The lobby of the hotel was buzzing with activity. The bellhop loaded their luggage on a cart, and they rode the elevator up to their suite. Marion said, "This is where we always stay in New York."

They entered the suite through the marble foyer. Cantrell said, "Go ahead, Kurt. Take a look around."

Kurt went into each room, and came back out to the living room. "This place is amazing. The bathroom alone is as big as the parlor in my house."

Cantrell asked, "What do you think of your graduation present?"

"This is more than I deserve and certainly more than I expected.

Thank you."

"You're welcome, but you earned it. You worked hard in college, and I expect you to do the same in law school.

"I have another surprise. This one is for Marion. Tonight we're going to Harlem's Cotton Club, the most famous nightclub in the country."

Marion said, "Oh, thank you, Uncle Russell. I can't wait. I've never been there, and I've always wanted to go. I adore jazz."

Russell said, "Kurt, do you know about the place? It's owned by gangster-bootlegger Owney Madden. He only lets whites in, but all the performers are Negroes. Ironic, isn't it?"

When they arrived, the club was humming with excitement. Decorated as a stylish plantation, the evening's show was a musical revue featuring dancers, singers, and comedians, all accompanied by the house band. Their table was up front near the stage.

Kurt thought it was exciting to be at the famed club and said, "I can certainly see I'm not in Akron, Ohio."

Marion was dressed in a red beaded silk dress with the fringed hemline a couple of inches below the knees. She wore patterned stockings and a matching beaded headband across her forehead that sparkled when it caught the light. As they sat down, she grinned and lifted up her skirt to show Kurt a flask tucked into her garter belt.

Kurt wore new shoes and a dark gray suit he bought for the trip and paid for with money from his bank account. It was only the second time he'd withdrawn money.

Kurt looked at Marion. She was smiling and having a great time. The band was in the middle of a number when Marion jumped up and started to dance in front of their table. She twirled over to where Kurt sat, threw him a kiss, and then turned around and shook her bottom.

Cantrell didn't miss how Kurt watched Marion. "She's something, isn't she?"

"I never knew how much fun she is. I'm having a great time. Thanks for asking her to come along." Marion had overheard. She gave Russell a knowing look.

As the evening wore on and they had more to drink, Marion moved closer to Kurt and chatted about what they were going to do for the rest of the trip. She talked about going to the Metropolitan Museum of Art, and he was impressed with how much she knew about art.

She saw how he looked at her and whispered in his ear, "I really like your style, Becker. I could get used to having you around." As she sat up, her lips brushed across his cheek, and it gave him a jolt.

During their time in New York, they dined at fancy restaurants, went to museums, and rode a horse-drawn carriage through Central Park. They saw a musical with Beatrice Lillie and Gertrude Lawrence at the Selwyn Theatre, where they had the best seats in the house.

By the time they caught the train home on Wednesday morning, Kurt had begun to see what Cantrell was talking about when he said Marion would be an asset in his career. She was sure of herself, knew how to talk to people, and had an ability to persuade people to do what she wanted.

She asked him where he lived and was appalled to learn he lived in a boardinghouse. "Why not move out? Russell owns an apartment building, and I'm sure he would let you live in one of the units. Isn't that right, Uncle Russell?"

"Sure, move in anytime. I have a couple of apartments available."

"Thanks, but for most of these next few years, I'll be in Cleveland at Western Reserve, and I'm not going to move out of the boardinghouse until I'm back in Akron for good." He thought of Antonia. He was conflicted because he realized how attracted he was to

Marion, but he *loved* Antonia. He decided for the rest of the trip, he wasn't going to think about Antonia. When he got home, this whole thing with Marion would blow over and seem like a dream.

Kurt felt as if he were in a trance. Captivated by the events of the weekend, he realized this was the kind of life he had always dreamed about. All those years of taking care of the boarders were a distant memory.

On the way home, he and Marion spent hours discussing everything from politics to what kind of food they liked. When they were almost in Cleveland, she edged up to him and passionately kissed him again. Kurt responded instantly and once again couldn't believe the sexual energy between them. He was heady with the excitement of the trip and suddenly said, "Would you go out to dinner with me next Friday?"

"Kurt Becker, I would go anywhere with you."

By the time they were back in Akron, he was in awe of Marion and her extravagant lifestyle. He was afraid he might be falling for her, but was struggling with what to do about Antonia. He rationalized that maybe he had begun to outgrow Antonia, but he felt guilty and was worried about telling her he was dating Marion.

He didn't want to hurt Antonia and decided he wasn't ready to tell her anything yet.

Grandpa said, "It wasn't a very nice thing for Kurt to do considering his history with my sister, but he was sure his fling with Marion wasn't going to last long enough to become a problem."

Chapter Twenty-one

❖

$\mathscr{C}$antrell was thirty-nine years old and by 1925, had become one of the state's better-known personalities. His confident swagger and phony charm made him a natural for politics. The year before, he won his first term to Congress as the Republican Representative from Ohio.

Cantrell's parents generously donated to his campaign, but at sixty-five years old, travelled for a good part of the year. They were absent from Hollingsworth House much of the time, but were usually home for part of the summer.

At breakfast one morning in June, his father said, "Sit down for a minute, Russell. I have something I want to say to you."

As Cantrell sat down, he thought, "Uh oh, that's never a good preface from my father."

His father said, "Your mother and I are very proud of you, son. But I must confess, there was a time when we thought you were never going to stay out of trouble. I don't want to count the times we extricated you from one of your predicaments. But that's behind us now. Both your mother and I want you to know how impressed we are by the fine man you've become."

Cantrell thanked him and walked out of the room laughing to himself. "Wouldn't he be surprised to find out what I'm really doing? My father and mother are such fools."

The compliment from his father made his day. Not only had his father actually praised him—rare indeed—but he got a charge out of knowing he was putting something over on his parents.

Cantrell had invested in numerous projects for Ohio's continued economic growth. For the past several years, he had spearheaded the fundraising for a baseball stadium in Akron. The dedication was scheduled for late July.

In the meantime, he was running a massive smear campaign against his opponent, and it was working. But he wanted more coverage in the press and asked his campaign manager to schedule an interview with Nick Henry, the iconoclastic political reporter at the *Cleveland News Tribune*.

Nickels tried to make arrangements to get to Washington to interview Cantrell in person, but one or the other always had a scheduling conflict, and they decided to do the interview by telephone. Nickels asked Cantrell's assistant to provide some photographs before the interview. Cantrell's office sent three photos—one of Cantrell sitting at his desk in Washington; one with his wife and children; and one standing at a dais giving a campaign speech.

Nickels studied the photo of Cantrell's office and took in the elegant furnishings and the original artwork, as well as the Congressman's expensive, custom-made suit. "I bet that desk is as long my living room sofa. It's obvious he's never known what it's like to need something you can't afford."

Their conversation lasted about thirty minutes and included many contentious moments. Nearing the end of the interview, Nick said, "I want to move on to another subject. Our investigative team has been digging into the murder of Councilman Lyle for over three years. It remains unsolved."

Cantrell was unable to hide the surprise in his voice. "It's puzzling that you would mention Lyle. What does it have to do with me?"

"Nothing directly, but the name Voigt keeps popping up. Isn't he your chauffeur when you're in Akron?"

"Yes he is, but I can assure you my driver knows nothing about a murder."

Nickels could hear him rustling papers on his desk and whispering to someone close by. Cantrell said, "I'm sorry, but in a few minutes I have a committee meeting, and we're going to have to wrap this up."

"Congressman, thank you for your time. I have a small request. Would you provide some specifics in terms of your campaign platform? Something more detailed than what you've been saying in your speeches? I would appreciate it if you could give it to me in writing by the beginning of next week. Is that enough time for you?"

Cantrell said, "Of course, I'll be happy to send you something, but I have to get going. Have a good day." He hung up without waiting to hear Nickels say good-bye.

Cantrell was rattled by Nick's mention of Lyle. He wondered how he was able to make that connection.

Nickel's article ran the end of June. "Cantrell talks less about what he can do than what he purports his opponent cannot. The people of Ohio want to know the specifics about his plans for our future."

The article also alluded to an ongoing investigation involving the Congressman and an associate.

Cantrell was determined to find out why Nick Henry was so negative about him. He had hoped their interview would create some positive press and was furious when it backfired.

✧

Cantrell and his wife Elizabeth had two daughters, ages one and three. Although Elizabeth was miserable in her marriage, she adored fussing over her daughters and was much more content now that she had a purpose in life. The only thing her husband demanded of her was that she and the girls make themselves available for photo opportunities and appear on the dais during his campaign speeches.

They never had sex anymore and slept in separate bedrooms. During lunch at the country club, she told her close friend in the strictest confidence, "Frankly, I'm glad he's out of my bed. I loathed having sex with him. He was always so rough with me, and I never enjoyed it. The sex was bad enough, but what made it worse was that he always smelled like one of his horrid cigars.

"There were a couple of times when he actually hit me. I told him if he ever did it again, I would move out. I know he's seeing other women, and I don't care. Let him do what he wants, as long as he leaves me and the girls alone."

When he was in town, Cantrell saw his daughters at breakfast but wasn't interested in spending much time with them, unless it had to do with his image. He had nothing to say to them, and children in general made him uncomfortable. He was usually in Washington, and Elizabeth refused to leave Akron.

Although Elizabeth didn't know exactly what Russell was up to, she was certain it wasn't good. When he was in town, he spent way too much time with his driver.

Voigt lived in an apartment Cantrell had added on above the garage. Elizabeth couldn't stand to be around Voigt. And she didn't like how he looked at her when her husband wasn't around. Whenever she spoke to him, he stared at her in a strange way and rarely replied. One time when she had come out to the garage to look for something, Voigt yelled at her to go back to the house. She had been afraid of him ever since.

Elizabeth said, "Russell, I don't want him living here on the estate. I don't understand why he's here when you're in Washington. When he looks at me, it gives me the willies. And that mangled ear of his is revolting. What's wrong with him?"

"Elizabeth, you're being ridiculous. He injured his ear in an accident when he was a boy. Give the guy a break. He's here because I want him here when I'm home. And you have no say in whether he lives here or not, so he will continue to live on the grounds because *I say so*."

Cantrell thought his wife was a scared little rabbit who would faint if she ever got a glimpse of what Voigt was really like.

Kurt's life was a far cry from the days of cleaning toilets and mucking out the chicken coop. At the beginning of the summer, after much prodding from Marion, he finally relented and moved out of the boardinghouse and into one of Cantrell's apartments.

"I have several unrented apartments, so it's not a problem. Pay the utilities and it's yours when you're home from school," Cantrell said.

Even though Marta tried to convince him not to move out, Kurt knew it was time to go. He was delighted to finally have his own place, and especially his very own, personal, private, nobody-but-me-can-use-it bathroom.

Chapter Twenty-two

❖

Summertime in Akron meant industrial league baseball, and tire manufacturers Goodyear, Firestone, General, B.F. Goodrich, and other Akron-based corporations sponsored employee teams. According to the *Akron News Journal*, "Cantrell Stadium will be dedicated on July 25, 1925 by Russell H. Cantrell, U.S. Congressman, prominent attorney, businessman, and noted philanthropist."

The article went on to say that the thirteen-acre stadium complex with over four thousand seats was built for the citizens of Akron. Local teams would play each other and also have the opportunity to play major league teams barnstorming across the country.

During the dedication, Goodyear's blimp, The Pilgrim, flew over the crowd. It was Goodyear's first civil airship, and the first to use helium. Kurt was fascinated with it. "Look at that, Marion. It's amazing it can stay up in the air. Isn't that something?"

Marion yawned. "This is so boring Kurt. I don't want to be here, sitting in this heat. I'm sweaty and uncomfortable. Can we leave now, please?"

"Not yet. We have to stay. Russell wouldn't like it if we left early."

Marion moved closer to him and said, "I'm looking forward to tonight, Kurt. I think you know what I mean," she said with a wink.

Kurt laughed and hugged her.

Kurt caught sight of Cantrell's wife, two little girls, and their nanny, an older, grandmotherly woman. Elizabeth looked as if she were ready to melt. "Look how frazzled Elizabeth is. I bet Russell is going to be steamed about how she looks in the photos. He's so hard on her, and I feel sorry for her. The only time he pays any attention to her and the girls is when he's campaigning and photographers are hovering around. But now that they have children, I'm sure she's in it for the long haul."

"Oh for goodness sake, she's ridiculous. I can't imagine why Uncle Russell chose her for his wife. I think if I went up to her right now and said, 'Boo,' she'd cry."

"I bet she's stronger than you think. I like her and think he treats her miserably."

✧

After the ceremony, Kurt made excuses and dropped Marion at her house, and then headed to a restaurant where he had arranged to meet Antonia. He still hadn't told Antonia about Marion and was dreading it. He didn't want to tell her, but so many people in Akron had seen him with Marion over the past few months. He had been careful to avoid Nickels and Charlie, but knew it was a matter of time before one of them saw him with Marion. He had decided his subterfuge had gone on long enough. It wasn't fair to Antonia.

Lately Antonia had noticed how detached he was and on several occasions asked him what was wrong. He put her off by saying he had a lot of work to do and a lot on his mind with law school. Because he was in Cleveland most of the time, it hadn't been necessary to explain why they weren't able to get together very often. When they had seen each other, Kurt felt ill at ease and really hated deceiving her. He could tell she knew things weren't the same.

He really didn't want to hurt Antonia, but he thought he was in love with Marion and planned to give her an engagement ring. Marion's father was pleased when Kurt asked for permission to marry his daughter. Mr. White had given Kurt a two-carat, emerald-cut diamond that had belonged to Marion's grandmother. Kurt had taken the ring to a jeweler and had the stone put in a more modern setting with smaller diamonds surrounding the large one.

When Antonia walked into the restaurant, Kurt was struck again by how beautiful she was. The fact that she was such a nice person and a good friend was not going to make this any easier.

She walked right up to him and kissed him on the mouth. It was a long, sensuous kiss, and he couldn't help but respond. She said, "It seems like years since we've been together. I've been looking forward to this night so much. I've missed you, my love."

After they sat down at their table, Kurt didn't know how to begin.

"What's wrong? You're so jumpy, you look as if you have the heebie jeebies."

"Toni, I have to tell you something I've been avoiding, but let's order first."

Antonia stood completely still and looked directly at Kurt. "I want you to tell me what's wrong right now."

He couldn't look at her. "All right. Um…Antonia."

"Kurt, you're scaring me. Just tell me. Whatever it is, it can't be that bad. We can handle it together."

"Toni, you know how much you mean to me. We've been together for a long time, and we're the most wonderful friends."

"Just say it." She had an awful feeling in the pit of her stomach.

"I'm sorry. This is difficult…but…I've been seeing someone else."

Antonia's face registered utter disbelief.

He said, "I have asked her to marry me. Her name is Marion White. There are no words to tell you how sorry I am. It just happened. It was nothing I planned. I want you to know that."

The color drained from Antonia's face, and she didn't say

anything. She refused to look at him.

She leaned over the table and spoke so softly he could barely hear her. "How could this happen? You can't throw away what we have."

He struggled to find words, opening his mouth, then closing it.

Antonia said, "You aren't thinking straight. I know a life with someone else can't be what you really want. We belong together. I want to know how long you've been seeing her."

"I'm so sorry. I've been seeing her for about a year and recently decided to make it official. It killed me to deceive you, and I can't be dishonest with you anymore. You mean too much to me. I know I should have told you much sooner."

Kurt looked at the floor. "This is one of the most painful things I've ever had to do. Please forgive me."

Antonia got up from the table and said, "Take me home. I won't stay here with you one more minute."

During the drive home she looked straight ahead and tried not to cry.

"I hope you'll be able to forgive me someday."

She didn't respond.

He tried to walk her up to the front door, but she batted him away. He asked if he could come into the house with her, but she frantically shook her head no. Once inside the house, she slammed the door as hard as she could. She collapsed on the floor and sobbed uncontrollably. Millie ran into the room and said, "Oh dear, what's wrong? What happened?"

She was crying so hard that she had trouble speaking. "Kurt has decided he wants to be with someone else, Mama. He broke up with me, and we're never going to get married. He's going…to…marry… Marion White." She continued to cry hysterically and couldn't catch her breath.

After Antonia began to calm down, she said, "Remember what I told you about that rich girl? Cantrell kept throwing Marion at him, and I knew she was going to be a problem. She put her sights on my Kurt, and wouldn't stop until she got him. I hate her. What am I going to do? I can't imagine my life without him. He's my best friend." She sat on the floor and wailed.

Millie was almost as distressed as Antonia. She thought of Kurt as a son, and she couldn't believe he'd hurt Antonia so badly. She couldn't find the right words, and instead went over to Antonia, pulled her up off the floor, and led her to the sofa. She pulled her daughter into her arms. "You'll get over this, my little Antonia. I know it doesn't feel as if you can, but you will. It is going to take time. But I want you to think about something. If he chose someone like her, maybe you're better off without him."

"I'll never get over him. I've loved him since I was a little girl. We were meant to be together. I can't believe he wants to be with that awful woman instead of me, but it's as if he's in a trance. I know him, Mama, and he's mesmerized by her money. He can't see beyond her bank account."

Grandpa Nicky said when he called home later, and his mother whispered to him what had happened, he took it as a personal betrayal. "I didn't think I would ever forgive Kurt. And when Papa heard about it, he was so disappointed in Kurt, he refused to let him visit anymore."

Chapter Twenty-three

❖

$\mathcal{K}$urt and Marion had become much closer and were having a really good time together. When she came up to Cleveland on weekends, his friends thought she was great fun. There was no question she liked to go to parties, and everyone looked forward to her visits. There were a couple of times when she drank too much, but so had everyone else, so it didn't appear to be much of a problem. His law school friends were caught up in her allure, which only confirmed for him that Marion was the right choice.

Kurt was heady with his new way of life and was amazed at how easily doors opened when he was with Marion. And one of the bonuses of being with her was that everyone got the impression he was wealthy too.

Kurt had reached out to Nickels many times over the last two years, but Nickels wasn't willing to let go of his anger. He wasn't sure if he could ever forgive Kurt for hurting his sister. Kurt worried their estrangement would never end.

But Marion didn't want Kurt to patch things up with Nickels. "You have new friends. What do you need those two for? That Tribe thing is childish."

"It's not as easy as you think, Marion. I've known Nickels and Charlie since I was a boy, and can't think of a time when they weren't an important part of my life. When you have people in your life you know you can always depend on, there's nothing like it. Don't you have any friends like that?"

"I haven't really thought about it, and I guess I don't think it's as important as you do."

"I'm going to do whatever it takes to mend my relationship with Nickels. I miss him, and I miss spending time with The Tribe."

Marion was glad Kurt wasn't speaking to Nickels. As long as they were at odds with each other, the less likely it was his sister Antonia would come back into Kurt's life.

✧

By the time Charlie was twenty-four, the Catholic Church no longer played an important role in his life. He stopped going to Mass and began to define his moral principles outside the church. To him, Catholicism had become more about politics and rules than spirituality. There were too many doctrines he didn't agree with and lots of unanswered questions, so he refused to blindly follow its teachings anymore.

Charlie had married Grace Allerton the year before. When he first told his mother about Grace, she was horrified and said, "She has two big marks against her. She's not Irish and she's not Catholic. Holy Mother of God. I can't believe you're going to marry a Protestant. Will she convert and go to Mass with you?"

"Mom, I don't go to Mass. And no, she's not going to convert."

His mother crossed herself and looked up at the sky. "Oh my sweet Lord, this isn't good."

"I'm sorry you feel the way you do, but I don't want to discuss it. I love Grace, and she's going to be my wife."

Since the marriage, Maureen's relationship with her daughter-in-law had improved, and now that Grace was pregnant, Charlie's mother had definitely warmed up to her.

When Charlie first discussed children with Grace, he said, "I love my parents and my brothers and sisters, but there was never enough of anything to go around—not enough love and attention or money and clothes. The only thing we had a lot of was chores. I'm not sure how you feel about it, but I only want two kids. I'm hoping that's okay with you."

"Yes, definitely. I feel the same way and only want two." Vivacious and friendly, Grace was an ideal match for someone as reserved and methodical as Charlie. She made friends easily, and she and Charlie had a large group of friends they associated with.

They bought a house in an up-and-coming neighborhood on the west side of town and had a great time fixing it up. They painted the nursery yellow and couldn't wait to find out if the baby was a girl or a boy. Charlie secretly hoped it was a boy. He imagined taking his son to Cleveland Indians games with Kurt and Nickels' boys, if they ever had any.

It had been six years since Charlie had joined the police force, and he had grown much more judgmental and opinionated. It came with the job. In January, he was promoted to detective, the youngest in the department.

When he discussed it with Grace, she said, "Tell me again why you like being a policeman."

"I like helping people. I like work that isn't routine, and more than anything, I like the excitement. Originally, I thought it would be the one job where there were distinct lines between good and bad, black and white. But being on the job has tempered any illusions I may have had. It's tough out there, and these aren't easy times for any of us on the force."

✧

Nickels came to dinner at Grace and Charlie's on one of the

evenings he was in Akron visiting his mother and sister. He really liked Grace and enjoyed spending time with the two of them.

To Charlie, Kurt's absence felt strange. He missed having the three of them together, but knew time was only thing that was going to heal the rift.

As they sat around the dinner table, Nickels asked Charlie about work. "I hear it's crazy out there."

"Crazier than I ever could have imagined. When I first joined the department, my beat was downtown. I worked nights mostly, and almost all of my arrests were run-of-the-mill drunks. Let me tell you about the time I ran in this one guy. He was walking down the street reeling from streetlight to streetlight. When I stopped him and suggested he go home and sleep it off, he told me to go screw myself and to leave him alone. The next thing I knew, he'd fallen backward onto the grass and was passed out cold. I called a wagon, and we took him to the station where we pushed him into a cell so he could sleep it off. The next morning he was so furious to find himself in jail, he banged on the bars and screamed for us to let him out. Turns out his wife was a fanatical member of the WCTU, and he was afraid she was going to find out he'd been drinking."

Grace said. "Pay attention, boys. It never pays to cross your wife."

Charlie and Nickels laughed.

Charlie had great instincts and street skills and was admired by the other officers. In one of his cases, he helped solve a murder involving a member of the Eugenics movement, a group that advocated trying to improve the genetic composition of a population. They believed immigrants, Negroes, Irish Catholics, and Jews severely threatened society.

Grace said, "Honey, tell Nickels about the Levin murder."

Charlie leaned back in his chair. "Now there's an interesting case.

When we first entered Robert Levin's home and found his body, we thought he'd had a heart attack. But when we rolled him over, we saw he'd been shot in the back. He had a ruby ring on his finger, a thick wad of cash in his pocket, and an expensive pocket watch, so we knew robbery wasn't the motive. Two days after we found the body, I interviewed George Barton—Barton's daughter Mary had been secretly seeing Levin. We're convinced Barton murdered Levin because he was Jewish and refused to stay away from his daughter.

"While we were talking to Barton, my partner was standing next to him. Suddenly Barton pulled a gun. I saw right away that his finger was on the trigger, so I shouted at my partner to move away. I dove across the room, clutching at Barton's legs to bring him down. His gun went off. Thank God the bullet lodged in the wall. After that it was easy to get him to confess. He'll spend the rest of his life in prison."

"Is that when you received a commendation for saving the other cop's life?"

"Yes, and that was a great moment for me, but what made me feel even better was that at the ceremony I heard one of the other officers say, 'If you partner with Bulldog O'Brien, you're in good hands. He'll go to the mat for you.'"

Nickels said, "I've always known that about you. I'm really proud of you, Charlie."

Charlie continued. "Thanks. But things have changed so much. Our residential neighborhoods are relatively peaceful, but downtown is reeling, and Akron is becoming increasingly dangerous—to a great extent, because of rumrunners coming into the U.S. from Canada. Prohibition be damned. These new criminals use murder, intimidation, extortion, and bribery to get what they want, and believe me, it's making my life much more difficult."

"And more dangerous," said Grace.

Nickels said, "In Cleveland, it's well known that much of the police force has been bought off."

Charlie nodded. "Yeah, it's a nightmare. The bootleggers give the officers a little whiskey and some money to make sure they look the other way. They consider it a cheap insurance policy. I'm suspicious of several guys on the Akron force, and it's really creating problems. Everyone knows it's going on, but it's not easy to prove it. What makes it worse is that we know elected officials are manipulating police appointments and promotions, while at the same time they're making a killing from booze, gambling, and vice. When you combine crooked politicians, racketeers, bootleggers, and judges with the crooked cops, you have a real hornet's nest.

"Federal revenuers are searching for a huge operation making bootleg liquor and distributing it throughout Ohio. Every night the Prohibition agents go out and look for smoke above the trees. They're pretty sure it's out in the woods somewhere in the country, but they don't know exactly where. Whoever is behind it has bought off a large number of police, so it's next to impossible to run an investigation. The people running the show are making buckets of money, and it's all tax free."

"This is really interesting. I think I could find a good column in this bootleg operation. Anything else you can tell me?"

Charlie said, "I'll tell you what we know. They're bringing in some of the booze across Lake Erie by boat. We believe they transport it in camouflaged trucks and distribute it throughout the state of Ohio and even into Pennsylvania and Indiana. They use those same trucks to pick up the liquor at a large bootlegging compound somewhere outside of Akron. Some big cheese is behind it, and everyone thinks we're getting close. When we finally break it, it's going to be big."

"Um…Nickels. There's something else I want you to think about."

"Uh oh, this sounds serious."

"I want you to think about forgiving Kurt. I understand why you're upset. We all agree he was a real cad to Antonia, but it's over now, and we can't change it. He's engaged to Marion, and Antonia has moved on with her life. I miss The Tribe and hope we can find a way to put this behind us. Promise me you'll think about it."

"You have to give me some time, but I'll think about it. He broke my sister's heart, and that's hard for me to forget."

"I'm not suggesting you forget it, but I'm hoping you can forgive him. I miss meeting you guys at The Canal, and I definitely miss having the three of us get together at ball games."

Grace said, "Speaking of Kurt… He and Marion sent us an expensive bassinet for the baby. They must have spent a fortune on it."

Nickels said, "He loves being around all that money, that's for sure. I've never known him when he didn't mention he was going to be rich one day, but maybe you should be careful what you wish for."

Charlie said, "I know what you mean. I don't think he's very happy. I have a feeling that once you have that much money, it no longer means so much. And, boy oh boy, that Marion is a wild one. I'm not sure how Kurt can keep up with her. Did you hear what she did last week?"

"No. What?"

"Grace's friend told her about it. Honey, tell Nickels about it."

"Okay, this is what I heard. Last week my friend was in a speakeasy, and Marion was there without Kurt. She was three sheets to the wind and jumped up on the table and began dancing provocatively. The three men with her kept encouraging her to dance and make a spectacle of herself. Apparently it was quite risqué. Someone who knew Kurt had the owner call him, and he rushed right over. When Kurt saw her up on display and dancing, he was so mad, he yanked her off the table and insisted she let him take her home.

"My friend told me he was screaming at her that she was making a fool of herself. She threw one of her tantrums on the spot, screeching at Kurt that he was no fun and being with him was like being with a boring old man. She went up to him, put both her hands on his chest, and pushed him really hard. He fell backward onto the table and everything went crashing. He got up, brushed himself off, and threw a roll of cash at the owner. Then he grabbed her by the arm and pulled her outside."

Nickels said, "I don't feel sorry for him. He was determined to live the high life with Marion, and look where it got him. I can't believe he still intends to marry her.

Nickels got up to leave. He shook Charlie's hand and said, "I'll think about what you said, Charlie. Like you, I miss The Tribe, but I'm not ready to spend any time with Kurt yet."

Chapter Twenty-four

❖

*K*urt had made it. He couldn't believe it was 1927, and he was finished with law school. He had always dreamed of being an attorney, and now he was only a bar exam away.

Kurt didn't want to participate in the graduation ceremony, but after his mother and aunt said they were disappointed and had been looking forward to it, he changed his mind. Marion wasn't there because she was in New York on another shopping trip with her mother. And Cantrell was in Washington, so it was just the three of them. Marion thoughtfully provided a car to bring Marta and Erna to Cleveland.

Kurt asked Charlie to come, but he was working a high-profile homicide case and couldn't get away. He invited Nickels, but didn't expect him to come.

Marta and Erna were extraordinarily pleased with what Kurt had accomplished. "Erna, can you believe Kurt is going to be a fancy lawyer? I'm so proud of him, I think I'm going to burst."

Erna was in a good mood, and excited about riding in a private car with a uniformed driver. "I always said he should go to college and law school. It's what he wanted from the time he was a youngster."

Marta looked at her in disbelief. "What? You said he should work in the factory for the rest of his life. You said he didn't need an education."

"I most certainly did not. Be quiet. Don't ruin this beautiful day."

Marta shook her head. She knew her sister would never change.

It was a wonderful day. Several people congratulated Kurt, including the dean of the law school. Kurt introduced the dean to his mother and aunt.

"You should be very proud of your son and nephew. He's a fine young man and an outstanding student. I thoroughly enjoyed our spirited debates over the past three years. He has a wonderful career ahead of him," said the dean. Marta and Erna beamed.

Afterward they went out for dinner. It was only the second time in Erna's life she had eaten in a restaurant, and she criticized the table setting, the wait staff, and the food. "This food is tasteless and needs some spice. I want to get into that kitchen and show them how to prepare a good meal."

"Relax and enjoy your time away from the boardinghouse, Aunt Erna. Be happy you aren't working today."

Erna harrumphed, "Shush. Just because you're a lawyer now doesn't mean you can tell me what to do." He didn't miss the trace of a smile on her face.

Marta was having a grand time, but wanted to get something off her chest. "Speaking of good cooking, we think it's high time you brought Marion over for dinner. We want to spend some time with the woman you're going to marry. We feel as if we don't know her at all."

Kurt was hesitant to bring Marion to the boardinghouse, but said he would talk to her about it and bring her over for dinner soon.

After moving back to Akron for good, Kurt told Marion about the dinner invitation and suggested they give their excuses, but she insisted they go. "They invited us, and it's rude not to go. After all, they're your family and I hardly know them. I'm curious to see the famous Stucke House you talk so much about."

Kurt had kept her away from Stucke House for the last three years.

He didn't want her to see it. When they pulled up in front of the boardinghouse, Marion was appalled and didn't try to hide it. "Is this… place…is this where you grew up?"

Considering the affluent lifestyle she was accustomed to, he knew it was a mistake to bring her to the boardinghouse. She had no idea what living with a diverse group of people was like, and her reaction to Stucke House and the neighborhood was exactly what he had expected. It was why he had avoided bringing her before.

"I know it's nothing like where you grew up, but Mama and Aunt Erna did their best to make it a nice home for me. Believe it or not, not everyone is born into wealth." He dreaded the evening and hoped Aunt Erna would behave herself and not say anything to embarrass him.

"Don't get all bothered and defensive. It surely can't be as bad on the inside as it is on the outside," she said as she looked at the house.

Marta and Erna had gone all out for the dinner. Because the boarders ate in the dining room, they set a beautiful table with their best linens in the kitchen. They started with a molded fruit salad and then served a pot roast with roasted vegetables and scalloped potatoes. Dessert was one of their famous Stucke House pies.

As soon as Kurt and Marion walked into the kitchen, Marta hugged Marion. "I'm so happy you finally made it to our home. We're glad to have a chance to get to know you better."

Marion squirmed to get out of her grasp. After she untangled herself, she formally said, "Thank you. Lovely to be here."

Kurt showed Marion around the boardinghouse and ended the tour in his old third-floor room, which was empty. She looked around the small room. "This is pathetic."

When they walked back into the kitchen, Kurt said, "Mama, rent out my room. I'm never coming back to live here."

She sighed. "I know. But I can't think of anyone else in that room.

To me, it will always be your room."

During the meal Marta watched Marion carefully, and was not quite sure what she thought of her. She was nice enough and pretty in her own way, but not nearly as friendly or beautiful as Antonia. When Kurt and Marion walked out onto the porch for a minute, she whispered to her sister, "She's definitely highfalutin, but since she's going to be my daughter-in-law, I suppose I have to give her some leeway."

At dinner, no one could stop talking about a young pilot named Charles Lindbergh. In May, he had soloed a non-stop flight from New York to Paris in his single-seat, single-engine plane, the *Spirit of St. Louis*. "Pretty soon we'll all be flying all over the country," said Marion.

Erna said, "I don't think that will ever happen. Ordinary people won't get in those contraptions and fly around in the sky. I'll stick to buses and trains, thank you very much."

Coming from two completely different worlds, the conversation among Marion, Marta, and Erna was forced, and Kurt thought they might as well be speaking different languages.

Erna asked, "Do you like to cook?"

"Oh no, of course not. We have a cook. Why would I want to cook when someone can do it for me?"

"Oh my, how nice for you. Do you sew?"

"Heavens no. Why would I want to sew?"

"We love to sew, and if I do say so myself, we're quite handy with a needle. We'll show you some of our best pieces sometime."

"I'd like to see them," Marion said. "You'll have to show me the next time I come by."

Marta said, "What do you do with your time, dear?"

Marion immediately became more animated. "I shop, play tennis at the country club, and at night, I love to go to parties and dance. Did Kurt tell you my father is going to sponsor him for a membership at the country club? Now that he's finished with law school, he's a shoo-in."

"That's wonderful, dear."

Marion showed them her engagement ring. The oohs and aahs were subdued as Erna took her hand and looked at the ring. "What a beautiful ring. Is it a real diamond?"

Marion laughed. "Of course it's real. The stone was my grandmother's. Kurt had it reset and added several smaller diamonds. Do you like the setting? Isn't it gorgeous? He has exquisite taste and knows what I like."

His mother and aunt nodded, but he could tell they thought it was a terrible waste of money.

He changed the subject. "What pie do you have for us tonight?"

"We have a surprise for Marion. We made a caramel pie."

"Oh, that's my favorite. Yummy."

Marta and Erna didn't understand someone like Marion. Later Erna said, "From what I can tell, rich women don't *do* anything."

When Kurt and Marion were on the way home, she said, "I'm relieved that's over, darling. I'm glad you never have to live there again." He was about to tell her she was off base when she added, "We should buy a little place for your mother and aunt so they can get out of that awful neighborhood."

She had surprised him. "What a lovely thought, Marion. I'll talk to them about it, but first I have to pass the bar and set up my practice. Russell put me on retainer like he promised, so at least there will be some money coming in."

"I told you we never have to worry about money. We have more than we could ever spend, especially when my trust matures. By the way, even though it was nothing fancy, that was a fabulous meal and the best caramel pie I ever tasted. You're right. They sure can cook."

Kurt had agreed to work for Cantrell after law school, but was not as enthusiastic about it as he was at first. There was something about Cantrell he didn't like, and he definitely didn't trust him. Lately he tried to avoid him as much as possible.

"Where have you been, kid? I haven't seen you in weeks. I know I'm in Washington a lot, but when I'm home, I expect to see you."

"I'm really busy, and haven't had a second to myself. Sorry about that."

"Let me lay it out for you, kid. You need to stay in touch with me and ask me what I need. You're my lawyer now, and you need to act like it."

"No problem. I'll make a point of it, but Russell, please don't call me kid anymore. I never liked it, and now that I'm your attorney, it doesn't sound right."

Without thinking, Cantrell clenched his fists and glared at Kurt. "I'll call you whatever I want."

He didn't like Kurt telling him what to do, but quickly slipped back into his charming persona. "Sorry if I seem short, but I have a lot going on. Of course I'll call you Kurt from now on if that's what you want." Cantrell was peeved with himself for letting the kid get under his skin.

Kurt smiled agreeably even though he'd seen Cantrell's clenched fists. He'd gotten another glimpse of Cantrell's volatile side, and he intended to be careful around him.

Cantrell saw himself as a man of the people. He believed his constituents needed someone they could believe in, and he was that someone. His job approval rating was high, and being a gifted speaker only enhanced his image. Cantrell had befriended the chairman of the Republican Party and had his hearty endorsement. He had recently spoken on the floor of the House and encouraged Congress to pass the Radio Act of 1927. Cantrell and his colleagues feared radio's potential to cause radical political or social reform, spread indecent language, and monopolize opinions. Essentially, the act limited free speech.

A dirty campaigner, Cantrell would stoop as low as he needed to beat his opponent. Of course he made sure that whatever disinformation he provided to the press was not traced back to him. Voigt was able to get the dirt on almost anyone, and Cantrell used it to his advantage.

Nick Henry wasn't fooled by Cantrell's slick veneer. He thought Cantrell was a good actor with no actual substance. In one of his articles, he wrote, "Congressman Cantrell, explain to the people of Ohio what it is you intend to do during your next term. We all know you are an excellent public speaker, but that is not enough."

Cantrell's aide drafted a response, which ran in the paper alongside a counterpoint by Nick Henry. Cantrell was aggravated, but didn't have the time to deal with the reporter he referred to as "that jackass Henry." His campaign manager assured him he would win the election by a wide margin.

Kurt asked Charlie if he knew why Nickels was so negative about the Congressman. Charlie said, "Nickels thinks there's something dirty about him and believes Cantrell is giving the people of Ohio a big load of crap. He doesn't trust him and thinks he's a liar and a cheat. He would love to see him lose an election, but Cantrell is over twenty points ahead of his Democratic opponent."

Kurt nodded. "To be honest, I get the same feeling sometimes. It's as if there's something lurking under the surface with him, as if he's always ready to explode. As for Nickels, I think it's important that Cantrell doesn't know his real name is Albert Jablonski, Jr. I can't explain why I feel that way, but I feel strongly about it."

"We feel the same way, and actually, now that you mention it, Nickels asked me to make sure to remind you again not to let his real name slip in front of Cantrell. It's even more important that Cantrell doesn't know he was the shoeshine boy at the country club. Nickels believes it will give Cantrell ammunition he doesn't want him to have. He doesn't want to jeopardize his position at the newspaper."

America's obsession with alcohol allowed the owners of speakeasies to charge any price they wanted, which meant when Cantrell and Voigt provided liquor to the speakeasy owners, they could charge a premium price. Voigt continued as the front man, while Cantrell pulled the strings behind the scenes. There had been a couple of tight situations, but other than Councilman Lyle a few years back, they hadn't come close to getting caught.

Everyone working for the enterprise considered Voigt the boss. They were afraid of him and went out of their way not to cross him because physical harm and murder were common in the business.

Voigt dealt with the workers as he saw fit. When one of the guys went against orders and drove a truckload of liquor over a heavily travelled road Voigt had specifically told him not to take, he cut off his middle finger and hung it in the office out in the country. He made sure other workers were around to watch him cut it off and hear his screams. "That finger is a reminder for all of you to follow orders."

A couple of months later, Voigt heard that Earl and Mike were talking shit about him. Voigt was concerned they might say too much in the wrong place to the wrong people. He invited the two of them to a nice dinner at the country house and led them to believe it was a reward for good work.

After dinner was served, Voigt went into the kitchen and told the help to leave. He sat back down at the table and kept the booze coming.

He waited for the two men to get sloppy drunk before he pulled his gun.

He pointed the gun at Earl and said, "Tie Mike to his chair."

Both men were terrified.

After Earl did what Voigt told him to, Voigt said, "Now sit down."

Voigt tied Earl to his chair. When Voigt pulled out a knife strapped to his leg, the two men knew this wasn't going to end well.

Voigt loomed over Earl. "Open your mouth." When Earl wouldn't open his mouth, Voigt grabbed his jaw and forced his mouth open. He pulled out his tongue and sliced it off. "That'll teach you to bad mouth me."

He threw the bloody tongue on the table.

Mike sobbed, "I won't say anything, I promise. I have a family. Please don't hurt me."

Voigt laughed, "You've already said too much." He cut Mike's tongue off, and threw it on the table next to Earl's. Both men were bloody and on the verge of passing out.

Voigt spent the rest of the evening torturing them. First Mike. Then Earl. He wanted Earl to watch because he was the biggest talker. Afterward, he strangled them and dumped their bodies into a communal grave on the edge of the property.

For months, the men whispered about what happened to Earl and Mike, but no one knew for sure. Mike's wife tried to get the police to look into his disappearance, but she didn't know where he went at night and couldn't give them any information. The police assumed Mike had been up to no good, and with no clues, the case got little attention.

✧

Cantrell was happy to let Voigt do all the work, but got frustrated with him once when he was sick. Voigt had ridden on one of the boats coming over from Canada before the lake had frozen over. It was a bitter cold and snowy night, and Voigt caught a terrible cold, which turned into pneumonia. While he convalesced, he was forced to slow down the bootlegging operation for a couple of weeks. Cantrell kept bugging him to get out of bed and get back to work, but Voigt was too weak.

Voigt coughed uncontrollably. "You have to give me a chance to get over this. Goddamn it, I nearly froze to death."

"We're losing a ton of money while you're lying around. When are you going to get out of that damn bed?"

"Jesus Christ. As soon as I am well enough. I contacted one of my most reliable men, and he'll take over for the next week or so. I handled it, so stop worrying. Don't you have enough goddamn money?"

"Never."

Chapter Twenty-five

❖

*K*urt wasn't deeply in love with Marion, but he believed as they shared their lives and grew old together, their love would grow.

They still had a lot of fun together. They went to the theater in Cleveland, poked around museums, and often went out to dinner. One thing was certain—they had no trouble igniting the spark in the bedroom. The sexual attraction they first experienced on the trip to New York was as strong as ever.

When they got in the car one night after dining out, she gave him a long, passionate kiss. Her tongue played around his as she reached down and rubbed him until he was hard.

He moaned.

"Do you like that?"

"Stop it Marion, we're right out here on the street."

"If you turn a little this way, I can get on your lap."

Kurt thought of Antonia, but he immediately pushed thoughts of her from his mind. He kissed and lightly nipped Marion's neck. Marion leaned her head back.

"You're such a little vixen, Marion."

"I'm your little vixen. You like that about me. Admit it."

After they made scandalous love in the car, they didn't want the night to end and went to one of Marion's favorite speakeasies. The crowd was loud and boisterous, but Marion shouted over the din. "My

trust fund matured last week, and now all my money is available to us."
When he asked her how much it was and she told him, he was
astounded. By the time they got home, he was really happy and figured
it was because they had such a good night out together.

✧

Antonia never talked about Kurt anymore, but Nickels told Charlie she
was in a terrible mood about Kurt and Marion's upcoming wedding,
and he suspected she secretly hoped Kurt would call it off at the last
minute.

Two weeks before the wedding, while Kurt and Marion were being
shown to their table at a restaurant, they bumped into Antonia seated
at a table with a group of her friends. Kurt's reaction was jealousy, and
the intensity of it surprised him. Throughout the meal, he couldn't take
his eyes off Antonia. Marion said, "Why do you keep staring at her? I
know who she is, Kurt. She's that Polack girl you used to think you were
in love with."

Kurt glared. "Marion, don't ever call her that again. You sound like
a bigot. Do you think because you have money, you're better than
everyone else?"

Waving her mother-of-pearl and silver cigarette holder, she
laughed. "Yes, actually, I do. But, darling, you better stop looking at her,
or trust me, I'll make a scene no one will forget."

Kurt hated it when Marion lost control, so he forced himself to
turn away. He knew he wasn't completely over Antonia and wondered
again if he was making a mistake by marrying Marion.

When Antonia caught sight of Kurt, she felt as if someone had
come up from behind and kicked her. It had been two years since Kurt
broke it off, and she was sure she was over him, but when she saw him
with Marion, it hurt almost as much as it did in the beginning.

During most of her free time, Antonia preferred to hang out with her group of friends. She dated a little, but wasn't interested in a serious relationship. She was too busy with school and working at the factory.

One of the guys in her crowd had repeatedly asked her out. She turned him down each time, but he was so persistent, she finally agreed to go out with him. She thought it might help her forget about Kurt.

They went out to dinner and a movie, and had a really great time, but he never called or asked her out again. When she saw him a few weeks later, she said, "I had such a good time and was hoping you'd call me again."

He said, "Every time I asked you out, you scarcely acknowledged me, and never considered saying yes. Everyone always talks about how nice you are, but I thought you were snotty. I kept asking, hoping you'd agree to go out with me, and every time you said no, it was another rejection. By the time you finally said yes, I had decided I wanted you to feel what it was like to have someone reject you."

She said quietly, "Oh, I do know what it feels like, but the difference between you and me is that I would never knowingly try to hurt someone."

After that, she was always polite to him, but went out of her way to avoid him.

She talked it over with her mother. "I'm afraid I'm never going to find the right person and fall in love again. I don't think I'll ever love anyone as much as I loved Kurt."

"Yes you will. Things are going to work out for you, you'll see. We never know where life is going to take us."

The night before the wedding, Marion's parents asked Marion and Kurt to go for a ride. They took them to Fairlawn Heights, a new upscale Akron neighborhood. When their chauffeured car pulled up outside a large front-entrance, brick colonial house with a beautifully manicured lawn, Marion said, "Daddy, what are we doing here? I have so much to do to get ready for tomorrow."

"This house is a surprise from your mother and me. It's our wedding gift to you, honey. We bought it for you last week, because Mommy and I want you and Kurt to start your life together in your very own home." Both of her parents had huge smiles on their faces.

Marion looked at the house, and half-heartedly thanked her parents.

Her father said, "Don't you like it? We spent a lot of time looking for the right place for the two of you."

Marion said, "Yeah, sure, it's fine. Can we go now?"

Kurt thought it was an extravagant gift, and since he was in no position to buy a house and certainly not one as grand as this one, he was happy to accept it. "It's very nice, and very thoughtful, Mr. and Mrs. White. What a wonderful gift. Thank you very much."

"Please Kurt, call us Mom and Dad."

He knew it was the custom, but didn't feel comfortable calling them Mom and Dad. He was going to marry their daughter, but he didn't feel he would ever really belong to their family, especially not in the way he had with the Jablonskis.

When Kurt told Marta the marriage ceremony would be at the country club, and they were going to be married by a judge instead of a minister, she wrung her hands and looked physically ill. "You must marry in the church. Marrying at the country club isn't right. A judge? No. No. No. If you won't marry in the church, I'm sure Reverend Reiter would agree to marry you at the country club."

"Mama, I know you're upset, but this is the way Marion and I want it. Neither of us wants to marry in the church. We are going to be married by Judge Towland, a friend of her family. I'm sorry. I know you don't like the idea, but I really want you and Aunt Erna at the wedding. There will be an orchestra, dancing, and wonderful food. It wouldn't be the same without you. Please try to understand, and tell me you plan to be there."

"I'm not happy about it, but of course we'll come. I would never miss seeing my boy get married. But I'm going to have a devil of a time explaining to Erna that you're not getting married in a church by a minister. I hope she'll agree to go with me."

"I know you'll convince her. It will be a wonderful day. You'll see. I want you and Aunt Erna to have new clothes for the wedding, so I'm going to take the two of you to O'Neil's Department Store where you can buy any dress, shoes, and fancy hat you want, no matter the cost. I'm only going to get married once, and I want my two best girls to look like a million bucks."

"You're too good to us," said Marta.

His mother and aunt were going to be horrified by the amount of liquor at the wedding, but Kurt knew Marion would never agree to a dry wedding. Because it was a private party, at a private club, and the booze had been stockpiled before 1920, alcohol wasn't an issue. And only a few people were aware that over the years, the club had secretly added bootleg liquor to its reserve.

The Whites spared no expense for their daughter's wedding. The ballroom at Rosewood Hills Country Club overflowed with white orchids, white roses, and white lilies. Marion insisted everything had to be white.

Marion's wedding gown was a floor-length, beaded, white chemise silk dress with a long train. The sleeves were trimmed in white fur. The hand-laced bridal cap fit closely over her bobbed auburn hair, and included a tulle veil with tiny clusters of small white Dendrobium orchids arranged around her face. She wore several strands of pearls of different lengths.

Marion walked down the aisle carrying a bouquet of white roses and orchids, and Kurt thought, "She looks beautiful. Marrying her is the right thing to do. Once children come along, she'll calm down. We'll have a good life together."

The reception afterward was lavish and went on for most of the night.

Charlie and Grace were there, but Nickels and Harriet declined the invitation. After Charlie asked Nickels to forgive Kurt, Nickels had phoned Kurt, and they spoke briefly. But Nickels wasn't ready to let it go completely. At least they were on speaking terms.

Marta and Erna were seated at a table with Charlie and Grace and two other young couples. Erna wore a copper-colored silk dress trimmed in dark brown velvet with decorative buttons. She wore a matching coat and a dark brown, tight-fitting hat with a narrow, turned-down brim. Marta wore a blue crepe de chine, with decorative ivory trim under the bodice and a wide-brimmed ivory hat with a wide blue ribbon that got in the way every time she talked to someone. Unlike the young women who showed their legs, the sisters wore their hems a couple of inches above their ankles.

Each sister pinned a temperance ribbon on her dress, and although they were dismayed by the amount of liquor, they did their best not to show it. They were particularly concerned with how much Marion was drinking. Marta whispered to Charlie, "Does she always drink so much?"

"I'm sure it's because this is such a grand occasion, Mrs. Becker."

Erna, on the other hand, was not so quick to hold her tongue. "Well, I think she's a bit wild. Not at all like his other girlfriend, that nice girl Antonia."

Marta cupped Erna's ear and whispered, "You didn't like Antonia because she was Polish."

Erna dodged the brim of Marta's hat and said, "I think she's looking pretty good right now."

Charlie thought it was a good idea to interrupt them. "Mrs. Becker would you give me the honor of this dance?"

"Oh my. I would like that, but I must warn you, I haven't danced in about one hundred years," she tittered.

When he brought Marta back to the table, he turned to Erna. "Now it's your turn Mrs. Stucke."

"Oh, I couldn't go out there. I haven't danced with anyone since my husband died," she said as she was getting up from her chair. Afterward, Erna said too loudly, "He's a nice boy, even though he's Irish."

"Shhh. Someone will hear you."

After dancing, Marta and Erna approached Russell Cantrell. When he saw them coming in his direction, he turned his back on them and began talking to one of the other guests. Marta and Erna patiently waited for him to finish. Realizing they weren't going away, he turned and said, "Mrs. Becker. Mrs. Stucke. How nice to see you again. I see you've finally made it to our country club. Isn't it a spectacular wedding?"

Marta said, "Yes, it is. Congressman, we wanted to thank you once again for everything you've done for us. You changed our lives."

"Oh, that. Think nothing of it. I was happy to do it. Have a good time for the rest of the evening, and watch for my announcement later. I have a surprise for Kurt and Marion."

He watched them walk away and thought, "If you only knew *why* I gave you the money."

It was a festive night, and everyone appeared to have a good time. Charlie was Kurt's best man and offered the first toast of the evening.

"Here's to one of the best friends a man could ever have. Kurt, Nickels, and I have been friends since we were kids, and I expect, will be until we're old men. We're like family to each other. Kurt, I believe you've caught yourself a live one, and the only advice I can give you is this: Don't try to tame her." There was an awkward pause and then everyone laughed. "Marion, you look especially beautiful tonight. May you always be as happy as you are right now."

After several other toasts, Cantrell came up to the microphone and raised his glass to Kurt and Marion. "Here's to the best looking couple in Akron. I hope your life together is filled with happiness, and for you, Marion, lots of shopping and parties." Marion had a huge smile on her face. Cantrell went on for a while and then said, "And one last thing. I haven't given you your wedding gift yet, because I wanted to tell you about it tonight." He waited for everyone to pay attention.

"I've booked you on a transatlantic voyage from New York to London where you'll stay in the best suite at the Brown's Hotel. I've also scheduled a side trip to Paris."

Cantrell was quite pleased by everyone's reaction.

Kurt and Marion danced their first dance, and later everyone danced the Charleston and shimmied to the popular song "I Wish I Could Shimmy Like My Sister Kate."

Later that night Nick called Antonia and asked her how she was doing.

She was sad, but said, "What's done is done. I sincerely hope Kurt and Marion will be happy, but we have to let this go now. He made his decision, and I have to get on with my life."

Grandpa said even though Antonia put up a brave front, she was devastated that Kurt had married another woman.

Chapter Twenty-six

❖

Built in 1834, Ohio's State Penitentiary in Columbus deserved its horrible reputation and was notorious for its primitive conditions. Originally intended to accommodate fifteen hundred inmates, by 1928 the prison housed more than three thousand. And like other prisons around the country, it was designed for discipline and punishment, not for rehabilitation.

The prison was so overcrowded, most inmates bunked two to a cell. Albo was one of the lucky ones who had a cell to himself.

In the hot Ohio summers, the prison walls retained heat, which created a stifling environment saturated with the smell of sweat of over three thousand men. In winter, the walls let the bitter cold seep in, and Albo's teeth chattered most of the time.

At night, inmates were locked in their cells, and during the day, they went to their work details and ate together in the dining hall. The food was unappetizing, usually something like cornbread, beans, and fatty bacon.

Albo sat down with his tray and stared at the food for several minutes. It made him sick to look at it. He daydreamed about Millie's cooking and thought he would give anything for one of her home-cooked meals. One of the guys at his table said, "Hey buddy, your food's getting cold." Albo jolted back to reality and began to choke the food down.

He said, "It not taste like anything. I not sure how much longer I can eat this food."

Required to work in one of the prison industries, he persuaded the administration to let him work in the kitchen where he was somewhat familiar with the routine. Inmates made everything from harnesses and shoes to barrels and brooms. They also worked in the laundry, library, and maintenance. Working in the kitchen was the one time during the day when Albo found some peace and could get away from his smelly, confining cell. The cook was a quiet man who liked Albo and made sure he got as much time in the kitchen as was allowed. And every once in a while, the cook gave him something extra to eat.

For the most part, Albo enjoyed the work, even though it often included cleaning up disgusting messes.

One day in May, the cook asked him to take a trash container outside and wash it out. There was no hose, so he had to take a bucket of water with him. When he took the lid off, he was horrified to see it was filled with rotting meat and teeming with maggots. The maggots began to fall off into the cuff of his pants and onto his shoes, and he shook his legs frantically to get them off.

He went back inside. "That can filled with maggots. I not know how to get rid of it."

The cook was unfazed. "Boil some water, add some bleach, and dump it in the trash can. That should take care of it."

He followed the cook's suggestion and went back outside with the steaming bucket.

Millie visited the next day. He explained to her what happened. "I poured the bleach mixture into the trash can, and the maggots clinging on the rim started to drop back into the squirming mass, one by one. Then it seemed as if the rest of them let go at once, and the wiggling mixture slowly stopped moving. I was gagging the whole time. After I finished, I still felt as if something were crawling on me. Since then, every time I leave the kitchen for the night, I make sure the lids on the trash containers are tightly closed and the meat is disposed of properly. It makes me almost retch to tell you about it."

Millie said, "I hate to think of you in this disgusting place, but it's almost over. Only a little over two years to go, and you'll be back home with us."

✧

Albo's morale was an ongoing concern, and Nickels thought if his father helped with a follow-up article on prison conditions, it might keep his mind on something other than his day-to-day hell. "Papa, if we work on this assignment together, I can visit you more often this summer."

Albo wasn't sure if it was a good idea, and Nickels said, "You'll be helping me out. Do it as a favor to me. Since I was promoted to columnist last year, I have a lot of flexibility in my work schedule, and have already had several meetings with my editor about writing the article. Will you help me with it?"

Albo said, "I'm not sure how much I can help, but I'll try."

After Nick's first article appeared, the Ohio Penitentiary had increasingly come under attack. Conditions within the facility were horrendous, and the public view of prisons was beginning to change. For his follow-up article, Nickels was given prison-wide access. He interviewed several administrators, including the warden and the superintendent.

Wholeheartedly in favor of Nick writing the article, the superintendent said, "Conditions here are so unacceptable, no matter how many pages you write, it won't give anyone the remotest idea of the wretchedness that the inmates have to endure. Anything you can do to bring attention to our problems would be greatly appreciated."

With prison conditions deteriorating drastically over the last several years, Ohio's Governor Webster was also interested in prison reform. He contacted the Cleveland newspaper's Editor-in-Chief and asked him to run an editorial he had written. After it ran, Nickels contacted Webster's office and asked if he wanted to tour the prison with him to see the conditions firsthand.

When Nickels arrived at the prison with Webster, the superintendent showed them around the facility. Even though he expected to see unsatisfactory conditions, the governor was dismayed by how bad they actually were. As prearranged with Nickels, the governor asked to meet with a prisoner named Albert Jablonski. "I want to learn about the prison from the unique viewpoint of a prisoner."

For privacy, it was arranged for Albo and the governor to meet in an attorney-client room. When Albo came into the room, Governor Webster offered his hand, and they shook. Nickels said, "It will be easier if I translate."

Albo explained about prison culture. "There is a group of prisoners who control most of what goes on. They break every rule. They're usually caught and punished. Everyday we're abused by the guards. There was one time when I was ordered to strip naked, lie down on the floor, and then crawl down the corridor. There isn't a week that goes by that I am not beaten and humiliated."

They discussed the details of everyday prison life, and when his conversation with Albo was over, the governor said, "I'm convinced I have to do something about the conditions as soon as possible. I promise I'll do whatever I can to improve life for you and the other inmates. Thanks to both of you."

✧

Millie missed Albo terribly and had a tough time seeing him in prison. Each time she saw him, she thought he looked worse than the time before. At fifty-one years old, he was pale and thin and had aged considerably. One of the problems in a prison system as large and as crowded as the Ohio penitentiary was that diseases spread rapidly. Albo told Millie a lot of men on his cellblock were sick with one thing or another, and she constantly worried he would catch something. She wasn't sure he was strong enough to fight it off.

Each time she visited, she worried about what she might see. One day when Nickels and Antonia went with her, they walked into the visiting area, and Albo wasn't there. She became flustered and asked the guard where he was.

"He had a little accident and will be here in a minute."

She gasped. "What you mean accident?"

"It's nothing to worry about, ma'am. Now please, go sit down and wait. He'll be here in a minute."

Nickels and Antonia saw their father limping down the corridor toward them. He had a bandage on his head. When he saw them, his face lit up. Albo walked in the room, and Nickels said, "What happened, Papa?" They always spoke in Polish so the guards wouldn't know what they were saying.

"Nothing. Don't worry. This is the way it is in here. There are fights all the time, and I got stuck in the middle of one. Those stupid guards don't care. They think it's fun to watch the men go at it, and then they always jump in to 'help.' Exactly like I told you last week."

Nickels said, "I want to know every detail, Papa. Don't leave anything out. The article isn't running for another two weeks."

"I'm hungry all the time, so I stole some meat from the kitchen. I couldn't help it. It smelled so good, and as usual, my stomach was empty. The cook didn't turn me in. It was another man working in the kitchen with me. He saw me take it, and he's jealous of my good relationship with the cook.

"They put me in the pit for two days. It's so small, you can't stand up, and when you're lying down, you can touch both walls with your hands. There is no mattress, and they feed us only bread and water. It's damp in there, and almost everyone comes out of the pit with a cold. It's completely silent, and I was totally isolated. I felt as if I were going crazy." From his conversations with other prisoners, Nickels knew the inmates dreaded time in the pit.

Albo blew his nose and continued. "When I got out, the first time I went to the mess hall, some of the prisoners taunted me and chanted 'stupid Polack likes the pit.' It made absolutely no sense, and I ignored them, but then this crazy guy at my table started yelling for them to back off. Suddenly all of them were fighting, and I was caught in the middle of it. The guards broke it up the way they always do—by hitting and kicking us."

Millie, who had said nothing up to this point, said, "But you had nothing to do with it."

"How would they know? I was in the thick of it and couldn't escape. They didn't know I wasn't fighting."

Millie was angry and raised her voice. "This is not acceptable. We must talk to someone about it. Albert, is there someone you've interviewed who could help protect your father?"

"Absolutely not. If the other prisoners heard he was getting special treatment, it would only make it more difficult for him."

Albo interrupted, "There will be no more discussion about it. We only have a short time to visit, and I want to talk about good things."

Two weeks later the first of Nick's two-part feature, "State Penitentiary Conditions Continue to Demand Reform" ran in Sunday's paper. He quoted the governor:

"I have asked the state legislature to draft a bill intended to relieve prison overcrowding and reduce the strain it places on the state budget. The state will work together with the Ohio prison systems administration

to come up with a plan that is fair to both the administration and the inmates."

The newspaper received more than one hundred letters about Nick's follow-up article, and it was picked up by several other Ohio papers.

✧

Charlie had continued to visit the prison, but Albo still refused to see Kurt. "I not forgive."

Charlie said, "I know what Kurt did was heartless, but you know him almost as well as I do. He's fascinated with money and always has been. It's like a drug to him. He made a terrible choice, and he'll pay the price someday."

"He his own worst enemy. I hope he find happiness with that rich woman, but Antonia much better for him. He find out when it too late."

Chapter Twenty-seven

❖

*C*harlie's homicide cases had become increasingly more difficult. The District Attorney was always happy when Charlie was the lead because not only did Charlie get the witnesses to talk, but he also made sure their statements were airtight. His reports were precise, and he was a good witness in court.

One night in 1929, when he and Kurt were at The Canal, Charlie said his ambition was to be Chief of Detectives someday. "No day is exactly the same, but that's one of the things I like about it. Sometimes I go on a stakeout and watch a suspect for hours. It can be really boring, but after I make an arrest, start the interview process, and bring in witnesses, time flies. To me, it's like solving a puzzle, and I don't stop until I find the evidence and information I need to arrest someone and get a conviction."

Kurt had passed the bar the year before, and with Cantrell as his principal client, his law practice was growing and starting to gain a good reputation. Cantrell had insisted Kurt concentrate on corporate law in law school and had said, "After all the money I spent on your education, I think I have a say in your career."

It had been four years since Kurt broke up with Antonia, and more than two years since his wedding. Things weren't going well with Marion. Sex was the only good part of their relationship.

Thinking Marion would settle down once they were married had been a huge mistake. She was wilder than when he first met her. She partied all the time and was furious with Kurt each time he refused to accompany her on one of her nighttime jaunts.

Whenever she scolded him, she stood with her hands on her hips. "You're such a stick in the mud, and absolutely no fun at all." In the beginning, he thought her pouting was cute. Now all it did was annoy him.

"I don't understand why you have to go out to a different juice joint every night with God-knows-who. Don't you ever want to stay at home and enjoy a quiet night together? When are we going to start a family? You know I want children. That can't be a surprise to you."

"I'm not ready to start a family. You act as if you're fifty years old, instead of twenty-seven. Why are you so serious all the time? Loosen up for God's sake."

"Marion, you're twenty-five years old. Most married women have several children by your age."

"I'm not most women. You ought to know that by now."

✧

Nick and Kurt had not yet seen one another face to face. They continued to speak on the phone a few times a month. Kurt had feared their phone conversations would be awkward, but was pleased when they eased right back into their familiar banter. They usually kept it neutral by discussing baseball and the weather.

The years of estrangement had been difficult for both of them, but especially Kurt because he knew it was his fault. Over the years, they had communicated through Charlie. Charlie felt as if he were stuck in the middle. He said to Kurt, "I speak to Nickels about it frequently, and it seems to me he's no longer angry. At least you've spoken on the phone for the past couple of years. Give it a little more time. Patience, my friend."

In one of his telephone conversations with Nickels, Kurt said, "The three of us need to get together. I know we all miss the camaraderie of The Tribe. Maybe the next time you're in Akron, we can meet at The Canal, like old times."

Nickels didn't say anything, and Kurt continued. "We're like brothers, Nickels. Brothers make each other mad and then get over it. I know I hurt your sister, but we have to figure out a way to put it behind us. What we have as friends is too important. The Tribe is a part of our lives."

Providence intervened when Nickels was given three tickets to an Indians game. He held onto the tickets for a week before he decided it was the right time and place for The Tribe to reunite. When he phoned Kurt, he said, "I was lucky enough to get tickets to an Indians game. Get yourself up to League Park on August eleventh for the second game in a four-game series against the Yankees. It should be a great game. I asked Charlie, too. I think it's time for The Tribe to get together. Let's eat some hot dogs and popcorn while we watch the Indians stomp the Yankees."

When he hung up the phone, Kurt was so relieved, he wept.

Charlie was elated Nickels had invited Kurt to the game in Cleveland. He was friendly with some of the guys on the force, but no one ever came close to the connection he had with Kurt and Nickels.

Thanks to an associate at the *News Tribune*, Nickels had tickets in a prime location. Their seats were next to the sports editor and right behind and to the right of home plate.

"I can't believe we're going to see Lou Gehrig and Babe Ruth," said Charlie as they walked into the park. "Take Me Out To The Ball Game" was blaring over the loud speakers.

Kurt stopped and looked up at the bleachers where the working-class immigrants and their kids were sitting. "Hey, take a look," he said as he pointed up at the stands. "That's where we used to sit."

"Yeah, and we loved every minute of it," said Nickels.

Kurt relaxed a little and was cautiously optimistic that, at last, everything was going to be all right with Nickels.

While waiting for the game to start, James Foster walked up to Kurt with an outstretched hand. They shook. "Kurt, nice to see you. Nice seats. How did you pull these off?" On the recommendation of Marion's father, Foster, a wealthy businessman, had recently become one of Kurt's clients.

"Jim, nice to see you. Let me introduce you to my friends, Charlie O'Brien and Nick Henry."

"Nice to meet you." Foster extended his hand to Charlie. They shook, and then Foster offered it to Nickels, who deliberately turned his back to him and talked to the sports editor. Foster, self-conscious and confused by the snub, hurriedly said, "Well…enjoy the game. I guess I need to find my seat."

Kurt wondered why Nickels had been so rude. It wasn't like him. After Foster walked away, he said, "What was that about? You refused to even acknowledge him."

"He's a pain in the ass. Remember when I was the shoeshine boy at the country club, and there was a member who razzed me every chance he got? I know I told both of you about him. He always went out of his way to taunt me.

"James Foster is that guy. He never walked by me without mocking me and calling me a stupid Polack or Polski. When you introduced me as Nick Henry, he had no idea who I was, but I never forgot him."

Charlie said, "Jesus, Nickels, remind me never to cross you. I don't want you to hold a grudge against me."

Kurt watched them, nervous about where the conversation was going.

Nickels looked directly at Kurt. "After you broke up with Antonia and married Marion, I didn't know how long it would take me to forgive you, or even if I ever could. My sister cried for weeks, and it tore me apart. But lately I find myself thinking a lot about you, and the three of us. We have too much history together to throw it all away. I realize you were caught up in Marion's allure, and it was as if you didn't have complete control over your actions. My life hasn't been the same without The Tribe. But, even though I'm no longer angry, I haven't forgotten what you did to my sister, and I never will."

"You know I didn't want to hurt Antonia, but I had to be with Marion. With hindsight, I see it was a mistake. My marriage is a disaster, and I'm struggling with what I'm going to do. Marion is a lunatic. She's out every night drinking and gallivanting with her rich friends, and most nights she comes home plastered.

"I realize now that when I went to New York with Russell and Marion and lived the good life for a few days, I fell in love with the lifestyle, not with the woman. It's taken me a few years to work it out and begin to understand it.

"In all this time I never stopped thinking about Antonia and what a fool I was to leave her for Marion. She's one hundred times the woman Marion is. Antonia is kind. Marion is mean. Antonia cares about others more than herself. Marion is self-centered. Antonia loved me unconditionally. Marion loves only herself. Antonia was my best friend, and I'm not ashamed to say how much I miss her."

Nickels grimaced. "I hate to say 'I told you so,' but you should have known better. After that extravagant trip to New York, you were swept up in the wealthy lifestyle and couldn't see anything but Marion's bank account."

"You're right, but she was so much fun and made me forget about the boardinghouse and growing up without money. What a colossal mess I've made of everything."

Charlie said, "Maybe you should think about cutting your losses. It's foolish to spend the rest of your life with someone you don't like."

"Do you mean divorce? I'm beginning to think that might be the only solution, but I hate the idea of it. I want to give Marion a chance to settle down."

"I hope it works out for you," Nick said. Charlie rolled his eyes.

The first inning was about to start, and anticipation was running high. This was the first year the Indians wore numbers on the back of their jerseys, and the three of them looked forward to seeing the new uniforms. Nickels said, "This game is going to make history because Babe Ruth is expected to break the home run record. Another historic game in Cleveland for The Tribe."

They weren't disappointed. During the game, The Bambino hit his five hundredth career home run, which was twice as many home runs as the player in second place. Kurt, Nickels, and Charlie were on their feet when Babe hit the record home run. The stadium erupted. Kurt, Nickels, and Charlie cheered along with the rest of the crowd.

The next day's headline was "Babe Ruth Hits 500th Home Run; Ball Is Found."

The article went on to say:

> The Babe reached a milestone yesterday in Cleveland when he smacked Indians starter Willis Hudlin's first pitch in the second inning far and wide over the right-field fence at League Park for his five hundredth home run. It is a startling figure, more than twice as many home runs as anyone in the majors has ever hit. The ball ricocheted off a Lexington Avenue doorstep and rolled to the feet of a young man who was walking to catch a bus home to New Philadelphia. The young man was brought to the Yankees dugout and presented with two baseballs and an autographed twenty-dollar

bill by Babe Ruth in exchange for the ball.

Kurt, Nickels, and Charlie were thrilled to see the Babe make history.

The Tribe was back together.

The 1930s

❖

*I*n October 1929, the frivolity and recklessness of the 1920s came to an abrupt end. The stock market crashed, and the world plunged into the Great Depression. With no hope of economic recovery, panic struck. Banks closed overnight, and many people lost everything.

Akron was severely affected. Despite the fact that forty percent of all tires bought in the United States were made in Akron, the rubber factories laid off twenty-five thousand workers, which resulted in the loss of jobs for thousands of other workers in related industries. Those who were able to hold onto their jobs often had to agree to reduced hours and wages.

With unemployment in the United States hovering at twenty-five percent, more than fifteen million Americans were unemployed. Ohio's unemployment rate reached a staggering forty percent.

The downtrodden flocked to the cities. Thousands of the unemployed who couldn't pay their rent or mortgages were thrown into the world of public assistance and bread lines. At the peak of the Depression, seventeen thousand families were forced out onto the street each month.

Many lived on powdered milk, dried beans, and potatoes. Men in bread lines stood five across waiting to sit down in a soup kitchen. The psychological impact was enormous. Unemployment and the inability to feed a family was a crushing blow, and self-blame and self-doubt were rampant.

For the working class, crowded living conditions were common.

Extended families shared living quarters, food costs, and even bedding.

People went to the movies to escape reality and amused themselves with free activities. They played board games, solved crossword puzzles, and played baseball in the streets. Listening to the radio was a huge source of entertainment and included newscasts, Radio Theater, the Grand Ole Opry, soap operas, sermons, and especially sports.

Chapter Twenty-eight

❖

The crash caused many people to become anxious and withdraw all their money from the banks in cash, which forced the banks to liquidate loans. "Bank runs" led to the failure of many banks, and Kurt lost every penny he had saved as a boy working at the boardinghouse.

But the Depression didn't affect everyone the same way. For the wealthy, the Depression affected them very little. When Kurt tried to discuss the loss of his savings with Marion, she said, "That pittance? Why are you so upset? For heaven's sake, we have more money than we could ever spend."

"I worked hard for that money, and when I was younger, it meant a lot to me. It meant my freedom from being poor someday. Every time I looked at my balance, I realized I wasn't going to be stuck living at the boardinghouse for the rest of my life. Even though what I saved as a boy doesn't seem like much to you, I was going to use that money to set up a retirement fund for my mother and aunt."

"You're being silly. If it upsets you that much, I'll have Daddy give you the money you lost, or better yet, we'll take it out of the trust fund."

"You really don't get it, do you? You never had to worry about money or food or what other people thought of you. You have no idea what it's like for most of the people in this country."

"No, and frankly, I don't care. I'm going out now. Don't wait up for me, it's going to be a late night."

Kurt was disappointed about losing his money and disgusted with Marion.

✧

People weren't buying cars, and there wasn't much work in the factories. Antonia and Millie were both let go in the second wave of layoffs in May. As they rode the bus home together, Millie stared out the window. "What are we going to do now?"

"Mama, we'll figure something out. We always do. It's going to be fine, you'll see." Antonia was frightened, and by the time they got off the bus to walk home, the gravity of the situation had hit her.

"Mama, maybe we should rent out a room to bring in some money. We're going to have a tough time without our paychecks."

Millie stooped over a little more than usual. "I don't want to. We'll think of something else. I don't want to explain why your father is in prison and have someone we don't know listening in on our conversations. I don't want anyone but you or me in my kitchen, and I want to walk around in my nightclothes if I feel like it. Your father will be home at the end of this year, and I don't want a stranger living in our home." Antonia realized she had never seen her mother look so downtrodden before, not even when her father first went to prison.

Millie said, "Tonight we'll talk it over and decide what we can live without and how we can get by."

They planned a garden for the backyard and bought some chickens so they could have fresh eggs. Nickels came down from Cleveland to build a chicken coop and help them plant the garden. He said, "Keep track of which chickens are good layers, and eat the other ones. If you have any eggs left over, sell them or give them away to the neighbors."

The garden provided fresh vegetables all summer. After Millie and Antonia canned what they needed for the winter, and gave some away, they sold the rest to the market. The pantry was soon filled with over four hundred quarts, including tomatoes, green beans, and pickles. They traded eggs for bruised peaches and cherries, and then canned them to use in pies and cobblers.

They learned never to throw anything away and reused everything they could. They ate warmed-over beans several times a week and made soup with chicken's feet. There was virtually no part of the chicken they didn't use. They preserved chickens so they would have some meat to get them through the winter months.

Millie sewed dresses and coats for herself and Antonia, as well as for customers outside the home. Word got around about what a good seamstress she was, but they soon found out sewing for others didn't bring in nearly as much money as they made at the factory.

About three months after they lost their jobs, Antonia asked her mother to come into the living room. "Sit down, Mama. I have something to tell you. I've decided to drop out of school, because we can't afford to pay the tuition anymore."

"You've worked too hard to quit now. Working at the factory all these years while going to school wasn't easy. Now you're getting an advanced degree in English literature, and I want you to finish. Then you can finally start teaching, which will really help us out. Promise me you won't do anything until I talk to your brother."

Once Nickels learned what Antonia was thinking, he said, "You have to finish. I know it's what Papa wants. Harriet and I discussed it, and we're going to send you and Mama a check each month to help out."

Antonia said, "But you and Harriet need that money."

This is what we both want. These are the times when we have to help each other. Harriet and I can live a little leaner if it means helping you and Mama."

Albo and Millie had invested in life insurance policies for each member of the family. When Albo's policy matured, Millie cashed it in. She managed to continue paying the premiums on the policies for herself, Nickels, and Antonia. When they matured later that year, she would cash them in.

Millie told Antonia, "All the money your father and I saved is gone. Our only income this year is the money from the insurance policies and my earnings from sewing, which averages only about thirty-four dollars a month. It's painful when I compare that to what we made at the factory when we were making more than ninety dollars a month. I don't know if I can ask for credit. I never charged anything before."

"But Mama, we don't have a choice. Thank goodness Nickels can send us a check each month. I don't think we could make it without his help."

"All right. I guess we're going to have to ask for credit, but we have to be very careful. I don't want to owe so much that we can't pay it back. And I draw the line at asking for relief. We're going to get through this without any help from the government."

To get by, they skipped payments on the mortgage principal and didn't pay the property taxes. They charged what groceries they needed, such as milk and butter.

The bright spot in their lives was when Nickels and Harriet came to visit with their three-year-old son Albert Jablonski Henry. They called him Bert.

"Bertie, give Babka a kiss." Bertie loved his Babka, and climbed right up onto Millie's lap. Being a grandmother brought her tremendous joy. After Bert was born, she told her son. "I think grandchildren complete the circle of life. You can't really understand your parents until you have your own children and become a parent yourself. Things you never really thought about or understood before become clear when you shift your focus from yourself to your child. Grandchildren are our family's immortality. Look at that dimple in his chin. It's exactly like your father's. I can't wait until his grandfather can meet him."

✧

Marta and Erna had grown too old and tired to continue running the boardinghouse. They weren't making much money, and the boon days of the factories were gone. "We decided to sell Stucke House," Erna told Kurt. "We found a little house on the outskirts of town, and we're going to move."

Kurt insisted on paying for the house and said, "It's the right time for you to do it." He knew they weren't able to keep up with the work anymore and had begun giving them money each month so they didn't have to take in as many boarders. They had lived frugally ever since Cantrell had paid off the mortgage and had refused to put their money in the bank, so they didn't lose anything in the crash.

It was difficult for Kurt to watch them grow old. Both of them had advanced arthritis and had difficulty getting around. Erna's knees were gone, and her legs were so bowlegged she walked with a waddle and used a cane. She no longer climbed the stairs, and Marta had to take care of anything on the upper floors.

They found a house built at the end of the last decade in the new style called "ranch." One-floor living would make it easier for Marta and Erna to get around. Kurt said, "I'll never let anything happen to you. You both were always there for me, through good and bad. You were the best mom and aunt a guy could ask for. I worked hard to make you proud of me and become a success, and I think I've done fairly well so far. Now it's your turn to have someone take care of you. In addition to the new house, I'll continue to give you a check each month. If you ever need anything, all you have to do is ask."

Erna said, "You're a good boy, Kurt. You've always done the right thing." His mother hugged him.

✧

Charlie had been promoted to Chief of Detectives and had twenty men reporting to him. He was tough on them and demanded they always give their best effort.

Because so many in Akron were frustrated by not having enough, the deepening financial crisis spawned more criminals, and the result was an increase in home robberies.

One night in February, a call came in from the Cantrell mansion. They had been robbed, and a maid was lying dead on the kitchen floor. Charlie and one of his detectives responded to the call. When they first arrived at the mansion, Charlie was bowled over by the size of it. "There must be over twenty rooms in this place. Cripes, it looks like a hotel."

They found Cantrell waiting in the foyer. He didn't seem at all concerned that a murder had happened in his home.

Charlie said, "Good evening, Congressman. I'm Charlie O'Brien, Chief of Detectives. I understand you've had some trouble out here."

"Thanks for coming. My staff has had quite a scare."

"Sorry to be here under such difficult circumstances. Please explain in as much detail as possible what happened."

"I was out at a fundraiser. When I got home, I heard loud voices coming from the back of the house. When I went back to the kitchen… please follow me…I found one of our maids on the floor in a pool of blood."

When they got to the kitchen, Charlie examined the corpse and saw her throat was slit, and she had bled to death. "Has anyone moved anything or touched her?"

Cantrell said, "Not to my knowledge. I think the butler checked to see if she was alive, but I told him to keep everyone out of here."

Charlie said, "She must have surprised whoever did this as he entered through the kitchen door. Where is your safe?"

"In the den, which is down the hall from where you came in." Charlie was amazed at how calm Cantrell appeared. He casually stood next to the gruesome sight of his maid lying in a pool of blood.

"Have you checked to see what's missing?"

"Yes. Somehow they managed to get the safe open, and took everything in it. All my wife's jewelry and quite a bit of cash."

"How much cash?"

"Around twenty-five thousand, give or take."

Charlie thought it must be nice to be so rich you don't know how much money you have in your safe. "How much is your wife's jewelry worth?"

"I'm not sure. I'll look in my files for the appraisals and get back to you tomorrow. The collection is worth a small fortune."

"Who else was on the premises at the time? I'll want to interview each of them."

Cantrell arranged for Charlie to talk to the rest of the staff, including Voigt, who had little to say and grunted his replies to the questions. Later, when they reviewed the case, one of Charlie's men said, "That guy Louis Voigt is weird. There's something creepy about him."

"Yeah, he's a strange one, all right. Hard to believe someone like Cantrell keeps him around."

To catch the Hollingsworth House killer, Charlie set up several stakeouts at the homes of wealthy Akron citizens, mostly in Cantrell's section of town. It took about a week, but they got lucky one night when one of his men caught a man breaking into a house not far from the Cantrell estate. The thief's partner was in a getaway car parked around the corner.

After Charlie grilled the partner in the police interview room, he confessed, but insisted he had nothing to do with the murder at the Cantrell mansion the week before. He agreed to testify against the murderer and revealed where his partner had told him he had hidden the knife used to kill the maid.

Charlie was proud to have solved the Hollingsworth House murder and robbery so quickly. When Grace asked him how he thought the trial would go, he said, "Both the DA and I have no doubts that a jury will send the killer to jail for the rest of his life. So many times, the guilty person isn't punished. It's rewarding when you have an eyewitness and the murder weapon, and everything works the way it's supposed to. I take great pleasure in saying, 'Case closed.' Now it's up to the courts."

Chapter Twenty-nine

❖

*A*s a result of the deepening financial crisis, Cantrell's bootlegging profits declined drastically, and whenever Kurt met with him, he was in a foul mood.

Kurt hadn't seen much of Voigt lately, but knew he was never far from Cantrell. On several occasions Voigt was present at their meetings, and after one of them Kurt said, "Russell, it seems strange to me that you would spend so much time with Louis Voigt. He doesn't seem like the kind of person you'd be associated with. I know he's your driver, but why would you allow him to sit in on our meetings?"

Cantrell had a peculiar smile on his face. "He's my chauffeur. I'm not sure what you're trying to say."

"He makes me uncomfortable, and I don't think it's appropriate for him to be involved in the private details of your businesses."

"Well, that's not your decision to make. I'm going to tell you what I tell Elizabeth. Don't worry about him. He's not all there—a little deficient in the mental department and a bit rough around the edges—but he's harmless. I rescued him when he needed rescuing, and now he's my puppy dog. Woof. Woof. I like having him around." Cantrell laughed.

Voigt was standing outside the door listening. Something broke in Voigt, and he knew he was going to have to settle the score with Cantrell. He paced and talked to himself. "No one is going to compare me to a puppy dog and laugh about it. Mentally deficient? What crap. I've run his operation too long for too little money and no respect to have him talk about me that way."

Kurt thought the whole situation was strange, but after that, he noticed Voigt didn't come to their meetings anymore.

◇

Kurt's law practice had grown so large that he brought in two associates to do the research and grunt work. His reputation was spotless, and he was known around town as someone who treated his clients with dignity and respect.

Kurt found it increasingly difficult to conceal his dislike for Cantrell. He was demanding and monopolized an inordinate amount of Kurt's time. He expected him to skirt the edge of the law, but Kurt wasn't comfortable doing anything illegal. As his attorney, he insisted on staying within the legal lines, but skirted as close to them as possible.

"When I tell you to do something in a certain way, that's what I want you to do. Do you understand?"

"Russell, I'm not a child, and I resent it when you speak to me as if I were. I have repeatedly explained to you that I will not knowingly break the law, not for you or anyone else. I know you paid for my education, but you have to realize I do have some ethics. I don't always agree with how you want to handle things, but as long as it's legal, I'm willing to do it."

Cantrell glared at him.

Kurt said, "Don't be angry. You need to realize when you paid for my education, you got yourself the best damn attorney available, and I'm going to make sure you get the best representation I can provide. Isn't that what you want?"

"Yeah, sure. I know you're right. You've saved me many times, especially when it comes to making sure my contracts and deals are ironclad. You're becoming an expert in contract law, which saves me a lot of money and aggravation. You understand how to limit liability and business risk. And you've helped me circumvent labor laws and get the most out of my investments in all my companies."

Cantrell thought, "At least in my legal businesses."

Since his election to Congress, Cantrell's investments had grown. He had made many valuable connections and learned of new opportunities, often at the moment they became available. He bought new companies and squeezed out the competition whenever he could.

Kurt asked, "When you have as much money as you do, when is enough, enough?"

"Let me tell you something. Money is like sex. The more you have, the better it feels and the more you want."

Kurt wasn't sure he believed that anymore.

Cantrell might have been a big cheese in Akron, but in Washington, he had become an embarrassment to many of his Republican colleagues. Nick Henry continued to criticize him, and in one of his columns, he got right to the point:

> *The people of Ohio need to pay attention and quit sending Cantrell to Washington. Many well-known Republicans disapprove of Congressman Cantrell. Through an unnamed source, we have discovered that Cantrell's Washington colleagues feel his many absences have become a problem. They know Congressman Cantrell spends more time on his other financial interests than on business in Washington. Here is a direct plea from voters: Get to work. We need real representation.*

After reading the column, Cantrell turned to Voigt and blew up. "Who the hell does this guy Henry think he is? I have no idea why he has it in for me, but I want you to dig up some dirt on him and find out what this is about. Then I'm going to crush him."

Voigt reported back within a couple of weeks. "I couldn't find a thing on him. It's as if he didn't exist before ten years ago. Do you want me to keep looking?"

"Yes. I want to know what makes him tick, and why he has it in for me. We already know he has a reputation as an ethical guy who can't be bribed, but we need to figure out some way to get to him and keep him in line. *And off my goddamn back.*"

✧

Kurt and Marion had been married three years, and each year their relationship got worse. Kurt wasn't ready to give up on it yet, but there was hardly a day they didn't argue about something.

One morning at breakfast Marion stumbled into the dining room for a cup of coffee. After the maid poured her a cup and left the room, Kurt watched as Marion poured some liquor into her cup. "Marion, your drinking is getting out of hand. Can't you have coffee in the morning without pouring booze into it?"

"Mind your own goddamn business, Kurt. I'll do what I want. Go do your lawyer stuff or whatever it is you do all day."

"Please, Marion, we should at least try to be civil to one another. We should do something together, just the two of us. Let's go out to dinner tonight."

"I can't. I'm going with Richard and some others to that new place downtown. Sorry."

"Richard who?"

"For God's sake, don't you ever listen to me? I've told you about him several times. He's independently wealthy—related to one of the rubber barons in some way or another. He's never had to work a day in his life. We have a lot of fun together."

"Marion, you're married to me."

"Darling, I know that. Of course I do. But you don't like to go out and party, so I'm forced to go out with Richard and some of his friends. I can't exactly go alone."

Kurt was annoyed, but tried to keep the conversation from blowing up into another screaming match.

"Marion, we need to spend some time together. I made a reservation at that new restaurant downtown. I want to sit across the dinner table from my beautiful wife."

"Oh, all right. When you put it that way, how can I say no? But I'm going shopping and out to lunch with Mommy today, so I'll meet you there, okay?"

"Sure. I made a reservation for eight."

"Okay. See you then. But now I have to bathe and get dressed.

Kurt thought about how Marion spent her days shopping and lunching with her mother or friends. She was never at home and would never deign to do housework or cook. She was a dreadful housekeeper who insisted on paying for a house full of help. He couldn't get over walking into his own home and finding the hired help cleaning or cooking for him.

When he spoke to her about it, she told him he was being absurd. "Why does it matter who cooks or cleans or where the money is coming from? Stop showing your boardinghouse roots, Kurt."

Although Kurt enjoyed wealth and all the material things it made available, the sheer excess of Marion's lifestyle had begun to bother him. He thought it might do Marion some good to have some boardinghouse roots. He made good money, and it irritated him that Marion tried to pay for everything.

He had stopped taking his wife with him whenever he went to see Mama and Aunt Erna because she always insulted them in some way. It was unintentional, but it was unpleasant to be stuck in the middle.

The last time he had visited, Mama asked him, "Why don't you bring Marion with you when you come to see us?"

"She's busy and can't make it."

"Doing what? As far as I can tell, she doesn't do anything. You know what I think? I think she needs to spend more time with her husband."

Kurt was embarrassed and didn't want to discuss it. "Stop it, Mama. I'll bring her the next time I come by."

That evening Marion was late arriving at the restaurant. After Kurt waited for more than forty-five minutes, the door flew open. With a grand flourish, she trounced in with two men and a woman trailing behind her. "Darling, you don't mind that I brought Richard and his friends, do you?"

Richard Stanley was tall, handsome, and exuded the self-assurance of someone who had known wealth his whole life. Kurt disliked him immediately.

Kurt didn't want to make a scene. He whispered to Marion, "How much have you had to drink?"

She laughed and turned to Richard. "I told you he would be provoked. Kurt, don't be such an old fuddy-duddy. We're having a great time getting the night started. Please call the waiter over and tell him we want to move to a bigger table."

Before Kurt had a chance to say anything to the waiter, Richard had already asked for another table. Loud and unconcerned that others in the restaurant were trying to enjoy their meal, Marion and her friends were well on their way to becoming totally inebriated. Each of them ordered bees knees martinis—illegal gin laced with honey and lemon to mask the smell of the alcohol.

By the time dinner was over, Kurt was the only sober one at the table. The evening was a disaster and certainly didn't accomplish what Kurt had intended. When he called the waiter over to pay the bill, he was annoyed to find Richard had beaten him to it.

He tried to get Marion's attention, but she was deep in conversation with Richard. "Marion? Marion? I want to go home. I have a big day tomorrow."

"Darling, you go on. I'm heading over to that new place with Richard and the others. I'll see you when I get home later." She got up from the table and headed out the door laughing and talking with her friends.

Grandpa said when Kurt watched the door close behind Richard and Marion, the absurdity of it hit him—the son of a teetotaler had married a drunk.

Chapter Thirty

❖

*M*arion's drinking continued to escalate. She partied every night and staggered into the house in the early hours of the morning. She slept most of the day, and then got up to do it all over again. Kurt was convinced she was a full-blown alcoholic.

When she drank, she had a vicious tongue. One morning in early April, when he came downstairs ready for work, Marion was sitting at the dining room table. She said, "You're nothing but a low-class wannabe, and I'll never know how I could have been so stupid to marry you. You've ruined my life."

Kurt knew in these situations it didn't matter what he said, because she would continue to rant. The best thing to do was keep his mouth shut.

"Aren't you going to say anything? I hate it when you don't answer me."

"What was the question? I don't believe I heard one."

"I don't believe I heard one," she mocked. She threw her coffee cup at the wall. It smashed loudly and the coffee left a brown stain on the imported wallpaper as it dripped down to the floor. She picked up a crystal vase from the sideboard and threw it at Kurt's head. He ducked, and it hit the edge of the door and shattered into thousands of tiny shards. The sound seemed to stun her. She looked at Kurt and at the mess and then crumpled into her chair, sobbing hysterically.

"You have to stop this ridiculous cycle, Marion. Can't you see that alcohol is a problem for you?"

"Are you saying I'm an alcoholic?"

"I'm saying at the very least you have a drinking problem. You need to quit drinking. I'm going to work now. I suggest you do some serious thinking."

He couldn't take her to work-related social events anymore, and the last time they had dinner with her parents, her father said, "You need to get control of your wife. Her mother and I are worried about her."

"I agree she has a problem, and believe me, I've addressed it with her several times. You know how hard it is to tell Marion what to do. She won't listen to a word I say."

She had stayed relatively sober while at her parents, but as soon as they got home, she changed her clothes and ran out to meet her friends for another night of boozing.

He thought back to the dinner with Marion and Richard and their friends. It became clear to him how much they all had in common and how little of that he shared with them. They had grown up with money and privilege, and Kurt finally realized it was a world he would never truly be part of.

The only resolution was divorce. Kurt and Marion were living separate lives and no longer shared a bed. He had taken a long, hard look at his life and didn't like what he saw. He now knew that from the start, his marriage never had a chance. When he first met Marion, he was in love with Antonia, and he never loved Marion the way he should have. He had been so sure he could make it work.

A couple of mornings later while Kurt was eating breakfast, Marion waltzed in from her night out. He knew it was useless to say anything, but he did anyway. "Where have you been Marion? Do you realize most people are just getting up and beginning their day now?"

"I don't care what other people are doing or saying, which is something you've never liked about me. But I have something important to tell you. I'm going to Reno for a divorce. I want to be with Richard. He's so much more fun than you are."

"Fun? Well, I guess that's all you've ever cared about. Having fun. I wish you much luck in that department. Marion, I can't say I'm surprised, and I have come to the same conclusion. It's the right decision for both of us for many different reasons. Our marriage was a huge mistake. We were never committed to one another the way a husband and wife should be, and we never loved each other enough to get through the tough times together.

"All my life I wanted to be rich. That day when I first went to the country club with Nickels I vowed someday I would belong. I wanted to be a success and have a lot of money, so when I met you and we started dating, I was intoxicated by your family's wealth and power. What I have come to learn is that the riches in life come from intangibles such as love, honor, and integrity."

Kurt looked directly at her. "I really tried to make our marriage work, but you haven't been interested. Why did you marry me?"

Marion had listened intently, and said, "I'm not really sure. I've thought a lot about it lately. I think it was because you were so handsome, and I knew you had a bright future ahead of you. And when Uncle Russell said you were head over heels for someone else, I wanted to prove I could get you away from her. And you can't deny the chemistry we had. That was powerful."

"Yeah, we were pretty good in that area. Thank goodness we never had children. It would make this so much more complicated."

Marion said, "You're right about that. I would make a rotten mother."

Marion said, "I'll come by later and have the maid help me pack up all my things. I'll put them in the front guest room, and a man will come by to pick them up."

Kurt said, "I hope you have a good life, and I want you to know I wish you no ill will."

Marion turned to go. "Same to you, darling. Are you going to run back to that little Polack girl now?"

"I will if she'll have me."

He watched her walk out the door and get into the Packard where Richard was waiting for her. Kurt felt as if someone had taken a huge weight off his shoulders. But he was sad that he had wasted so much time with the wrong woman.

Kurt and Marion both thought it was probably the easiest divorce on record. The legal paperwork presented no problems, and there was no drama when it came to dividing up their material things. Marion gave Kurt the house. "I don't care a twit about it. I never liked it anyway. It was a wedding gift from Daddy and Mommy, and I didn't want to hurt their feelings." They kept separate bank accounts, so that presented no problem.

When he told Mama and Aunt Erna, they were upset about a divorce in the family, but said they never liked Marion anyway.

When he told Nickels and Charlie, they both said they weren't surprised and thought it was about time.

Kurt couldn't stop thinking about Antonia and wished he could turn the clock back. She had never married, but he often saw her around town either out on a date or with friends. Nickels told him she hadn't been serious about anyone since Kurt broke up with her. Kurt hoped the love and connection they used to have were strong enough to reawaken her feelings for him.

A week after Marion left, he discussed it with Charlie and Grace. "I wonder if she'll ever forgive me completely. What a fool I was to marry someone else. I don't like the person I was with Marion. I've learned so much about what's important in life. It scares me to think Antonia might not give me another chance."

Grace said, "If the feelings are still there, you'll know it. Give her time and whatever you do, don't push her. She'll be hesitant around you because she'll be afraid you'll hurt her again."

Charlie said, "Kurt, I know the way you are when you want something. You're like an express train. There's no stopping you until you reach your destination. But this time with Antonia, you're going to have to be patient and move slowly."

Chapter Thirty-one

❖

It was April 21, 1930. Albo sat in his cell daydreaming about his early release. After close to ten years in prison, he would appear in front of the parole board for the first time in November. It had seemed like a lifetime and was often intolerable, but it was almost over. He could think of nothing other than going home and sleeping next to Millie, hugging his children, and eating one of his wife's home-cooked meals. And he was finally going to meet his grandson Bertie. He hadn't been able to meet his grandson because only school-age children were allowed to visit the prison. The few photographs he had seen of Bertie were never enough.

The crowded prison now housed more than four thousand inmates. Construction crews were working on an expansion, and wood scaffolding lined the side of the building where Albo's cellblock was located. "They hammer and saw all day long. Make my head pound. It sound like jackhammer outside door. Can't stand the noise," he said to the guard.

"Too bad. Get used to it."

"Not me," thought Albo. "I'm getting out of here for good."

That night, when he was already locked in his cell for the night, he was certain he smelled smoke. He detected a faint gray tinge to the fading light. He heard some shouting in the distance and the sound of doors slamming open and shut. The noise began to escalate, and he sensed something was terribly wrong. A guard ran down the corridor, and yelled to another guard. "Open the level-two door. We need to get out of here."

Someone shouted, "Where are they going? What's happening?"

Albo was frightened.

The intensity of the activity increased, and guards ran by his cell screaming to each other, "Get out. Get out *now*."

A fire had broken out on the wooden scaffolding outside Albo's cellblock and was rapidly spreading throughout the prison. Albo and hundreds of other inmates shouted and banged at the bars of their cells. They yelled for the guards to let them out. Smoke and deafening noise filled the cellblock, and Albo was having difficulty breathing.

Guard after guard raced down the corridor, passing his cell, ignoring him and all the other prisoners. They refused to unlock the cell doors, and even more egregious, continued to lock up prisoners who weren't in their cells. Albo was frantic. "Wypuść nas stąd. Co się dzieje? Pomocy." *Let us out of here. What is the problem? Help.*

The fire reached the roof and was spreading through the entire complex. The heat was unbearable, and Albo tried not to panic.

The screaming didn't sound human anymore.

Outside, prison officials had cordoned off the towering prison walls, while squads took up vantage points in guard towers. Soldiers from Fort Hayes, a local military post, were also on the scene. Prison guards mounted machine guns at the gates and on the walls, and troopers with bayonets were ordered to shoot to kill. Like marching ants, a troop of National Guardsmen flowed into the prison yard, and thirty minutes after the fire started, the prison was completely surrounded.

Inside, prisoners who weren't locked up began to riot. When the firefighters tried to enter, they couldn't get in because prisoners were throwing rocks at them. Prisoners ran up and down the corridors looking for implements that would help them release the other inmates. Albo saw two prisoners run down the corridor chasing a couple of guards. They caught one of the guards, threw him down, and grabbed his keys.

Albo's heart rose as he realized the prisoners had begun their own rescue efforts. He heard the shouting as they tried to get the prisoners out of their cells. There were heroes that day. Some inmates miraculously escaped, gasped fresh air, armed themselves with sledgehammers and crowbars, and rushed back into the burning building to try to rescue other prisoners. They knocked locks off, spread steel bars, and ripped away cell doors. They helped guards and scrambled into the inferno to drag or carry screaming men to safety.

Albo called out, waiting and hoping they would make it to his cell. But the sound of their voices got farther and farther away.

Although a handful of guards attempted to save the prisoners, most ignored them. Fifty inmates made it out of their cells before heavy smoke stopped the impromptu rescue. There was a loud explosion as part of the roof caved in.

Albo heard the screams, the curses, and the howls. He imagined men in their cells, how they must be watching the fire dart up the timbered walls, how they must know they faced a fiery death. He felt a calmness wash over him, quenching the intense heat. He knew he wasn't going to make it out. He kneeled by his cot and prayed, "Please God, watch over my family and keep them safe." His last thoughts were of Millie, Albert, Jr., Antonia, and his grandson Bert.

By the time the fire was under control, more than three hundred men were dead and many seriously injured. On the upper tiers of the prison, the trapped men were dead or dying. Some shrieked from pain, and some were unconscious, overcome by poisonous smoke.

❖

Nickels first learned something terrible was happening when a report about a fire at the penitentiary in Columbus came over the Associated Press Teletypewriter in the newsroom. He felt the hair rise on the back of his neck and rushed to call the prison. He couldn't get through. "Oh Papa, please be all right."

The Teletype continued to spew out information, including the growing number of casualties. He knew he had to get home to be with his mother and sister.

He told his boss he had a family emergency and left immediately for Akron.

By the time he got home, reports were so dire, he knew he had lost his father. When he walked into the house, neither his mother nor Antonia had any idea their world was about to fall apart. His mother gave him a big hug. "What a wonderful surprise, Albert. What are you doing home this time of day? I thought you were working."

"I have an assignment that brought me down this way, and I thought I would spend the night here."

"Wonderful. I'm going to get dinner started." She gave him a hug and went into the kitchen.

As soon as Millie left, Nick said, "Turn on the radio. There's something going on at the prison, and I don't want to scare Mama, so keep it low."

"What's going on?"

"Just listen. It's not good."

The news report droned on, repeating the same information over and over. Nickels and Antonia paced back and forth across the living room until Millie called them to dinner.

As they ate, they tried to keep the conversation normal. Nickels talked about his latest assignment at the newspaper, and fortunately, Millie asked a lot of questions about what he was doing. The minute they were finished, Antonia jumped up to clear the table.

Millie said, "What's wrong with you tonight?"

"Nothing."

Millie said, "Well, you're not acting right. You two go in the living room. I'll wash the dishes and clean up the kitchen."

As soon as they were back in the living room, Nickels turned the radio back on.

"Our poor Papa. I hope he's safe."

When Millie came into the room, Antonia quickly turned the radio off. "What are you listening to? You two are acting very strange. Are you upset about something?"

"You're imagining things, Mama. Why don't you go to bed early? You look tired."

"I am a little tired."

After Millie went upstairs, the phone rang, and Nickels answered. He had called the warden directly to find out if there was any news about Papa. The warden told him it was too soon to know anything definitive, but he would get back to him as soon as they sorted everything out. "I expect it won't be until morning. We have a disaster here."

"Please call anytime—day or night. We're desperate to know if my father is okay."

Nickels and Antonia stayed up all night.

Antonia said, "Why doesn't he call? I'm frantic to know about Papa. I have a horrible feeling."

Nickels hugged her. "So do I."

Around six in the morning, the phone rang. Nickels answered it immediately.

Antonia watched her brother's face as he listened to the caller. When she saw her brother's eyes fill with tears and his chin begin to shake, she knew Papa was gone. Antonia cried, "Oh no. Oh, please, no."

Millie walked into the living room and saw Nick and Antonia crying. "What's going on? You need to tell me what's happening."

Nickels had trouble finding the right words. When he finally spoke, his voice was barely audible. "Sit down Mama. I have some very bad news." The look on his face frightened her.

"There was a fire at the prison, and many of the inmates didn't make it out." He let her think about what he had said.

"Mama, Papa is gone. He died in the fire."

"What? Don't say that. It's not possible. Why are you saying such an awful thing?"

Nickels and Antonia stood close to her. Both were sobbing. When she looked at them crying, she knew they would never make up something so terrible.

Millie slumped down and pounded her fists on her thighs. "Albo, my Albo." She said his name again and again until she was hoarse. "My wonderful husband, how can I live without you? He was almost home. No. No no no."

Nickels and Antonia sat on either side of their mother. They held hands and cried together for a long time.

Afterward Millie wouldn't move from the couch. "Leave me alone. Please leave me alone. I want to be alone." Her face was swollen from crying, and as they walked into the kitchen to give her some privacy, they could hear her moaning softly, "Goodbye my wonderful husband. I will miss you more than life itself."

Nickels called Kurt and Charlie to tell them about his father's death.

Kurt was distraught about Albo. He said, "I'm so sad about your father. And I'm sad I never got to see him again. I'd hoped that after you were able to forgive me that your father would too. I realize now that he wasn't ready."

Nickels said, "He was starting to come around, but he said he needed more time."

Kurt said, "I'll never be able to tell him to his face how sorry I am for what I did. I can't believe I'll never be able to talk things over with him again."

Nickels gave him the details about the funeral and told him he would see him there.

Grandpa Nicky said my great grandmother Millie was never the same after my great grandfather Albo died in the fire.

Chapter Thirty-two

❖

*T*t was a gray, cloudy day, and Antonia was unhappy the sun wasn't shining for Papa's funeral. She was having trouble holding herself together, but for Mama's sake, she knew she had to. Nickels arrived the night before, and of course Kurt and Charlie were coming. Although she had seen Kurt a few times over the years, for some reason she was really nervous about seeing him today.

Millie insisted on displaying the casket in their home like in the old country. The funeral home would transport it to the cemetery while they were at the church service.

As they waited for everyone to arrive, Millie hugged Antonia. "Everything is going to be all right, even though it doesn't seem like it ever will be again." Antonia didn't want to let her mother go.

"I know Mama, but I'm so sad. Papa did nothing to deserve this, and I keep envisioning him in that terrible fire."

"Hush. We're going to talk about good things today like Papa always wanted. We're going to remember the special times we had with him."

Friends and relatives began to pour into the house. They hugged, cried and fondly remembered Albo.

Nickels was standing with Charlie when they overheard one of his father's friends talking about the country club murder. "We know Albo didn't kill that girl. It's a shame no one proved it. What a tragedy for him to die like he did before he could prove his innocence."

Charlie said, "Nickels, over the past few years, myself and some of my guys have been trying to prove your father's innocence. It's not easy to find information, but we're working on it. There's someone out there who killed Catherine Block, and let's face it, they also killed your father. They're as guilty of Albo's murder as they are of hers. Maybe they didn't light the match, but they might as well have. We're not going to stop until we can prove he didn't do it."

"I appreciate everything you're doing, Charlie. It's only a matter of time."

Kurt walked into the Jablonski's thinking of Antonia and not knowing what to expect. But as soon as Antonia saw him, she walked over and thanked him for coming. "We're so pleased you could be here, Kurt. My father thought the world of you, and over the years, he said many times that you and Charlie were like sons."

Tears welled up in his eyes when he thought about Albo. "We're all devastated by his death, especially the way he died. I can't stop thinking about how I hurt him and your family, and how I'll never get a chance to see him again and apologize. I wanted to tell him I learned from my mistakes, and I'm a better man…" He didn't know what else to say.

She rubbed his shoulder and told him it was okay.

She looked around the room. "Where's Marion? Is she with you?"

"Marion and I are getting a divorce. She's in Reno with her *friend* Richard. They deserve each other."

He could see she was surprised.

"Toni, I can't express how sorry I am about your father."

He noticed a faint smile. "I forgot you call me that. You're the only one who ever did."

"Oh, I apologize."

"No need to. I actually like it. But, excuse me. I need to go help my mother serve the food. I promise to talk to you later." He watched her walk away. He loved the way she walked. It always seemed so effortless, as if she were gliding instead of walking.

After Antonia went to help her mother, Nickels approached Kurt. "Did you tell her you and Marion broke up?"

"Yes, I just told her."

Nickels said, "I can see how you look at her, and I want you to know you're not going to have a second chance to break my sister's heart. Be careful, Kurt. If you hurt her again, I'll never forgive you. That's a promise."

"You're absolutely right. I was a total cad and wish I had never broken up with her and hurt her so badly. I promise you I'll never hurt Antonia again. The thing is…I haven't been able to get her out of my mind since Marion and I split up. Oh, Jesus—let me be honest—she's never been out of my mind.

"I don't know if she'd ever consider taking me back, and I won't blame her if she doesn't, but I want to start seeing her again. It would mean a lot if you would give your approval. I give you my word that I'll go slowly."

"We can talk about this later. Today is about my father, and right now I need to speak to some of the others."

Millie handed out mourning cards, which was the signal to everyone that it was time to go to the church.

✧

Millie, Nickels, and Antonia were amazed by how many people were in the church for the service. Albo would have been surprised and pleased to see how many people were there. Fellow parishioners, friends from the Polish community, and even members of the country club were there. Albo had touched a lot of lives.

Antonia walked down the aisle and sat in the first row. Her mother sat on her right, with Nick and Harriet on her left. Bertie was in Cleveland with Harriet's parents.

Near the end of the Mass, the pastor walked down the center aisle. He leaned over and quietly told Nickels that after the prayer, it was time for him to speak.

The room became silent as Nickels approached the front of the church.

He looked out at all the people and cleared his throat.

"I welcome every one of you to this celebration of the life of Albert Henrik Jablonski, Sr. My father was a man no one can replace, especially in the hearts of my mother, my sister, and myself.

"My father was a likeable man of strong conviction. His life was a positively charged force field that you couldn't help but feel when you were around him. He was a man who was proud of his wife and children. He was a man who was proud to be Polish.

"My father was the man I hope someday to become. His strength was a quiet one, defined primarily by his unfailing ability to rise above his limitations in his effort to take care of those around him.

"One of the lessons I learned from Papa was the value of hard work. He worked hard and played hard, always with great concentration. I remember one time I asked my mother, 'Why does Papa work so much?' He woke up everyday and went to the first of his two jobs to provide for our family. I can count on one hand how many times he was sick. Even if he didn't feel well, he got up and went to work.

"One of my most vivid memories of him was the day he met my friends Kurt and Charlie. We had a club we called The Tribe. My father asked us about it, and we knew he was genuinely interested. That's one of the things he taught me—be sincerely interested in others. I think that's why I became a writer."

His voice began to crack, and he stopped speaking until he could compose himself. He looked down at Mama and Antonia who were both quietly crying.

Nick took a deep breath and continued.

"I remember one winter when he took Kurt, Charlie, and me ice fishing on Lake Erie. We trekked up to Cleveland on the trolley bus with all our gear and made our way to the harbor. Papa cut a hole in the ice, and we couldn't wait to catch a fish. We sat there in the cold and wind for what seemed like an eternity. Finally, Kurt asked him, 'Mr. Jablonski, are we going to catch a fish?'

"My father looked at him and said, 'Maybe we will, or maybe we won't, but we definitely won't if we don't try.' We sat on that cold ice all afternoon and caught nothing. But you know what? We had a great time.

"You—his family and friends—are all that he would have asked for today. He lived his life the best he could. He never had enemies, nor did he ever intentionally harm anyone. It's almost unbearable to think that our family was within months of being reunited. It's true my father was loved, and seeing all of you here today is testimony to how many of you know he was innocent of the crime he was convicted of ten years ago.

"Papa and Mama came to America from Poland for a better life. He never lost that dream, and to the end rarely complained about what happened to him. I pledge to all of you here today that we will continue to try to prove my father was innocent. I don't know how or when, but we won't stop until he is completely exonerated.

"I am fortunate that he was my father, and there are no words to express his influence in my life. It is through his example I learned to be the father and husband I am today."

When he finished, most were crying. As he made his way back to

Millie and Antonia, no one made a sound. Then Kurt began to clap. And then Charlie, followed by another, and another. Soon everyone was crying and applauding, including the priest.

Family and close friends drove to Glendale cemetery where the family had arranged for Albo to be buried. As they gathered around the freshly dug grave, Kurt stood next to Antonia.

Having her next to him felt right, and he was more determined than ever to recapture what they once had. He impulsively reached down and took her hand and was elated to feel her fingers tighten around his.

They held a brief graveside service, and as they were leaving the cemetery, the sun peeked out from behind the clouds.

"There's my Papa," said Antonia.

Chapter Thirty-three

❖

*A*fter Albo's funeral, Kurt earnestly began trying to win Antonia back. At first she refused to go out with him, but Kurt wouldn't give up. He brought her flowers and candy. He scoured bookstores to find interesting books for her.

Millie said, "You not hurt my baby again."

"I promise I won't. I made a huge mistake, and I know it. I'll give Antonia as much time as she needs to trust me again. I want this to be right. And I want her to understand I'll never do anything to hurt her again."

Kurt and Antonia had many conversations about their relationship. Gradually she opened up to him and let her guard down. A year after they began seeing each other again, they were out to dinner when Kurt said, "Toni, you're the love of my life, and I'm never letting you go again. Do you think you'll ever be able to trust me completely?"

"I want to Kurt, but you have to be patient with me. When you first told me you were going to marry Marion, I thought I would die. My heart felt as if it was broken in two, and I didn't think I would ever get over you. But after some time, and much reflection, I began to think maybe there was a good life for me that didn't include Kurt Becker. But when I ran into you and Marion at the restaurant that time right before your wedding, the old wounds opened up again, and I felt as miserable as when we first broke up."

"I was awful to you, and I will never be able to express how sorry I am. But I want you to know I'll wait for you as long as it takes. I told you we'd be together someday, Toni. What I didn't know was my stupidity and Marion White were going to come between us."

"When I was a little girl, the first time I met you, I liked you immediately. I sensed even then we had a special bond. When I was sixteen, and we went to the World Series game, I knew you were the one I wanted to spend my life with. I dated a little over these past few years, but I never came close to the feelings I had for you. I decided I wasn't going to get into a serious relationship or marry if I couldn't find the kind of love we had.

"I can't believe we're together again. I know it's going to work out. We were destined to be together," she said. "I wish I could tell Papa. He'd be so happy for us."

"That's one of my biggest regrets. I wish things could go back to the way they were. I missed talking to him and seeing him those last few years.

"You're ten times the woman Marion ever was or could be. I was money hungry, and I admit it. From the time I was a little boy, all I ever wanted was to be rich and successful, but what I didn't realize was how steep the price was for marrying Marion, and how much I stood to lose."

"I believe everything happens for a reason. I think you're a better person for marrying Marion."

Kurt was stunned. "What? Why would you say that?"

"I mean it. If you hadn't been with Marion, you wouldn't have the insight you have now. You wouldn't know money isn't the most important thing in the world. Being with Marion is what it took for you to appreciate the real riches in life. I think we'll both cherish what we have together this time around."

He apologized over and over again. "I made such a big mistake, and I'll never forgive myself for how badly I hurt you."

She insisted he stop apologizing. "You've probably told me you're sorry a hundred times. Enough. It's all in the past now, and we need to look toward our future. To me, it feels as if we've always been together, and the rest of it was just a bad dream. Mama always told me it would work out."

They left the restaurant, and went back to his house. They sat down in the living room, kicked off their shoes, and began to kiss. He pulled away and said, "Toni, you make me feel like a teenager. I get excited when I hear your voice. I want to make love to you. I am trying so hard not to push you. I hope you know that."

"Oh, Kurt. You've been a perfect gentleman." She hesitated for a minute.

She said, "I want you so much, but I'm not sure if I'm ready."

"Take all the time you want. I don't want to push you. When the time is right, we'll both know it."

He reached for her, took her in his arms, and began nuzzling her. He couldn't stop himself. He kissed her ear, and whispered, "I love you so much, Toni. I feel as if I'm home again."

He ran his hand down her neck, between her breasts and over her stomach. When he touched the inside of her thigh, she pressed her body into his, and his lips lightly traced her face until his mouth and tongue reached her parted lips. They kissed passionately, and when she moaned, he thought he would lose his mind. Even her smell was intoxicating.

Antonia laughed out loud.

He was surprised. "What's so funny?"

She grinned. "I decided I'm ready."

He laughed and led her into the bedroom. They hurriedly undressed each other and lay down together. He covered her body with his, and finally, after all these years, they made love.

Afterward, they knew they were exactly where they were always meant to be.

Chapter Thirty-four

❖

One day in April 1932, Kurt walked into his office, and his secretary handed him a stack of messages. As he went through them, he spotted one from William Oxnard, Albo's defense attorney from twelve years ago. Oxnard was in the Cantrell Pavilion at City Hospital and asked Kurt to stop by and see him. The message said it was urgent. Kurt wondered what Oxnard wanted.

After the debacle of Albo's plea agreement, Oxnard disappeared, and no one had heard a thing about him. To Kurt's knowledge, he no longer practiced law and hadn't for years, at least since the time of Albo's conviction. Kurt entered Oxnard's hospital room, looked around and thought, "Is this the right room? That shriveled, white-haired man can't be Oxnard."

He heard a shaky voice. "Thanks for coming. I'm sure you didn't want to."

He recognized the voice as Oxnard's and was shocked at his condition. "I really don't know why I came. But I have to admit I'm interested to know why it's so important for you to see me."

Oxnard struggled to sit up and motioned Kurt to come over and help him. When Kurt touched him, he realized Oxnard was virtually skin and bones. Oxnard said, "The doctors tell me I don't have much time left, and I have something I must tell you before I die.

"I have lived with a monstrous lie for all these years, and I can't live with it for one more minute."

"What are you talking about?" Kurt wanted to leave. Oxnard coughed and began to talk in a raspy whisper. Kurt said, "I can't hear you. You have to talk louder."

"I'll try. I'm having trouble getting the words out. This isn't easy to say."

Although Kurt had nothing on his calendar for the morning, he said, "Christ, just say it. I have a meeting to get to."

Oxnard cleared his throat. "What I have to tell you is…" Oxnard stopped to clear his throat again, and it irritated Kurt.

"Spit it out, old man."

Oxnard nodded. "You have to understand, this is difficult. Back in 1920, I know many of you were certain Albert Jablonski didn't kill Catherine Block. You were positive he was innocent."

Oxnard cleared his throat again.

"You were right. The real killer set him up. Then he threatened and bribed me to make sure there wouldn't be a trial. He was afraid the evidence wouldn't hold up in court. I was forced to pressure Jablonski to plead guilty to second degree murder by persuading him he would get a reduced sentence."

Oxnard sounded as if he were choking.

"I took that money and knowingly sent an innocent man to jail for the rest of his life. It's important you understand how it happened. He had his man choke me and break my finger," he said as he held up his hand and showed Kurt his crooked pinky finger.

"When he physically harmed me, I resisted and wouldn't give into his demands, but then he threatened my family, and I had to do what he wanted. I had to protect my family. Please try to understand."

Kurt felt a slow burn spreading through his body.

"When I heard that Jablonski died in the prison fire, I knew what

I had to do. I couldn't live with it anymore, but I kept putting off my confession. Now there's no more time."

Kurt couldn't hide the horror in his voice. "Who really murdered her?"

Oxnard struggled to catch his breath. "Russell Cantrell murdered Catherine Block. They were having an affair. She was pregnant and planning to expose him, which would have ruined his precious reputation and political aspirations. Cantrell had his thug Voigt plant the bloody towels and golf club in Jablonski's locker at the country club. After that it was easy. Who would believe a potato-peeling Polish immigrant when he insisted he had nothing to do with it? Cantrell had it all figured out. And it worked exactly as he planned."

Kurt couldn't move. He was glued to the floor. "You bastard. You fucking bastard."

Destroyed by Oxnard's revelation, Kurt lurched toward the door and then turned around and glared at him. "How stupid could I have been? May you rot in hell for what you and those evil excuses for human beings did. You put an innocent man in jail, and his death in the fire will torment his family for the rest of their lives. Do you realize he was a few months away from getting out?"

Kurt turned to leave, and Oxnard gasped, "Wait. I never touched the bribe money. I stashed it away. I want the Jablonski family to have every last penny of it."

"Do you think that will mean anything to his family?"

Oxnard said, "No, but it's a lot of money. I want them to have it."

"How much?"

"One hundred thousand."

Kurt walked down the hospital corridor and out onto the street. His thoughts slammed around his brain, and he was in deep distress as he walked toward his car.

Kurt flashed back to the day of the murder and remembered how agitated Cantrell was during the entire four-hour round of golf. There was so much conflicting information and so much wrong with that day, but at the time, Kurt chalked it up to bad golf.

He thought about the encounter outside the Grille Room when Catherine Block hurried past with Cantrell right behind her. Cantrell wouldn't even look at him.

He remembered seeing Cantrell in the locker room a little later and how weird it was that he had changed his clothes and that he was sweating profusely.

He remembered on the first tee that Cantrell said he was going to have to work after the match, and then later in the locker room, he said he was having dinner with his wife.

He remembered going to the parking lot and seeing Cantrell sitting up front in his car waiting for Voigt to get in. They sped right by him, obviously in deep conversation.

It suddenly dawned on him that Cantrell didn't give the tuition and mortgage money out of a sense of altruism, but because he was afraid Kurt knew something about the murder.

Kurt went home, shed his jacket and tie, and rolled up his shirtsleeves. He went to the liquor cabinet in the dining room where Marion kept her booze, poured a stiff drink, and sat down at the table. After the first gulp, he was surprised by how much he needed it. He had never cared for alcohol, and was never much of a drinker. He raised the glass to eye level and watched the caramel-colored liquid swirl around as he stared right through it. How could he have been so stupid?

He jolted back to reality, set the glass down, and envisioned the conversation when Cantrell told him he would pay for college, law school, and the mortgage.

It was blood money. All the pieces began to fall in place, and Kurt understood that Cantrell thought he kept his mouth shut because of the money. He was angrier than he'd ever felt before and vowed to make him pay. He said, "Fuck you, Russell Cantrell. I'll get you for this. I don't know how or when, but you screwed with the wrong people."

✧

A few days later, after carefully thinking everything over, he visited Oxnard in the hospital one more time. "I have a question. How did you find out who really murdered her? How did you know it was Cantrell who killed her and not Voigt?"

"Voigt came to visit me every year. He considered it an 'insurance policy' so I wouldn't tell anyone about the country club murder. He relished telling me about all the havoc he and Cantrell created over the years, including Catherine Block's murder.

"Voigt bragged to me about it. He was proud of what his boss had done. He said, 'Cantrell got rid of that bitch because she was going to blab. All I did was clean up after him, and put the stuff in the Polack's locker.' Most of the time Voigt did the dirty work, but he was quite insistent that Cantrell murdered Catherine himself.

"He also bragged about other murders, other crimes. They've killed several people over these years. Voigt laughed about how no one could ever prove who did it. I dreaded his visits."

"Neither of them has a conscience, and Voigt in particular enjoys hurting people. He told me listening to people scream while he tortured them was as good as an orgasm. When I reacted with disgust, he laughed like a madman. There is no way of knowing how many people the two of them have murdered. Cantrell may play the part of a respectable Congressman, but he's as bad as Voigt, maybe worse. The two of them together are deadly."

Oxnard's voice was so weak Kurt had trouble hearing him. "Voigt thought if he told me the truth, it would scare me. He wanted me to be afraid of Cantrell. And it worked. I was so afraid of him that I never practiced law again."

"Why didn't you leave Akron?"

"I wanted to, but Voigt told me to stick around and warned me if I left they would find me and my family. I couldn't take that chance. My life has been a living hell. My relationship with my wife and children has never been the same, but at least my family is safe, although I'm worried about what might happen to them when I'm gone."

A couple of days later, Kurt took his secretary to the hospital. Oxnard dictated a confession that vindicated Albo and implicated Cantrell and Voigt. Kurt notarized it and sent it by mail to his office so it would have a stamped date on it. At the right time, it would be opened in front of a judge.

Oxnard died the next day.

Chapter Thirty-five

❖

Kurt was sitting in his kitchen at the round oak pedestal table when Charlie breezed in the back door.

"Hey Kurt." They shook hands and briefly hugged.

"Where's Nickels?" Charlie asked.

"He's on his way. He called to tell me he's working on a big story and will be a little late.

Charlie said, "We're both curious about why you asked us to get together on the spur of the moment. What's so urgent? And why here at your house instead of The Canal?"

Before Kurt could say anything, Nickels came in the door. The three of them shook hands.

"Hey, you guys, what's going on?"

Kurt asked them what they wanted to drink. Charlie said, "Where's your maid?"

"When Marion left, I let all the help go. I never liked having them in the house. Now I sit in the kitchen instead of the dining room, and serve myself. What can I get you?"

After Kurt poured all three of them a scotch, he began. "I have some information you need to hear from me in person. When you hear what it is, you'll understand why I wanted to meet in the privacy of my home instead of The Canal."

Charlie said. "Tell us what's going on."

Kurt took a sip of his drink. "A week ago William Oxnard contacted me and asked me to come and see him. He was very sick and in the hospital. Do you remember him?"

Nickels was immediately riveted. "Of course I do. He was my father's attorney. Why did he contact you? Why would he want to talk to you instead of me? What's going on?"

"Oxnard was gravely ill and had something he wanted to tell me before he died. Give me a chance to explain."

Nickels and Charlie were on the edge of their seats.

"I'm going to say it straight out. Oxnard knew all along that Albo was innocent. He knew Albo didn't kill Catherine Block because Russell Cantrell murdered her."

Nickels bolted out of his chair. He swept his hand across the table, and his drink flew across the room, shattering against the wall. "That bastard. Oh my God, I can't believe this." His hands were clenched in fists, and he looked as if he would explode.

He paced around the room and kept saying, "That bastard," over and over again.

Kurt said, "Take a deep breath, and please sit down, Nickels. You need to hear the rest of this."

Nickels sat down, but he couldn't sit still. Kurt explained how Cantrell framed Albo.

"Cantrell was having an affair with Catherine, and she was pregnant. When she started pressuring him to divorce his wife and marry her, he killed her to shut her up.

"Cantrell and Louis Voigt framed Albo. They coerced Oxnard into getting Albo to plea to second-degree murder to avoid a trial and any further examination of the evidence. They knew the case would fall apart in court. Cantrell couldn't afford for anyone to look elsewhere."

"Oh God," Nickels cried. "I knew it. There was something about that bastard Cantrell that always bothered me. I never liked him. Oh, Papa." Tears ran down his face.

Charlie and Kurt sipped their drinks and didn't say anything.

When Nickels pulled himself back together, he said, "I guess I shouldn't be surprised. We always knew someone framed my father. The fact that it was Cantrell and Voigt who ruined my family makes sense. It's hard to believe I interviewed him on several occasions and never knew I was talking to the man responsible for my father's imprisonment, and ultimately, his death."

Nickel's voice cracked. "Damn them all. Cantrell, Voigt, and Oxnard."

Charlie said, "This is unbelievable. The only thing I can think is that we have to do something. We have to make them pay."

Nickels said, "Oh, he's going to pay. I'll make sure of that."

Kurt interjected, "Hear me out. Be furious at Cantrell and Voigt, but let me tell you about Oxnard. He was in an impossible position. Cantrell and Voigt tortured him. They choked him and broke his finger, and yet he still wouldn't agree to do what they asked. When they threatened his family, he did what he thought was necessary to protect his wife and children. He abandoned his career and never got over what he did. Voigt visited him once a year to remind him to keep his mouth shut.

"Nickels, the reason Oxnard spoke to me was because he knew we are close friends and that I'm an attorney. He also wanted to exonerate Albo and asked my advice on the best way to do that. I have a notarized letter in my office safe that provides irrefutable proof of Albo's innocence. When all is said and done, your father's name will be cleared."

Nickels said, "Oh God. Two years. Why didn't he tell us two years ago? Two years, and my father would be alive today. I'm so floored, I can't think. I hear what you're saying about Oxnard. You say you don't want me to blame him, but it's tough not to. What he did wrong was to keep everything secret all these years. At the very least, he was a coward…"

Kurt interrupted. "He died the day after he dictated the letter. He knew there were no words he could say to your family other than, 'I'm terribly sorry.' Cantrell ruined his life too."

Kurt continued, "After I talked to Oxnard, I figured something else out. I'm ashamed to admit this, but I'm certain the money Cantrell gave Mama, Aunt Erna, and me was his idea of hush money. Even worse, I'm pretty sure he thought I knew he was paying me to keep my mouth shut. My career is a sham. It makes me sick to think of all the money and aggravation I've saved that bastard Cantrell over the years.

"When he came over to the boardinghouse and offered to pay the tuition for my education, I was so relieved not to have to work and go to school at the same time, I refused to question his motives. Why didn't I see a red flag when he paid off the boardinghouse mortgage? It's unforgiveable, and I feel partially responsible for what happened to Albo. Why didn't I put two and two together?"

Charlie said, "Kurt, you know it's easy to look back and see the clues once you know the real facts. We don't blame you, do we, Nickels?"

"Of course we don't. The two people ultimately responsible for what happened to my father are Russell Cantrell and Louis Voigt, and I'm going to make sure they pay."

Kurt said, "I have a golf game scheduled with Cantrell next week. I don't know how I will get through four hours with him."

Kurt, Nickels, and Charlie didn't speak for several minutes.

Kurt broke the silence. "The reason I asked you to meet me here wasn't only to tell you about Oxnard's confession. Now that we know for sure it was Cantrell who framed Albo, we have to do something.

After Oxnard told me, my first thought was that we have to get even. That despicable animal got away with murder for the past twelve years, but we're going to show him what happens when The Tribe bands together. We need to figure out a plan, and we're going to have our first strategy session. Agreed?"

Nickels and Charlie both said yes.

Kurt refreshed their drinks.

Over the years Charlie had gained tremendous self-confidence and by now was considered a star in the Akron Police Department. Kurt knew he could count on Charlie's help and appreciated the specific skills he brought to the table. His ability to organize and plan was definitely going to come into play as they figured out how to retaliate against Cantrell.

Charlie said, "When I think of Albo and all the times he was there for me when I needed him, it makes me sick. I remember one time when I was almost fourteen and tried to talk to my father. He was drunk as usual and started screaming at me. I came over to your house, and as soon as your father saw me, he asked me if something was bothering me. After we talked, I felt so much better. I never tried to talk to my father about anything serious again. I loved Albo. Whatever we decide to do—legal or not—I'm in."

Nickels said, "Remember all those years ago when we used to sit under the boardinghouse stairs, and we knew we could always depend on each other? That's how I feel right now. It's always been the three of us together. I want you both to know how much it means to me that you are going to be in on this with me, no matter what. Especially you, Charlie. Being a cop, I know this won't be easy for you."

"I wouldn't be anywhere else," said Charlie. "Your father meant the world to me—to all of us."

Kurt said, "There's one more thing to tell you, Nickels. Oxnard never touched the bribe money Cantrell insisted he take. Oxnard wants the money go to your family."

"What? Are you fucking kidding? We don't want that money. It has my father's blood on it."

"I know you're angry, you have a right to be. But think it over. It's a huge amount and will make your mother's elderly years much easier. You don't have to tell her where you got it."

"I don't know. I'll have to think about it. I can't think about it now."

Charlie said, "I know it doesn't seem right, but in a way, it doesn't seem right not to take it. Considering everything Cantrell took from you, I think it's a form of convoluted justice that you end up with his money."

"Like I said, I have to think about it. I'm not saying no. I guess it really would make Mama's life easier, and heaven knows she's had a tough time over the past twelve years. How much is it?"

Kurt said, "You won't believe it—one hundred thousand."

Nickels and Charlie were stunned by the amount.

Kurt said, "You don't have to decide now, take your time. I have the money in my safe and it's yours if and when you want it. If you decide you don't want it, we'll donate it to charity."

Four hours later, Kurt, Nickels, and Charlie were all a little drunk.

When they began formulating their plan, they realized that to pull it off, they needed Antonia. Nickels hesitated to include her, but Kurt and Charlie persuaded him they would keep her safe and make sure she was never alone with Cantrell.

"My sister is a strong and resilient woman, but this is a little different. I recognize we need her to make this work, but I worry about her."

Kurt said, "I agree, but we can't do this without her. We'll watch her and keep her in sight at all times. I've found her again after all these years, and I'm not going to let anything happen to her."

They agreed to meet again at Kurt's house in a week. Kurt said he would explain everything to Antonia and bring her to the next strategy session. After Charlie and Nickels left, Kurt locked the door behind them.

✧

When they met again the following week, each of them had ideas on how they should proceed. Antonia was shocked to learn what they were thinking, but said that she would go along with whatever they finally decided. "Not a day goes by that I don't think of Papa. We can't let Cantrell get away with what he did. If we go to the police, we'll have no idea if Cantrell has them in his pocket or could get to them with a bribe. Charlie, I'm sorry to say that, but you know it's true. We have to take care of this ourselves."

They discussed various scenarios for the rest of the evening. Charlie's inside knowledge of police department procedures was critical to the plan, and he helped them understand how a police investigation would typically proceed.

Finally they believed they had a plan that would work.

Nickels signaled for everyone to stop talking. "Now is the time to back out if you don't want to be involved. Especially you, Toni. Are you sure you want to be a part of this? I want each of you to tell me whether you are in or out."

Everyone was in.

Charlie suddenly quoted Ty Cobb. "Baseball is a red-blooded sport for red-blooded men. It's no pink tea, and mollycoddles had better stay out. It's a struggle for supremacy, a survival of the fittest."

Kurt said, "Very appropriate."

They had a plan, and they would put it into action in June at

Cantrell's fancy campaign fundraiser at Hollingsworth House.

"It's genius. Zemsta for Papa." said Nickels.

Antonia said, "Oh yeah."

"What does that mean?" asked Kurt.

"Revenge for my father."

"That's perfect," said Charlie. "We must all agree to keep this a secret forever. No one other than the four of us can ever know."

Nickels extended his hand, palm down, and one by one, The Tribe stacked their hands on top of the other. "Come on Antonia, you too," said her brother.

"Zemsta."

Chapter Thirty-six

❖

 $\mathcal{K}$ urt and Cantrell had an early tee time at the country club on a sunny day in late April. They'd golfed together every now and then over the past five years and usually used the time to discuss business. Kurt was agitated about having to spend the round trying to pretend that nothing was wrong.

The first few holes were uneventful, but when Kurt found his swing, he began outshooting and outscoring Cantrell on every hole. Cantrell never liked to lose, and Kurt could see he was annoyed. Over the next few holes Kurt saw him roll the ball up in the rough for a better lie a couple of times, and drop a ball when he couldn't find the one he hit. He was used to Cantrell's creative scoring, and usually ignored it, but this time he couldn't stop himself from calling him on it.

On the next green, after they putted out, and Cantrell told him his score, Kurt said, "Did you add a penalty stroke for the lost ball you dropped in the rough back there?"

"I didn't lose a ball."

"Russell, I saw you drop a ball when you couldn't find the one you hit."

"Are you saying I cheated? Watch yourself."

"I'm saying you need to adjust your score for the lost ball."

"I didn't drop a ball, and have no idea what you're talking about. You're up."

Kurt thought, "Well, I guess that saying is true: 'Golf shows your character.'"

Cantrell said, "What's with you today? You're not acting like yourself. Is something wrong?"

"I'm fine, but there's a bunch of work sitting on my desk, and I'm a bit preoccupied."

Kurt wondered how he was going to get through the rest of the round without strangling him.

As the game progressed, Kurt shot one of the best games of his life. "This is one time I'm not going to let him win, and I'm going to enjoy every minute of it. Even with his constant cheating, he's not going to beat me today."

Standing on the final tee, Kurt said, "Russell, I'm assuming you heard about that prison fire in Columbus two years ago, but I wonder if you're aware Albo Jablonski was one of the casualties."

Cantrell's expression didn't change. "Of course I know about the fire. I'm working with the governor to cosponsor a bill that addresses prison crowding and conditions. It's expected to pass without dissent. Once it becomes federal law, states will be required to maintain prisons according to standards put forth in the legislation. Who the hell was Aldo Ja-whatever-his-name-was?"

"*Albo Jablonski*. His name was Albert Jablonski. Don't you remember him? He was the Polish immigrant who worked in the kitchen here at Rosewood Hills. He pled guilty and went to jail for Catherine Block's murder."

Cantrell shrugged. "Don't remember him at all."

Kurt wanted to punch him.

"His family is struggling to come to terms with his death. They believe he was innocent, and his son is determined to find the real killer. You remember Nickels, the shoeshine boy, don't you? He's been looking into the murder for the past two years, and has discovered some important inconsistencies in the evidence."

Cantrell remained stone-faced. "Didn't that happen about fifteen or twenty years ago?"

Kurt looked directly at Cantrell. "*Twelve years.* It's been twelve years since the murder."

"How does he expect to prove it now?" Cantrell was staring off at something in the distance.

"Russell. Are you with me?"

Cantrell swung around and grabbed the golf club his caddy was handing him.

"You're up Russell. Believe it or not, you have the honors." He chuckled loud enough for Cantrell to hear, and was glad to see he'd rattled him.

Kurt beat Cantrell by seven strokes. When the match was over and they were in the locker room, Kurt laughed to himself as he watched Cantrell count out the money to pay off their bet.

Cantrell walked out the door, and growled, "I'll catch you next time. Louis is waiting for me out in the parking lot, and I have too much to do today to stop in the Fountain Grille."

Kurt took his time before he left the locker room. He didn't want to see Cantrell again today and wanted to avoid him as much as possible until The Tribe's plan was launched. When he reached the parking lot, he expected Cantrell to be long gone, but as he neared his car, he heard Cantrell and Voigt loudly arguing. The two men were trying to keep their conversation civil. It was difficult to hear exactly what they were saying, but Kurt could tell it was starting to get heated.

"Why would you mention to anyone about us working together? I thought we agreed never to let anyone know you were anything but my driver. You have a couple of drinks in a bar and start bragging to everyone within hearing distance that you are much more than Congressman Cantrell's chauffeur? What were you thinking? I can't afford to have people think of you as anything other than my driver."

Voigt looked as if he were ready to hit Cantrell. "I'm sick and tired of being treated like a second-class citizen. You treat me as if I'm your servant, when what I am is…your partner." By now he was screaming and his face was flushed red. "I'm your partner, goddamn it. Do you understand? I do all the work, and you take all the money. I'm sick of it."

"Why you…"

Voigt interrupted. "I want a big bonus for all the years we brought in huge profits."

Cantrell was amazed. In all the time they'd been together, Voigt had never complained or asked for more money. "What's wrong with you?"

"What's wrong is that I don't like how you treat me. You think I'm your puppy dog? Who the hell do you think you are? I figure you owe me something after everything I've done for you."

Cantrell went berserk. "Everything you've done for me? You must be joking. I literally pulled you out of the gutter. Without me you'd be rotting in jail, or worse yet, dead."

When Cantrell spotted Kurt and several others gaping at them, he said, "Get in the car Louis. *Now*. People are watching."

It wasn't lost on Kurt that several members were listening to Cantrell and Voigt argue. "We couldn't have set this up if we'd tried."

When they were in the car, Cantrell could see how furious Louis was. "I built that apartment over the garage for you. You live there rent free, and enjoy all the amenities of the estate. Doesn't that count for something?"

"With all the money we've made from all the work I did? That's a drop in the bucket. Without me, you wouldn't have had a bootlegging business."

"What do you want? I'm listening."

"I want money. A lot of money. At least two hundred thousand. And I want you to buy me a house, and put a nice new car in the driveway."

Cantrell knew there was no appeasing Voigt. He could ruin him if he wanted. "All right, I'll get you a house and car, but you have to give me some time. I'm going back to Washington in a couple of days. Find a small place you like. Once you have it picked out, I'll give you enough money to buy the house and car and have some left over."

"What about the two hundred thou?"

"I'll give you fifty thousand and no more. I think that's more than fair when you add in the house and the car."

"Are you kidding? Do you realize how much you made because of me? Let's face it. Fifty thousand is nothing to you. You've made millions because of me," he sneered. "Make it two hundred thousand. Consider it the price you have to pay for me to keep my mouth shut."

After fourteen years together in their odd, yet symbiotic, relationship, Cantrell couldn't believe how much Voigt had grown to resent him. But he was trapped. Voigt knew too much and could ruin him many times over. Not only did he help with the illegal businesses, but he was also privy to Cantrell's many illicit affairs.

Cantrell typically had a couple girls stashed away, and when he tired of them, he bought their silence. He had learned a tough lesson with Catherine Block and made sure not to get anyone pregnant again. At the first hint of possessiveness, he dumped them. Sometimes Louis drove them to a new town and gave them enough cash to start a new life.

Voigt knew who the women were, and the dates when Cantrell

was seeing them. Cantrell was sure Voigt could provide a detailed list of names and dates to the press.

Cantrell was disappointed in Voigt's drastic change in attitude. Over the years, he had come to depend on him, and believed he was the only person he could really trust. He realized Voigt must have had these feelings for a very long time.

"Fuck him. Who needs him? I was fine before I met him, and I'll be fine now." But somehow, Cantrell felt as if he had lost the only real friend he'd ever had.

In May, Kurt, Nickels, Charlie, and Antonia met one last time at The Canal to put the finishing touches on Zemsta. Each of them was nervous about what they were planning, and after they had worked out all the final details, Kurt asked them again if they wanted to go forward with the scheme.

"I'm dead serious about this. Does each one of you want to continue and follow through with Zemsta?

"Nick?"

"Definitely."

"Charlie?"

"Absolutely."

"What about you, Toni? Are you sure?"

"Yes, I'm doing this for my Papa."

Chapter Thirty-seven

❖

After twelve years of Republican leadership, the Democrats believed FDR would help solve the crippling financial problems created by the Depression. Cantrell tried to stem the Democratic tide with the slogan "Reduced Federal Spending and Renewed Prosperity." Expecting an important endorsement, he wished he could get that jerk Nick Henry off his back.

Nick's last column was particularly harsh and lambasted Cantrell about how many days he actually spent in Washington. When Cantrell read the column at breakfast, he crumpled the newspaper and threw it across the room. Elizabeth laughed and said, "Another negative column by Nick Henry about the great Congressman Cantrell?"

His face twisted in anger. "Shut up Elizabeth."

Elizabeth couldn't stand to be around her husband, and spent more time away from the mansion with their daughters than she spent living there. She laughed again. "By the way, I'm going to be out of town during your fundraiser. Raise lots of money, darling."

"I need you here. I need your support. You know having you here is vital to my image."

She smiled slightly, turned her back on him, and walked out of the dining room.

He yelled at her. "Come back here. You will do what I say."

Elizabeth kept walking.

✧

It was a cool June night when Kurt and Antonia arrived at Hollingsworth House for Cantrell's lavish reelection fundraiser. Russell never did anything small, and with more than four hundred on the invitation list, it was the season's must-attend social event.

Cantrell was there to greet them as they walked into the grand foyer. "Well hello, Kurt. I'm glad you could make it. Introduce me to this pretty young lady."

Kurt laughed to himself when he saw how Cantrell looked at Antonia. "I knew he'd go for her," he thought.

Russell took their coats and handed them to a maid. Kurt introduced Antonia as Toni Jones. He watched Cantrell ogle her from head to foot.

"Lovely to meet you Congressman."

"The pleasure is all mine, Toni, but please, call me Russell. Come on in, a wonderful combo jazz band is playing out on the sun porch, and there's lots of delicious food. Help yourself to something to eat."

Kurt noticed that Cantrell's wife Elizabeth was absent and asked where she was.

Cantrell seemed momentarily uncomfortable, but said, "I insisted she take a much-needed trip. She works so hard on all her charities, and deserves a nice long cruise. I can handle this little party on my own. Now what can I get you two?"

The house was festooned with elaborate flower arrangements. Waiters were weaving through the crowd with loaded canapé trays. The champagne was flowing.

"This is elegant," Antonia said to Kurt. "I've never been to a party as extravagant as this."

Antonia wore a classy, mid-calf, black cocktail dress that emphasized her figure. Her hair was swept back in a chignon to show off her long neck. Her nails were painted red, and she was wearing red lipstick. "You look fabulous, Toni. You're the best looking woman here. He won't know what hit him," Kurt whispered. "I already caught him looking you over, inch by inch. He can't resist a pretty face and nice figure, especially if it's a new conquest."

As they walked into the reception room, Cantrell took Antonia's arm and moved in close to her, "You're so gorgeous, you take my breath away." Antonia looked up at him coyly. "Why thank you, Russell. How's the election going?"

Cantrell smiled, puffed on his cigar, and launched into a detailed explanation about voting districts and percentages. Kurt knew this was the right time to excuse himself, "Be right back. I have to visit the facilities. Take care of my girl for me."

Cantrell led Antonia out on the veranda. He wondered how long Kurt had been seeing her. "She's exactly my type—young and good-looking. I need someone new. I'm tired of Sandra. She's boring and getting too attached."

Cantrell couldn't take his eyes off Toni's fabulous figure, which he thought curved in all the right places. "How do you know Kurt?"

Antonia expected questions and was prepared. "I met him through mutual friends at a Christmas party. We've dated for about six months."

"Is it serious between the two of you? Kurt hasn't mentioned you to me."

"Serious? Define serious," she said as she tilted her head to the side.

"Oh, sorry, I guess I'm probing. It's the attorney in me." Just then, his campaign manager came out on the veranda and told him he should come back into the party, because others were asking for him.

Cantrell said, "Give me a minute. I have to take care of this."

Antonia was relieved to move back into the house and get away from him.

Cantrell came back within a few minutes and said, "Okay. Now what were we saying?"

She wanted to spit in his face, but instead she smiled sweetly and encouraged his attention.

Making certain no one saw him, Kurt quickly headed down a long hall on the other side of the mansion and snuck into the den. He jimmied open the desk drawer and took out Cantrell's forty-five caliber, semi-automatic pistol. Cantrell had once proudly showed Kurt his gun, making a point of saying he always kept it loaded in case he needed it in a hurry. Kurt carefully wrapped the gun in the monogrammed handkerchief he had swiped from Cantrell's office and tucked it into the back of his pants. He took one of Cantrell's cigar butts from the ashtray on the desk and put it in his pocket.

"Thank God that's done," he thought. "Time to get back to the party." He was about to open the door when he heard Antonia and Cantrell coming down the hall. He stepped behind the drapes right before they walked in. His heart was pounding so loudly, he was sure they could hear it.

"What a beautiful home you have. You're such an important man, Congressman. It's an honor to be here to support your reelection campaign."

Cantrell beamed. "I want you to know I play as hard as I work. But that's enough about me. I'll admit I'm intrigued by you, Toni Jones, and I want to get to know you better."

"What about your wife? I have a feeling she might not approve of us getting to know each other better."

"Oh, she won't find out. As I said, she's on a transatlantic cruise. I love it when she travels. It makes my life so deliciously uncomplicated."

Antonia was thoroughly disgusted, but was appeased by the thought that he was going to finally get what he deserved. She was amazed by how easy it was to pretend to be interested in him.

"I promise I'll think about it. But right now, I'm famished and beginning to feel light-headed. Let's get back to the party. I need to find Kurt and get something to eat," she said as she maneuvered him toward the door, intentionally brushing her hip against him.

"Toni, wait. Can we chat for a few more minutes? I really enjoy having you all to myself." He put his hand on the small of her back and began to rub in small circles. It made her skin crawl, but she looked up at him and smiled. "You flatter me too much. Why would a distinguished man like yourself be interested in someone like me?"

Cantrell ate it up. "You underestimate yourself. Do you know how beautiful you are?"

Listening to their banter was nauseating. Kurt was hot and sweaty and getting more aggravated by the minute.

Cantrell said, "What's that? Did you hear that?"

"I didn't hear anything." Toni was alarmed. She'd heard the curtains rustle and knew it was Kurt. "Come on, I really must have something to eat. You don't want me to faint from hunger, do you?"

"But then I could swoop you up in my arms, and *that* I would like very much."

Kurt wanted to bolt out of the curtains and crush him.

Cantrell said, "Let me grab the notes for my speech."

He picked up the notes from his desk and led her toward the door, never taking his hand off her. "Okay, let's get back to the party. People to see and people to get money from. Then we'll spend some time getting to know each other better," Cantrell said as he winked and ushered her out of the room.

She loathed his proprietary touch. "He's so damn sure of himself. I can't wait to see the look on his face when this is over."

Kurt waited for a few minutes and then went back to the party. He found Antonia munching on hors d'oeuvres and talking with an obviously enchanted Cantrell. She saw Kurt and said, "There you are. I'm not feeling well and need to get some fresh air. Would it be all right with you if we stepped outside for a few minutes?"

Cantrell spoke directly to Antonia, never looking at Kurt. "Don't leave. The party is just getting started, and it's almost time for my speech."

"We're not leaving, but the lady needs some air. We'll be back shortly."

Cantrell was so entranced by Antonia, he seemed almost surprised when Kurt spoke. "Sure. But you both need to come back to the party. I'm counting on your support."

As they walked away, Kurt looked back over his shoulder and saw Cantrell staring at Antonia. "I knew he would fall for you," Kurt whispered to Antonia. "This is going exactly as we planned."

Outside, they found Nickels and Charlie waiting behind a tall hedge in the garden. "Glad you made it. We've already checked out Voigt's apartment." Nickels said in a hushed voice. "I hope this works."

"It has to work. We're only going to get one chance," Kurt said.

Kurt handed the cigar stub and the gun in the handkerchief to Charlie, who had instructed them to be careful about leaving fingerprints. Kurt said, "Here's what you need. We have to get right back to the party, so no one notices we're gone. See you at The Canal later."

By the time they rejoined the party, more people had arrived, and even though the room was enormous, there wasn't much room to move. Cantrell was deep in conversation with his campaign manager George Hart and a couple of his guests. Tapping a spoon against a glass, Hart wanted to get the attention of the crowd. "Attention everyone. I'm going to make a toast."

He spoke a few brief words and then said, "Here's to Congressman

Cantrell winning reelection in November by a wide margin. "

Cantrell grinned as everyone clapped loudly. "Thank you. Thank you. I'm going to keep this short, but first I want to tell you how much I appreciate your support. This year is a big year for us. Our economy is improving and we're going to put the dark years of this dreadful financial crisis behind us." He went on for about ten minutes, and concluded by saying, "Every one of you who votes in November has a say in the future of our state and the country. Now please, enjoy yourselves. Eat some of the delicious food our cook and kitchen staff prepared."

Antonia glanced at Kurt's face and immediately knew something was wrong. He signaled with his eyes for her to look across the room where Harry Boyer was standing. "Oh no," Antonia said as she immediately turned her back to Harry. He had gone to high school with Kurt and Antonia. "He can't see me or it will ruin everything."

"I'll go keep Harry busy and give you some more time alone with Cantrell. Make sure you reel him in," Kurt whispered to Antonia.

As soon as Kurt walked away, Antonia caught Cantrell's eye and smiled seductively at him. He immediately walked over to her. "I can't stop looking at you. Do you have any idea how captivating you are?"

"Please stop. You're embarrassing me. Let's talk about something else. I want to hear more about who you are as a man, not a politician."

They chatted for a long time, and eventually the party started to wind down. Cantrell had to say goodbye to his guests.

Cantrell stood at the mansion's imposing front door eyeing Antonia as she and Kurt were leaving.

Suddenly someone bumped into Antonia, and she cried out when Kurt jerked her arm and pulled her toward the valet. As he quickly dragged her to the car, she said, "Let go Kurt, you're hurting me. What are you doing? You've never touched me like that before."

"I'm sorry, sweetheart, but Harry is the one who bumped into you. I knew if you turned around to see who it was, we were in trouble. Russell was standing right there watching you. I didn't mean to be so rough."

"Did Harry see me?"

"No, I'm sure he didn't. If he had, he would have said something. I had a long conversation with him earlier, and he waved goodbye to me. He didn't see your face."

As soon they were in the car, they both leaned back on their seats and took a deep breath. "I didn't realize how much I wanted that to be over," she said. "I didn't feel the least bit nervous while I was there, but now I'm shaking all over."

Kurt put his arm around her. "You were fabulous, but I can't believe you went into the den with him by yourself. We told you to make sure you were never alone with him."

"The only reason I went with Cantrell was because I knew you were there. Thank God you were able to hide before we walked in."

"You were talking loud enough for me to hear you walking down the hall. So…did it work? Did he ask you to meet him?"

"Yes. It was easy, and it went exactly as you thought it would. I listened attentively to him. I pretended to be fascinated by everything he said. Oh, and I definitely played hard-to-get. I guess you know him pretty well because that's all it took. The only thing I had trouble with was trying not to show how much he repulses me."

"He's a disgusting person, and I'm glad he's going to get what he deserves. I knew he would instantly latch onto you. He's a womanizer who's had too many affairs to count. He never stays with a woman for long because it's the challenge that intrigues him. Now *you* are his latest conquest. It gives him a thrill to know you're my girl and that he's skunking me. If I didn't know how serious this is, I would get a big kick out of fooling him. Did you arrange to meet him where we planned tomorrow evening?"

"Yes. I casually mentioned the Portage Hotel, and he was in such a hurry to talk to one of the big donors, he told me to stand outside the hotel's side entrance on Main Street. He's going to pick me up around eight."

"Well done, Toni. Now let's go meet Nickels and Charlie at The Canal. Part one of Zemsta accomplished."

Chapter Thirty-eight

❖

The next evening was overcast, but not raining. Nickels and Charlie entered the Cantrell property from the secluded south entrance, which led directly to the stables, where they hid until it started to get dark. They picked up the stable blanket from under a bush where they'd put it the night before and ran toward the garage.

Earlier that afternoon Voigt backed Cantrell's brand new Lincoln into the estate's multi-car garage. Cantrell pilfered close to four thousand dollars out of his campaign funds to pay for the high-end, ultra-luxury car. He ordered customized hubcaps and an oversized trunk to go on the rack at the back.

Kurt knew that since their argument, Voigt rarely chauffeured for Cantrell. Cantrell had casually mentioned it when they last met. "I'm enjoying my new car so much, I like to drive it myself. I'm not ready to give the wheel to Louis." Kurt played dumb.

Nickels and Charlie smashed the back right taillight on the car and confirmed the trunk was firmly attached to the rack. Nickels said, "Thank God we didn't have to put the trunk on. The car is so new, it's still attached. Come on, let's go. We have to get up to Voigt's apartment right away. We only have thirty minutes before Cantrell leaves for what he thinks is his tryst with my sister."

"Hold on for a minute. I want to think about this. Are we sure we're approaching this the right way?"

"Don't you think it's a bit late to have second thoughts? The plan was put into action last night, and Cantrell believes he's meeting Antonia tonight. Are you backing out? Never mind. I'll do it myself."

"Don't worry, I'm not backing out. We're going into a dangerous situation, and it's important not to rush it. That's how mistakes are made. Believe me, I've seen it happen too many times."

Charlie's experience as a cop had kicked in, and according to plan, he would take the lead. Nickels knew Charlie had resolved any conflicts he had about what they were about to do. He trusted him completely.

"Yeah, okay. I thought you were going to abandon me at the last minute." Nickels took a deep breath. "Thank God you're still in this with me. I really didn't want to do it alone."

Voigt had the night off and was thinking about the day when he would have his own place and a lot of money. He thought about how much he hated Cantrell and how much he wanted to get out of the crappy apartment Cantrell had put him in. He said aloud, "It was bad enough having to work with him all these years, but living next to him is too much. He'll be sorry if he doesn't give me the money. I'm leaving Akron for good, and I won't look back."

Nickels and Charlie looked up at Voigt's apartment. The lights were on, and they saw him moving around behind the curtains. They put on leather gloves and crept up the stairs to the apartment. When they tried the door, they were reassured to find it wasn't locked. "One less thing to worry about," Nickels whispered. He slowly turned the knob, and they inched into the apartment. Voigt was standing in the kitchen drinking bootleg liquor. His back was to them.

Charlie had the gun pointed at him when Voigt heard them and turned around. "What the…? What the fuck do you think you're doing in my apartment?"

"Shut up and stay where you are, Voigt," Charlie said.

Voigt was completely stunned, but wasn't worried. He knew his gun was right behind him and within easy reach. "What the hell?" he said as he slowly put his hand on the counter.

The three of them stared at each other for a few seconds. Charlie spoke first.

"Remember when Catherine Block was murdered at the country club back in 1920? You planted the bloody towels and golf club in a kitchen worker's locker to frame him and to throw suspicion off that piece of slime you call a boss."

Voigt's expression didn't change. "I don't know what the fuck you're talking about. You're friggin' nuts. Get out of here now, or I'll make you leave. And trust me, that won't be pretty."

Nickels said, "That kitchen worker? His name was Albo Jablonski, and he was my father. Cantrell decided it would be a good idea to pin the murder on my father to take the heat off himself. Then the two of you tortured and bribed Oxnard to make sure it wouldn't go to trial.

"Not only did my Papa go to prison for a murder he didn't commit, but he died in that horrendous prison fire. You and Cantrell ruined the life of an innocent man. We're here to make sure both of you pay for what you did."

Voigt laughed loud and hard. "How do you two pussies think you're going to do that?"

Nickels was having trouble keeping his temper in check. "You're not even human. Did either one of you ever stop to think about the life of Albo Jablonski?"

"Shit. You think we cared about that Polack? What difference did it make if one more stupid immigrant went to jail? He was nothing. And the same goes for all the bohunk immigrants and snakes in this town. They're all worthless."

Nickels snatched the gun from Charlie, which gave Voigt the time he needed to grab his gun on the counter and aim. In that split second when Nickels saw Voigt was going to shoot him, he pulled the trigger. The bullet hit Voigt in the stomach, and he dropped to the floor with a loud crash. Voigt tried to stem the flow of blood. He looked up at Charlie and rasped, "Wait a minute, ain't you a cop? I recognize you. You were here the night the kitchen maid was killed."

"Yeah, I'm a cop, you asshole. I'm here to make sure we finally get justice for Albo Jablonski and for Catherine Block. Now shut up."

Voigt was lying in a pool of blood and looked as if he were about to pass out, but his hand was still on his gun, which was underneath his body and hidden from view. Voigt said, "Don't do this. I'm sure we can work something out." He was having difficulty speaking. "I'm getting a lot of money. I can tell you all the things Cantrell has done, and then I'll disappear."

Charlie said, "No deal."

Suddenly Charlie saw that Voigt was trying to cock his gun. Without hesitation, he grabbed the gun from Nickels and shot Voigt in the temple. The bullet went through his head and lodged in the floor. Voigt's body jerked once and then stopped moving.

For several seconds Nickels and Charlie froze.

Charlie said, "Hurry up. We have to get this son of a bitch out of here. Pick up Voigt's gun. We'll get rid of it later."

They cleaned up what they could with a shirt they found hanging on the back of a chair and wiped the handkerchief in the blood. They left the cigar stub on the floor in a corner. They wanted it to look as if Cantrell dropped it by mistake.

They wrapped Voigt in the stable blanket, looked out the window to make sure no one was around, and carried him down the stairs and into the garage. He was so large that they had trouble stuffing his body into the trunk. "He's huge," said Nickels. "Are we going to be able to get him in here?"

"Be patient. It's a matter of finding the right angle."

Finally, they had Voigt positioned in the trunk. They slid the gun in next to the blanket and closed the lid, leaving a snippet of the bloody handkerchief hanging out on the opposite side of the broken taillight.

"Thank God the car was backed into the garage. When Cantrell gets in, he won't see this," Nickels said.

"Yeah, and good thing this is an oversized trunk. That guy is huge. Did you see his hands?" Charlie said.

They had ten minutes before Cantrell was due to show up.

"Let's get out of here."

They hurried out of the garage and ran toward the south entrance where they left their car. Both of them were out of breath by the time they got there. Nickels gasped, "I can't believe we shot a man in cold blood."

"He got what he deserved."

Grandpa Nicky said by the time he and Charlie were in the car, he had finally stopped shaking.

Chapter Thirty-nine

❖

*C*antrell was dressed in a new dark blue suit with wide lapels that emphasized his shoulders. The latest style, it came in sharply at the waist, and he was sure he looked good in it.

He whistled as he entered the garage and slipped into his new car. He ran his hands over the leather seats and steering wheel. He thought about Voigt and realized it was time for them to part ways. The bootlegging business was only a dribble, and word was out that the Prohibition amendment would be repealed next year. He decided to give Voigt the money he asked for, including enough to buy a house and a car. "Good riddance," he thought. "I hope he moves far away from Akron. In fact, I think I'll make that a condition before I give him what he wants."

Cantrell was definitely looking forward to a night out with Toni Jones. He thought, "I need to go slowly with her. If I rush her, I might scare her off. She's not like most of the women I see." He laughed to himself when he thought about Kurt. "Wouldn't he be pissed to know I'm meeting his girl tonight? The hell with him. Maybe I should cut my losses with him, too. He's getting a little too cocky, and I don't like it."

Cantrell had a feeling tonight was going to be the start of something special.

While driving downtown, it crossed his mind that it was odd Toni had chosen the Portage Hotel as the place to meet. The hotel was located in one of the busiest downtown areas. But he'd been in such a hurry when they made arrangements to meet, he'd readily agreed to pick her up at the Main Street entrance.

When The Tribe came up with their plan, they picked the Portage Hotel for the tryst, because Charlie knew they were having problems in the area, and the police were watching that section of town. Charlie had checked a couple of days ago to make sure they continued to heavily patrol it.

As Cantrell neared the hotel, he looked in his rear view mirror and saw two motorcycle cops motioning him to pull over. "Goddamn it, I'm already late. What the devil do they want?"

One of the policemen walked up to the car, and Cantrell rolled down the window. "What's going on, officer?"

"Sir, you have a broken taillight."

"That's not possible. This is a new car. I've only had it a couple of weeks."

"Well, sir, if you don't believe me, get out and take a look."

Cantrell got out and walked around to the back of the car. "I wonder how that happened. I'll get it fixed tomorrow. Thanks for alerting me, Officer."

He was already late for his date with Toni, and didn't want to waste any more time, so he began to walk back to the front of the car. Suddenly one of the policemen noticed the small piece of fabric hanging out of the trunk. "Hey, what's this?" As he leaned it closer to look at it, he said, "This doesn't look right. Is this blood?"

The other policeman moved closer, looked at it, and said, "It sure looks like blood to me."

This was no longer a traffic stop. The officer turned to Cantrell and said, "Open your trunk."

"I'm not sure you know who you're talking to. I am Russell

Cantrell and a United States Congressman. Give me a ticket and move along. I'm on my way to an important meeting."

"I don't really care if you're the Pope. Open your trunk now."

Cantrell angrily took the keys out of the ignition and stomped back to the trunk. Something about this wasn't right. "Here are the keys. Go ahead and open it. I have absolutely nothing to hide."

The patrolman opened the trunk. "What the hell is this? What's in the blanket?"

Cantrell said, "I have no idea."

The cop had the handkerchief in his hand. "This is blood, no question about it."

Cantrell saw his initials on the hanky, and started to sweat. He thought, "Someone's trying to set me up."

When the other officer tugged the edge of the blanket, it uncovered Voigt's hand and part of his arm. The officer jumped backward.

When Cantrell saw the huge hand, he knew who it was. No one but Voigt had hands as big as that. He had no idea what was going on, but it wasn't good. He wasn't sure how to handle it. He knew this was about to get really complicated. He thought, "I'll have them locate Kurt. Let him get me out of this."

"Oh Jesus. We have a body here. Step aside, Congressman." The cop turned to his partner and said, "Radio headquarters and have them locate Bulldog O'Brien."

The partner said, "I saw him go into The Canal a few minutes ago. I'll tell them to call him there."

It was twenty past eight, and Kurt, Nickels, Charlie, and Antonia were sitting in their regular booth at The Canal. Nick and Charlie had changed their clothes and wiped down their shoes. They were on edge waiting to hear about whether the third part of the plan worked.

Nickels said, "Antonia, are you sure he said he would pick you up around eight?"

"You've asked me that at least ten times. The answer is yes. Stop worrying. This is playing out exactly as we planned."

Charlie said, "I talked to one of the traffic guys tonight, and he mentioned that they were definitely watching the area around the Portage Hotel. There's no question they're going to spot Cantrell's broken taillight, but I have to admit, my stomach is in knots. It's hard to believe everything hinges on one rear taillight."

"This waiting is like slow torture," said Kurt.

Antonia looked at her brother and said, "I can't stop thinking about Papa. Do you think he would approve of what we're doing?"

"I've thought a lot about that. To be honest, I'm not sure, but no one other than Papa knew what he really went through in that hellhole. He was beaten and humiliated on a daily basis. When he sat in his cell and realized he wasn't going to make it out of the fire, I wonder if he thought about the person who had set him up and had taken so much from him."

"We can never tell Mama."

"God, no."

Just then, the waitress came over to their table to tell Charlie there was a phone call for him. "This is it," Charlie said.

You could feel the tension in the air. When he came back to the table, he said, "They've found the body. Get it together, and don't blow it. Remember to say as little as possible."

"This is outrageous," Cantrell said. "I had nothing to do with this. I have no idea how this body got in my trunk."

"I've never heard that before."

One of the policemen tried to unwrap part of the blanket without pulling it completely out of the trunk. They needed O'Brien on the scene before they did anything more. He tugged a corner of the blanket and exposed Voigt's bloody head with the bullet hole in his temple. Cantrell feigned surprise, "Oh my God, that's my chauffeur, Louis Voigt. This is terrible. Who could have done this?"

Both the officers stared at him, and it was obvious they didn't believe him. They stepped aside and talked quietly for a few minutes.

When they came back to Cantrell, one of them said, "Turn around. We're going to cuff you."

"I most certainly will not turn around, and I refuse to allow you to put handcuffs on me." The police and Cantrell continued to argue for several more minutes, until Cantrell said, "I won't say another word. I want to talk to my lawyer. His name is Kurt Becker."

"We're waiting for our Chief of Detectives to get here. O'Brien will decide how we're going to handle this and what we're going to do with you. In the meantime, we're going to handcuff you. We'll let him know you've requested a lawyer."

As Kurt walked up to the car with Charlie and Nickels, Cantrell was tremendously relieved to see him. Antonia was hidden behind the men, and Cantrell couldn't see her. "Kurt, thank God you're here. Tell them to take these infernal things off."

Kurt stared at him and said nothing.

"What's the matter with you? Tell them to take these handcuffs off. Why are you looking at me like that?"

Kurt remained silent. He turned to Charlie. "I'm not his lawyer."

He slowly turned back to Cantrell. "Effective immediately, I resign as your attorney."

"What the hell are you talking about? You know I didn't do this. This is a set-up. I own you, Becker, and I forbid you to resign."

Kurt turned his back on him, which made Cantrell even angrier.

The police had found the gun stuffed in the side of the trunk and were holding it up in front of him. "Is this your gun?"

"Uh…yes I believe it is, but I didn't murder my chauffeur. I'm being framed. Why can't you see that?" He was panicking.

"Kurt, I demand you tell them you're my attorney. Tell them to take the handcuffs off."

Kurt ignored him.

Charlie told the officers to take Cantrell to Summit County Jail and lock him up. "We have more than enough evidence to get a search warrant. Get the coroner over here to examine the body. Then locate a judge, so we can get a team out to search the Cantrell estate right away."

Kurt said, "Make sure you search the apartment above the garage. That's where Voigt lived."

Charlie looked at Cantrell. "You might want to find a new attorney as soon as possible. This doesn't look good for you."

As the police were getting ready to transport him, Cantrell said, "This is a travesty. I'm a United States Congressman. Whoever did this won't get away with it."

"Oh yeah?" said Nickels, as he moved in close to Cantrell. He whispered, "Like you did when you murdered Catherine Block? You remember her don't you?"

Cantrell was shocked. "I don't know what are you're talking about."

It slowly began to dawn on him what was happening.

Kurt positioned himself in front of Cantrell and spoke low enough so the police couldn't hear. "You bastard. You paid for my education and the boardinghouse mortgage because you were afraid I saw you with her that day. You were buying my silence because you thought I knew you murdered her. If I had paid attention, I would have known you were the one who really killed her. And I would have turned you in. I loved Albo Jablonski like a father."

Cantrell no longer looked so big and powerful.

Nickels said, "I hope you enjoy sitting in a prison cell for the rest of your life. You're finally getting what you deserve, and I hope you rot in hell. I only wish my father were here to see it."

Kurt looked at Nickels, and let out a huge sigh. Cantrell watched them.

Then Cantrell saw Antonia. "What the…?" He was completely confused. "What's going on? What are you doing here?"

Kurt said loud enough for everyone to hear, "Hey, Nickels, maybe you'll win a Pulitzer Prize for the *Cleveland News Tribune* when you write an exposé about the venerated Congressman Cantrell and his long fall from grace."

Cantrell's eyes grew wide as he gaped at Nickels and Antonia standing next to each other. When Kurt mentioned the newspaper, it suddenly all made sense.

Nickels was Nick Henry. Toni Jones was his sister Antonia. And Albo Jablonski was their father.

Epilogue

❖

*A*ntonia and Kurt married in a small ceremony in September 1932. My father Albert Jablonski Henry—Bertie—was five years old at the time. Antonia's life-long friend Rosemary was matron of honor, and Grandpa was Uncle Kurt's best man.

Grandpa Nicky said he had never seen two people more in love. On the day of the wedding, when Kurt took Antonia in his arms and kissed her, there wasn't a dry eye among them.

After much cajoling, Millie agreed to live with the newlyweds. Antonia didn't want her to be alone, and Kurt was happy to have her.

Marta was also there, but Erna had died of cancer in late summer. Marta missed her sister terribly, but the house she and Erna bought wasn't far from the one where Kurt, Antonia, and Millie lived, and she could see them as often as she wanted.

Nickels decided to accept Oxnard's money and established a trust in his father's name, which was administered by Antonia. It not only paid for the education of all the Jablonski grandchildren, but also offered scholarships to the children of Polish immigrants. He knew Papa would approve. In addition to Bertie, he and Harriet had two more children.

My grandfather never won a Pulitzer Prize, but he won many awards, and his column was nationally syndicated. He wrote two books, one of which made the nonfiction best seller list. Grandpa wrote an article about a year after Cantrell went to jail and exposed him for the murder of Catherine Block. He never got around to writing a book about the murder. He always said it was too painful, and he was too close to it. He asked me to give it a try someday after he was gone.

Kurt's law practice became well known statewide, and he continued to practice until his retirement in 1957. He and Antonia had three children.

Charlie left Akron to take a job with Cleveland's Police Department and went on to become their police commissioner. When he retired, the governor attended the ceremony. He and Grace had two children, exactly as they had planned.

Marion and Richard married and divorced. The last anyone heard of her, she was on her fourth marriage.

Kurt, Nickels, and Charlie weathered conflicts, weddings, and divorce. They were there for each other for births, graduations, vacations, and reunions. They made a pact to be there for each other, and that's what they did.

✧

After Voigt's death, the authorities connected him to several murders, but the murder of Headmistress Kruger was never solved.

The Feds never located Cantrell's bootlegging operation. Prohibition was repealed in 1933.

Cantrell's dramatic fall from prominence played out in newspapers and on the radio. In 1936, there was a small blurb in the second section of the Akron newspaper.

> *Russell H. Cantrell, a former Congressman and once-prominent attorney and businessman, convicted for the 1932 murder of his chauffeur Louis Voigt, was found dead in his cell at the state penitentiary in Columbus today. He was fifty years old. Cantrell was serving a life sentence and had been held in solitary confinement since his 1932 arrest.*

Cantrell was also implicated in the 1920 murder of Akron socialite Catherine Block, but was never tried for the crime. Upon his death in 1932, attorney William Oxnard left a notarized confession, which thoroughly exonerated his client Albert Jablonski and implicated Cantrell and his chauffeur Louis Voigt. Jablonski perished in the 1930 prison fire at the Ohio State Penitentiary.

Many also thought Cantrell was involved in the murder of Akron City Councilman Stephen Lyle in 1922, but it was never proven.

"Foul play was not suspected in Cantrell's death," the prison's warden reported. "It is believed he died of a heart attack."

If you liked *Zemsta*, please post a review on the site where you purchased it. I would be very grateful.

About the Author

❖

Victoria Brown grew up in northwestern Pennsylvania and lived in the Boston area for 20 years. She has two grown daughters and is now basking in the sun in Boca Raton, Florida with her two mini-dachshunds and a cat named Puppy. This is her first book. For more information, go to www.woodchuckpublishers.com

Acknowledgements

❖

I never would have written *Zemsta* without the encouragement of my sister Rebecca Ewing.

I also owe a huge thank you to Eileen Landy who served as my editor and helped me work out endless plot conundrums. Her advice throughout the entire process was invaluable.

My cousin Lois Downey helped with all the Akron references.

Suzanne Rynne provided insight into large Irish Catholic families.

Maciej Tarnawski was my source for all things Polish.

Thank you to Judy James at Akron-Summit County Public Library for research assistance.

Thanks to beta readers Rebecca Ewing, Lisa Kreider, Emily Smith Ewing, Lucy Cushman, and George Teren.

A special shout-out to proofreaders Kaitlin Kenned, Rebecca Mullen, and Stuart Harris.

Thanks also to Gayle Kidder who converted the file to a variety of e-book formats.

I tried to stay as historically correct as possible. My mother, Virginia Brown, grew up in Akron. Although she is a decade younger than the characters in *Zemsta*, she remembered a lot about the times and was a wealth of information.

I researched slang, technology, and much more about the 1920s.

Did they have ignition keys?

Was "stick in the mud" a phrase at that time?

What swear words did they use?

If you find something you believe is inaccurate, e-mail zemsta@woodchuckpublishers.com. I will correct it in future editions.

The Akron Police Department actually had ninety-eight uniformed police officers in 1920. That was also the year they named the first Chief of Detectives.

The fire at the Ohio State Penitentiary actually happened on April 21, 1930, the same date as in the story. Three hundred and twenty-two men died in the fire, and one hundred and fifty were injured when the guards wouldn't let them out of their cells.

There is no Rosewood Hills Country Club in Akron.

Cantrell Baseball Park is fictitious, but a municipal baseball field was built in Akron in 1925, the same year as in the story.

City Hospital did exist and is now called Suma Akron City Hospital. There never was a Cantrell Pavilion.

The triple play by Bill Wambsganss in the 1920 World Series happened as it was written. The same is true of the 1929 game when Babe Ruth hit his 500th home run.

Contact: zemsta@woodchuckpublishers.com.

Questions for Discussion

❖

1. The author introduced The Tribe as young boys. How does this add to the story? Discuss how their childhoods might have influenced them.

2. Why is Cantrell so damaged? Discuss his parents' role in developing his character.

3. Discuss Cantrell's relationship with Voigt.

4. Name the many ways life was different during Prohibition.

5. Why did it take Kurt a year to tell Antonia about Marion?

6. Do you feel Kurt's obsession with money is his only character flaw? At what point do you think he realized money was his downfall?

7. Although the country club murderer is revealed to the reader from the beginning, discuss the ways in which the author manages to create suspense.

8. Why did Charlie go along with the scheme to murder Voigt and pin it on Cantrell?

9. Discuss why Kurt, Nickels, Charlie, and Antonia were willing to murder Voigt. Why didn't they murder Cantrell instead?

10. What does it take for people to do something they wouldn't normally be capable of?

11. The author creates an authentic sense of time and place by including many period details. Discuss some of the most memorable images and their importance to the story and to your own experience reading it.

12. Discuss how the city of Akron is important to the story.

Made in the USA
Charleston, SC
17 May 2012